THE WELL OF SOULS

CORDELIA KELLY

BCP

For Mom

You've been with me from the very start, my champion and greatest supporter

Duchesne Island

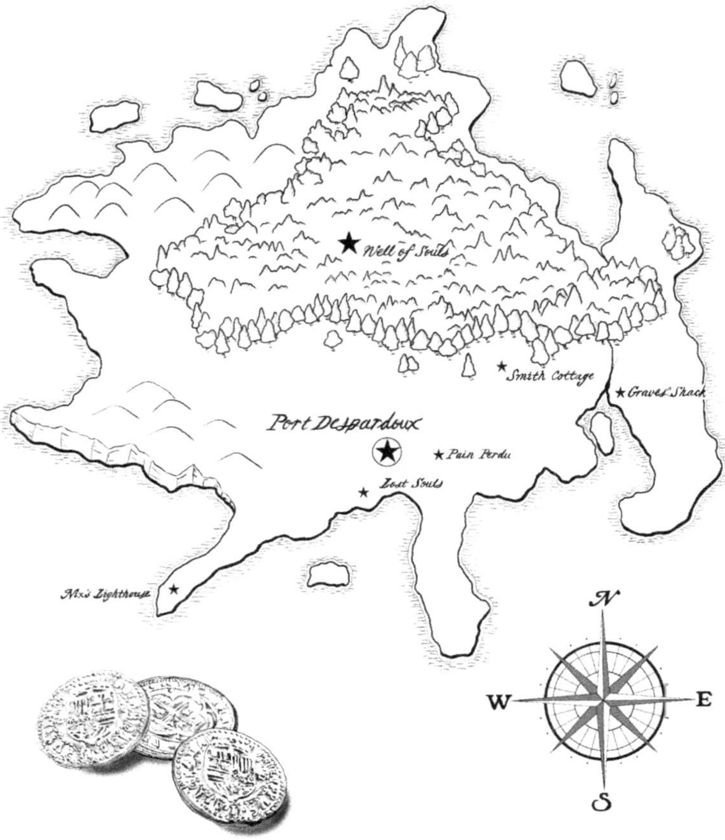

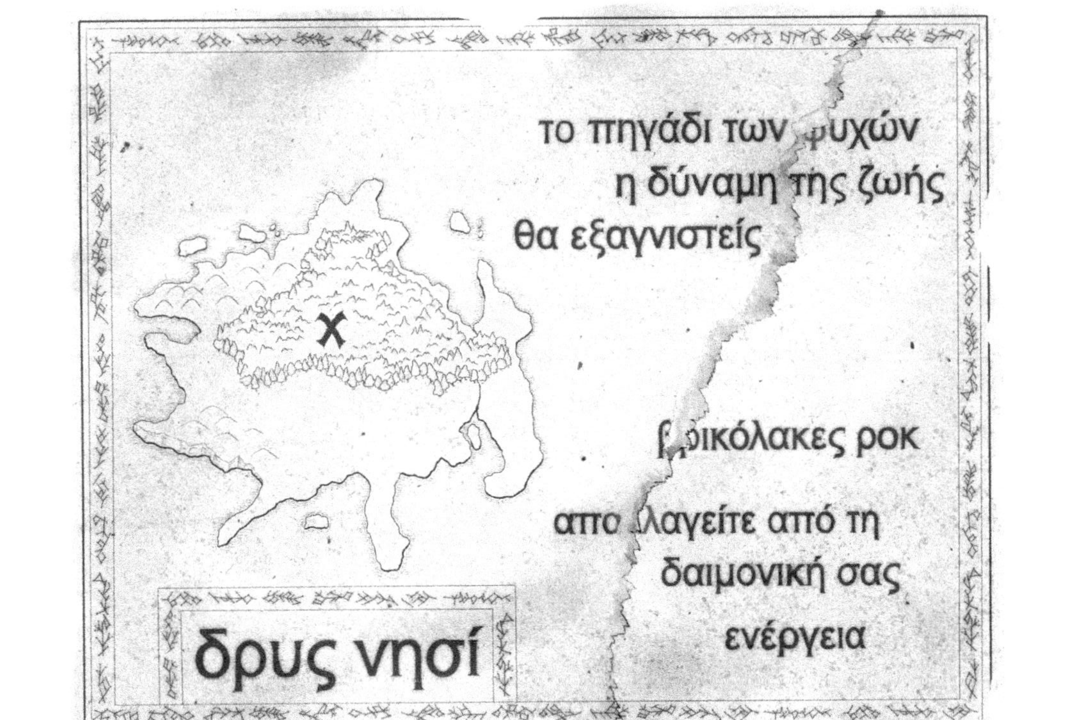

το πηγάδι των ψυχών
η δύναμη της ζωής
θα εξαγνιστείς
β,οικόλακες ροκ
απο λαγείτε από τη
δαιμονική σας
ενέργεια
δρυς νησί

THE WELL OF SOULS

A Port of Lost Souls book

Cordelia Kelly

ONE

Every hour, Lola became increasingly hungry. Being cooped up inside this boat with the fishermen – or *edibles*, as Beau liked to call humans – was torture.

The deck of the ship rolled under Lola's feet and male voices cried out on the deck above her. She tilted her head to listen. The crew she had caught a ride with exclaimed over the unseasonal squall. A few cursed the last-minute passenger they had picked up on their way to Nova Scotia.

That would be Lola. She could tell from their resentful stares that her presence made the men uncomfortable. They wouldn't know why, of course, but they blamed her for the odd behaviour of the Atlantic.

Men of the sea had remained superstitious long after the age of rationality took over, especially when it came to women passengers. In this case, they had every right to be. Since Lola had boarded, they had been plagued by terrible weather, storms blowing up and half-submerging them in waves.

But she had good money to pay, and the fishing industry not being what it used to be, the captain wasn't in a position to turn her down. They were on track to arrive early at their destination, even with this detour. Every storm they encountered pushed them unerringly in the right direction. *Unnatural*, the men muttered when they thought Lola was out of earshot. They glared if she came too close and refused to speak in her presence.

The sooner she was off this boat, the better for everyone. She needed to keep a low profile, and a boat of dead fishermen wouldn't go unnoticed.

She paced her cabin, barely two steps from one side to the other. It was not that she minded small spaces. How could she, given her line of work? But her hunger beat steadily against her, in the ever-slowing thumps of her sluggish heartbeat. It wouldn't pick up again until she fed. And the longer she was trapped on this boat, the more tempting the feast surrounding her.

She dug sharp nails into her palms, pins of pain distracting her from her suffering. Focus on the goal. She smoothed the ancient scrap of parchment laid across the worn desk. The stolen blood in her veins thrummed as she studied the map, pried from the bowels of a Spanish galleon.

The Well of Souls. This map was centuries lost; the treasure it promised lost for far longer than that. And Lola was going to find it, or die trying. She hadn't been given any other choice. Her immortal life had already been declared forfeit.

The parchment had been torn in half, but this half had the all-important map, faded over the centuries. A message in archaic Greek was barely legible: *Seek not for glory, nor for wealth. To only the worthy will the treasure be made great, and the power will be theirs.* Her fingertips played over the markings scrawled down the side, unlike any lettering she had encountered before. The dots and lines almost appeared to be constellations, but not of any stars she knew.

She had risked so much for this; she couldn't afford to lose focus now. What remained to be seen was whether the risk was worth it. They were close now, she could sense it. Land wasn't far off.

She rolled the parchment with every care, returning it to its container. It nestled at the bottom of her backpack. Everything else she had brought with her could fit around it. In some ways she packed like a typical sixteen-year-old girl: t-shirts, leggings and lip gloss. She was low-tech compared to the modern-day treasure hunter, relying instead on demonic instinct. But she doubted many humans carried with them a sack of ancient doubloons found scattered on the bottom of the Caribbean Sea. Loose change, in Lola's circle.

Still, she slipped her hand into the sack of coins, the weight heavy and pleasing. She had fenced what she could for cash in Havana, but she had been in a hurry. And transactions left a trail she couldn't afford.

She slipped on her raincoat and bag and climbed onto the deck. The spring storm this far north was fresh, like a slap in the face, one she relished. Though it was daytime, the thick cloud cover above them allowed her to be outside, shielding her from the harmful rays of the sun.

Land approached, barely visible in the veil of mist that curled around the island. The muffled flare of a lighthouse blinked, cautioning them to be wary. Anticipation tingled through her at the thought of setting foot on the fabled island.

Duchesne Island, haunted from one side to the other.

The boat lurched, and several men around her shouted in alarm as the boat veered too close to the jagged shoals.

Lola felt no fear. She was driving this boat, whether they knew it or not, and the heaving of it thrilled her. As she thought about it, the boat swung high into a wave, and everybody on deck but her was thrown off balance. If she wasn't careful, she'd bring the entire ship down with her. The pull of the sea always dragged at her.

All vampires shared an affinity with an element, and water was hers. Her demonic energy resonated and strengthened when she was near the ocean. It allowed her to nudge the currents in the right direction, taking them to their destination faster than naturally possible. But using her powers like this weakened her and made her crave even more the life-giving blood her body demanded.

She shook out her hands and calmed her thoughts, allowing the waves to settle around her. Several of the fishermen shot her dirty looks as they righted themselves, as though they knew she was responsible.

The captain of the vessel came to stand next to her, his eyes on the nearing island. Like his men, he was cautious around her. "Are ya sure you wanna be out in this weather, missy?" the captain called. She figured he meant he wanted her out of sight, so as not to antagonise his crew.

"It suits me fine, *capitaine*." She exaggerated her French accent, purring around the vowels. It usually buttered up tough old salts like him. She held back the snarl she wanted to unleash. She was always expected to play nice, to go along and keep her head down. It was maddening.

If Beau was in her place, he would have eaten them all and sailed into harbour on his own. But Lola needed to get to Duchesne Island under cover, without anyone finding out. Especially not Beau.

"It's a nasty one." He tugged at his hood. "Ya might be better off below deck."

The air smelled of ozone and held a weird quality as they pulled into the harbour, like the tingling before a lightning bolt strikes the Earth. The charge prickled over her skin and buzzed through her blood. The island they approached was magical to the core. "We'll be there soon," was all she said, ignoring the captain's sigh.

"We'll be putting in here at Port Despardoux for the rest of the night," he said. "We'll wait out the storm before heading to Halifax."

"It'll calm down by tomorrow."

He nodded, as though expecting this. "There's an inn near the docks, in case yer lookin' for some'er to stay."

She studied him from the corner of her eye. "Kind of you."

"Things're quiet here until the tourists come. And Sunday, besides. Most places'll be closed up. Pub on Saturdays, church on Sundays."

Lola snorted. "That's true in places all over the world. I'll figure it out."

The captain gave her a searching look, his cloudy grey eyes meeting hers for the first time. "Can't figure why a slip of a girl like you'd come here. She's a pretty enough place, but there're rumours, you know. Some say she's haunted, if you believe in that kind of nonsense."

She barely held back the wild laughter that threatened to erupt from her. "I believe in all that nonsense."

The boat juddered to a stop as it pulled in. As the men shouted to those on the wharf and threw out lines to the dock, they went out of their way to avoid Lola, falling over ropes and crates to keep their distance. The captain kept his gaze on her, probably wondering how she had convinced him to come to this curious place. "Some kind of ghost hunter, then?"

"Actually, I'm hunting something else."

He clicked his tongue. "Seeking out the legends, then, of buried pirate treasure? Yer not the first or the last, and yer joining a flock of fools if you ask me." He paused, then pointed. "The old treasure pit's over that ridge there, deep in the oak forest. Uncanny, that; oaks aren't supposed to grow here. It's a mystery." He scratched his beard. "But all the legends about hidden treasure and pirates' curses are only stories. The treasure of Duchesne Island was found long ago and spent. There's no gold left on the island, just fishermen like us doing their best to fill their bellies."

"You would be astounded what you can find if you scratch the surface." With a curving half-smile, she held up a coin with two fingers. "For your troubles, *capitaine*."

She placed it into his callused palm and pulled the hood of her coat over her tangled hair. As he gaped, she cocked an eyebrow at him. "And for your silence. I was never here, and neither were you."

He eyed her shrewdly, as though wondering whether there were more gold coins to come. "Men'll talk. Sailors can't keep secrets."

Fury boiled inside of her, her patience at a breaking point. She pretended she was Jacquotte, her former boss. Nobody ever talked back to Jacquotte. A small amount of her power shone through her eyes, just a hint at what she was, and what she could do if pressed. "They can if they're dead."

She winked as the captain blanched and strode down the gang-plank. The men straightened and watched her pass, silent in her wake.

She hesitated at the edge of the dock. If the tales were true, the moment she stepped foot on this island, she would be cursed. She didn't know the nature of the curse, but if she didn't find the trea-sure of the Well of Souls, she was doomed anyway.

She trod lightly onto the faded wooden boards. A buzz of energy rippled through her, and then it was gone. Her fate was decided, one way or another, and she was going to see this through to the end.

Few people were on the wharf. Only the men working the docks braved the elements today. All sensible humans sought shelter from the blistering wind. Under the howl of it, the hollow thunk of boats hitting the wooden docks sounded, rhythmic with each slapping wave. And above wheeled the gulls and their lone-some cries as they reeled overhead in the gusts.

Wooden lobster traps were piled along the edge of the dock, damp nets reeking of fish guts. Lola licked her mouth, tasting salt. It made her think of blood, and how very hungry she was. Her fangs slipped out over her bottom lip.

She turned to raise a hand to the captain, who inspected what he held in his hand: gold, authentic, and possibly Spanish. Then a heavy mist rolled in from the hills, devouring her and the rest of the wharf, camouflaging her movements. The last thing Lola heard before marching toward the crest of the ridge was the rumblings of superstitious men caught in the jaws of a supernatural spell.

Two

The nocturnal pull twitched at Lola's senses. She hummed to herself, holding up a hand to admire the play of pink in her skin, the tangle of capillaries underneath. *Very life-like.* Her hunt had been satisfying.

It had also earned her a place to stay, although she would have to be careful of the locals discovering her. The fishing shack belonging to the man she'd fed from was barely more than a lean-to, but it provided shelter from the sun. And running water, *dieu merci.* After feeding on a local, she had slept like the dead for the entire day.

As evening approached, she had woken, and now she unpacked her few belongings. The shabby dresser was one of the few pieces of furniture not entirely in shambles. She'd mainly brought skin products: rich creams and serums designed to keep this body youthful. It was essential to keep up proper skincare when your skin was always on the verge of rotting off.

She brushed the snarls out of her hair tangled with sea salt, and at last it bounced, curly past her shoulders. Her regime of creams helped smooth her skin, but nothing healed like human blood. She was new again, the same as she had been for the past eighty years.

She never aged; she never changed. She was a sixteen-year-old girl, for eternity. Her shoulders slumped forward at the thought. All those years she'd survived, all the years stretching out in front of her, sometimes she wished it would all go away.

If Beau could only see her now, the way his lip would curl as he took her in. *You think too much*, he'd told her. *It's going to get you killed one of these days.*

Did he gloat now at how dead right he had been?

She shook her head, ridding herself of these bleak thoughts. Better if Beau simply forgot about her, though she didn't much trust in happy endings. Not for her, anyway. But she would worry about that another time. The sun was setting and the evening stretched ahead of her. Perfect. She was ready to explore, and she knew exactly where she wanted to go.

The shack she holed up in was along the northern edge of town, on the shoreline where a creek from the forest trickled into the ocean. The waves slapped against the rocks of the creek bed in a slew of brackish water and decomposing seaweed. It wasn't the type of place people would come looking for anything, not if they could help it.

A wooden bridge that looked nearly as old as Lola spanned the creek and headed towards the centre of Duchesne Island, towards the forest the captain had told her about. Oak trees that shouldn't exist. Lola picked out the gravel path that headed up to the ridge and over into the quiet space of the woods at night.

Once she was surrounded by the oaks, she could see why they would be considered mysterious. They were skyscrapers above her, the leaf cover a hundred feet above, their sturdy trunks like fortifi-cations. The roots curled out of the earth, forming arches she could duck under. They were strange, these trees, certainly centuries old. When she put her hand to the bark of one it prickled under her skin. She brushed her hand along her jacket to wipe off the feeling that sank into her palm.

Underneath everything, a vibration scratched the air, trying to get her attention like a chant beyond the edge of hearing. The call chafed her, lured her deeper into the forest. She should be wary. Although she didn't understand what the call meant, she would bet her last gold coin it had something to do with the Well of Souls treasure and the legends that swirled around the island.

Nobody knew exactly what lay at the end of the Well of Souls. But the myths told of a power so strong, it would render a demon invincible. Lola needed to become invincible if she was going to survive what was coming after her.

The path pounded into the forest floor was littered with brave saplings peeking into the air. Lola bounded past all of these as the chant picked up its tempo. She slowed at a bend, knowing she approached the centre of the calling.

The tree rose in a perfect half-moon, claiming more space than should be allowed. The trunk twisted and writhed, stooped like a wise woman. Thousands of branches spread out in all directions. Some were so old and heavy they rested on the earth, weathered with moss and home to an ecosystem of forest creatures. Tiny buds haloed the upper branches in glowing spring green. The mist coiled through the twigs as if this mighty oak breathed.

Roots stretched out like spokes of the wheel, reaching aeons into the earth. Lola blinked, not knowing where that thought had come from. Trembling, she approached the tree. A shimmer of feeling curled inside of her, unknown and foreign. It felt very like wanting, a warmth that radiated through her. But she didn't know what it was she desired.

She laid her palm on the bark and drew in a sharp breath. She could feel its heartbeat, thrumming an ancient tattoo. She snatched back her hand and stared at it, wondering if she had been stained by all the life inside. What magic was this?

Disoriented, she stumbled back, then caught a scent and stilled. A man approached; he smelled like cinnamon and fresh morning dew. She unleashed her demonic energy, her senses sharpening until she could make out his heartbeat. It was far younger than that of the tree. With agonizing slowness, she crept around the tangle of roots, keeping herself in the shadows.

He was her age, on the cusp of adulthood. He walked with an easy gait and was tall, with tawny-brown skin. His black hair was on the long side, a style reminiscent of another time, but it suited him fine.

Lola chewed her lip with a fang, considering him. He looked delicious. Though she had recently eaten, she couldn't help her response. If she got too close, she knew she'd want to sink her teeth into him, know what he tasted like on the inside.

But she couldn't start bingeing on the population of a small island, because people would take note. Especially a young person; their disappearances were always noticed. She would have to be discerning. From here on, it would be best to hunt local wildlife only. Though it never satisfied her hunger to the same degree, she could survive on it.

The teen could be helpful, though. It would be wise to bring on a local as an ally and guide. The strategy had worked in the past. No need to kill when the participant was willing, and swaying men to her way of thinking was a talent of hers.

Lola fluffed out her hair and unzipped the top of her jacket, ready for battle. She would do what she needed to get the treasure. If she could access the power it promised, she might never have to run again.

A wooden thwack sounded, harsh and out of time with the lullaby of nocturnal murmurs. Lola peeked over the root. The young man was throwing rocks at the tree, the beautiful wise old tree. His face was crinkled; frustration marred his every movement. He wound up, all fluid lines and potential energy, about to make another pitch.

"What are you doing?" Lola's tone was sharper than she had meant. Startled, he turned toward the sound and his throw went wild. The rock came flying right for Lola, and she whipped out of the way. The stone only grazed her hair, but it could have been messy if she hadn't been who she was. She whirled to face him, taking a steadying breath to regulate her voice. She didn't want to push him away.

His gaze slowly travelled from her face, down her body to her thighs, and she figured she wouldn't have any problems.

She couldn't have designed better lighting. The last of the twilight illuminated her face and she touched on some of her supernatural abilities, bringing a faint glow to her skin. She shook out her hair, and her smile dimpled as he froze, speechless.

She approached. His face was handsome, almost beautiful. His features were finely chiselled, with a strong jaw and dark eyes ringed with black lashes. He had the look of the Latino actors on the telenovelas she had spent time watching in Havana. Her smile stretched wider. Swaying this particular local was going to be fun.

She began the rally, modulating her voice so it sounded more like a modern teenager. "What the hell? Is throwing rocks at people's heads fun for you?"

Her taunt shook him out of his stupor, and he loped toward her. "Sorry, you came out of nowhere. I didn't mean to biff that at you." His voice was deep, and his chest was pleasingly wide.

Lola cocked her head. "I'm not hurt. But what do you have against trees?" She pointed at his target, where pockmarks from the rocks were clustered in a tight bullseye. Her fingers hovered over the wound, unwilling to touch the pale weeping sap.

"I – nothing against trees; I love trees." He hovered a few feet away, stealing glances as though unsure she was real.

She caught his eye. "You're hurting it."

He laid his hand over the bark. "I didn't mean to. I'm sorry." He leaned against the tree, failing to appear nonchalant. He crossed his arms over his chest, then braced a hand against a branch that proved a little too low, then settled on jamming his hands in his pockets. Lola bit back her smile.

"Where are you from?" he asked. "It sounds like you have an accent."

"From France, originally." She gave her Rs an extra roll to show off. "But that was a long time ago."

"French, eh? That's cool. I speak a little, not very much. I speak Spanish, though. Not that you asked." She giggled, which coaxed a shy smile from him. "Right, shut up about me. What about you? What are you doing here?"

"I'm visiting," she said. "I heard Duchesne was an interesting place."

"Tourists don't usually show up for another few weeks."

"I like to get an early start."

"That's cool. Are you with your parents?"

Lola narrowed her eyes. These rambling questions were going to get annoying. She ignored them and glanced up, eyes half-hidden under heavy lashes, and held out her hand. "I'm Lola." His callused palm was warm under her cool touch. Her thumb grazed over the fleshy pad, taking in the uptick in his heartbeat.

He swallowed hard. "I'm Gael. Gael Smith. I live 'round here. You're on my property, actually."

Her eyebrows shot up. "So, I'm a trespasser?"

"Oh, but it's okay. You can be here. There's not much here other than trees."

"Right, the trees. That brings me back to my question. What has this tree ever done to you?"

"Oh." Gael pushed his hand through his hair. His cheeks flushed pink and she could practically taste the blood rushing to his face. "I was just letting off steam."

"It seemed more than that." She rolled her hips as she walked to a nearby root, taking a seat and crossing her legs. She pulled out a cigarette, lighting up and blowing out a long string of smoke. "You looked like you wanted to take out an army with your arm."

Gael sat next to her, watching her smoke with fascination. "Smoking is, like, super bad for you. Hasn't anyone ever told you?"

She looked at the burning tip of the cigarette and knocked

away some ash. "It's a terrible habit, I know, but I can't seem to quit. I've been smoking far too long."

"Seriously? What are you, fifteen? You can't have been smoking that long."

"I'm not that young." She gave a flirty pout, and Gael grinned. He was an easy mark; she couldn't believe he had fallen into her lap. "You don't believe me?"

He fell into the flirtation. "Not even a little bit."

"That's hardly what a girl wants to hear. Now, Gael, time to confess. You clearly have a grudge against the universe." She pointed to the pockmarks on the tree with her cigarette. "Where's that coming from?"

Her words seemed to remind Gael of something she had distracted him from, and his shoulders slumped. His lips flattened to a grim line. "Oh, that. It's...life stuff."

She put her accusing cigarette down and leaned towards him. If she could get him to trust her, he'd be more willing to help her later. She widened her eyes, doe-like, designed to make men melt. "Listen, I know you don't know me at all, and it would be insane to share anything with me. But maybe there's a reason I went for a walk through the woods this evening, and maybe there's a reason I met you. Keeping all that crap in can lead to serious bad vibes, not to mention crimes against trees." The edge of his mouth quirked up. She had him. "Besides, sometimes there's no one better to tell than a complete stranger."

Gael cupped his hand over his mouth as he contemplated her. "I'm worried I hit my head and you're not actually real."

"I'm as real as you." Lola knocked her knee against his.

Her touch seemed to steady him, and he nodded. "Just tell a complete stranger everything going on in my messed-up head?"

She nodded. "Better than therapy, because I listen for free."

He let out a drawn-out sigh, staring into the darkness of the forest. "My little brother has cancer," he said after a moment. He glared at Lola's cigarette, and she subtly set it to the side. "Diego.

He got sick last year. Things have gotten really bad since then. He has to go to the mainland for his treatments, and my mum goes with him, of course. But she lost her job because she can't be there all the time, and it's only the three of us, so...we've been struggling." His lips twisted around the words, as though reluctant to share them, while his hands clenched and unclenched.

His face jerked away, his words rushing out now the dam had been broken. "My mom's had to take on odd jobs to pay the bills when she can, mainly as a cleaning lady, which is not her at all. She used to be this well-known archaeologist, and now she's cleaning up after the rich snots on the island who haven't lifted a hand to help her out. I'm doing what I can, taking on part-time work at the wharf with the fishermen, but short of dropping out of school and working full time, it's not enough. And I don't want to drop out of school, you know? Getting my degree, maybe a scholarship, it's a way to get the hell off this island. But Mum needs the help, and Diego..." He trailed off, rubbing a hand over the back of his neck.

She guessed at what was driving his emotions. "It's not selfish to want to finish school."

His gaze darted towards her, then away. "I don't know. It seems pretty selfish to me."

"I'm sure your mother wouldn't want you to drop out of school. You're far too hard on yourself."

He slapped a fist into his palm, then gave a rueful smile. "No, she told me she'd kill me if I ever considered it. But I wish I could do more for her."

Lola surreptitiously put out her cigarette in damp moss and leaned forward. "It sounds like you love them very much." His story touched her, somehow, pressing deep and heavy in her chest. What would it be like to be loved like that?

She frowned and flicked her fingers, ridding herself of the feeling. Where had that come from? She had work to do. She couldn't afford to be distracted.

Gael let out a shaky laugh. "I don't even know why I'm telling you all this. My best friend barely knows any of it, and here I am pouring my heart out to you." He squinted at Lola. "I don't know if you know this, but there is supposed to be spooky shit that happens on this island. Like phantoms and sirens and beautiful dryads that appear out of the mist. Are you sure you're not one of those?"

Lola tossed her hair back, shifting closer to him. "Just an ordinary girl, in the right place at the right time. What is this place, anyway? *C'est incroyable.*" She raised her arms as if to encompass the entire tree. She caught Gael's gaze drift to her upraised chest before darting away. His ears turned red at the tips.

"This is the treasure tree. It's actually kind of famous. You might have heard of it."

"*This?* This is the treasure tree of the famous Duchesne Island treasure? I've definitely heard of it." A smile lingered on her lips. "A treasure was found here a long time ago, I understand."

"Yup. By my great-great-great-whatever."

"Really? That was your family?" She peered at him. Interesting. Perhaps it wasn't just good fortune that had driven her to him. Here was exactly the man she wanted to speak to. What forces were conspiring to help her – and more importantly, why?

"Yup, old Grandpa Smith. He and some other kids dug right here and found themselves a chest of pirate treasure." Gael shifted, his leg bouncing with contained energy. "If only there was some of that treasure left. We could use it right now."

Lola took several steps to a place equidistant between two great roots, where the earth sank into a slight depression. She brushed her foot over the dirt. "Right here?"

"That's the spot. You see that branch overhead? They found a rotted rope and pulley system there, dangling over the earth like an arrow. I guess from the first person who buried it."

Lola shot him an assessing look. Gael was going to be an asset; he just needed a little push in the right direction. "Did you ever wonder if there was any more?"

"That's an old sailor's tale. I'm guessing you've heard that too? The shaft was too well built, and the treasure was buried too far down to *only* be hiding a chest full of gold. I wouldn't be picky, though. I think a chest full of gold would be plenty good enough."

Lola hummed, as though considering. "Just thinking out loud, but imagine if my family was desperate for money, and I also happened to be the owner of a mysterious, famous treasure site. In that case, I might want to dig around to see what I could find."

He narrowed his eyes. "You're one of those treasure hunters, aren't you? God, you wouldn't be the first. People are constantly trying to buy the land."

"Why don't you sell it?" Lola asked, genuinely puzzled. It would be an obvious solution to this family's miseries.

"Something complicated about the deeds to the land." Gael's tone went flat, as though he'd repeated this many times before. "Only a Smith has the right to dig here. So even if somebody did find something, it wouldn't belong to them. So, it's not worth trying."

Lola closed her eyes. She was losing him; she'd have to get more creative.

She stood in front of him, one hand on her uptilted hip. "Well, Gael Smith, I figure you are one of those Smiths that deed is talking about. And it so happens I am in the market to offer you some help. I have some experience with this kind of thing." He stiffened, and she hastened to add, "I'm not interested in the treasure."

He glared, unconvinced. "Then what's in it for you?"

She gave him an impish smile and held out her hand to help him to his feet. She didn't step back as he rose, so they were only inches apart. She tilted her head up, delighted to watch the tips of his ears redden again. "The adventure, of course."

He was still for several heartbeats, and she could feel the heat rise from his body. He wanted her, but she wanted him to want more than that. She wanted him to want the treasure, for this to be his idea. That everything he had ever wished for was coming to him, if only he was willing to dig for it. As she gazed into his eyes, she noticed his irises were rimmed in the same gold as Spanish doubloons. She was certain she had him, then his brow crinkled. "Hey, you've got something on your neck. Is that...blood?"

Without taking her gaze from his, Lola put her hand over her offending throat. "I must have scratched it in the woods. Or, you know, maybe someone threw a rock at my head."

"Oh." Gael stumbled back over a root. The tension of the moment broke, like a candle snuffed out in the breeze. His face fully aflame, he righted himself. "I'm really sorry about that."

"I'm not. It got you to talk to me, didn't it?" She let her smile take full effect. "And, if you're willing, I'll be back again tomorrow, shovel in hand. What do you think?"

Gael rubbed the back of his neck, a bemused smile on his face. "I think I hardly have a chance, if I'm up against you."

Not a single one. "I'll be here at sunset." She eased into the surrounding darkness before he had a chance to think it over.

Out of sight, she scrubbed at her neck, cursing the oversight. She really needed a shower. And, apparently, a shovel.

THREE

Port Despardoux, once a thriving port town, had been bypassed centuries ago for bigger cities on the mainland. Now little more than a fishing village, it came alive in the summer as tourists flooded its beaches, eager for a glimpse of the supernatural phenomena for which the island was famous.

The town hall, resplendent with a grandiose clocktower, faced the equally overdone art deco hotel on the other side of the square. Most of the buildings here were brick, wrought iron decorations spilling from rooflines and flowers overflowing from window boxes.

The scent of roses and lilacs wafted from the florist's tubs on display, mingled with fried seafood from the restaurant next door. Lola wrinkled her nose against the heavy scents, both unwelcome to her hunter's senses. She had preferred the rain-fresh cedars of the forest.

A gazebo stood in the grassy square, pastel colours and gingerbread curlicues evoking a grandeur from times past. Lola gazed at the empty building, imagining this deserted space filled with families out for a picnic, teenagers playing football on the grass, and sunlight everywhere. Of course, music would be playing, maybe the high school band choking out something brassy. Or no: something softer, a single fiddler playing, the lonely notes hovering in the air in the evening sun.

She shook her head at the image, unsure where it had come from. Her mind had been buzzing since arriving on Duchesne, odd images floating past her mind's eye. Whatever phantoms roamed this island, they were haunting her as well.

She ambled down the cobblestoned Main Street. The buildings jutted out at unusual angles against the steep road, more weathered here, with faded clapboards and wooden shingles. From the second floor above one of them, a statue of a pig-tailed girl leaned out of the window as though calling out to someone. Lola shivered at the metal eyes gazing unseeing down on her.

The shop itself specialized in the occult, playing up the island's haunted reputation. A faded sign promised tarot readings and books on local ghost stories. She paused to admire the window display. Part of the shop was devoted to tokens for St. Elmo, the patron saint of sailors. The rest was taken over by skulls, jars of potions and artifacts from the island, eerie in the dim lighting. It was possible some were genuine items, filled with otherworldly energy, but likely they were nothing more than trinkets for tourists.

The lanes were lined with bicycles, the easiest way to get around in a crowded space like this. The tight streets of the old town would make driving a nuisance.

As the captain had warned her, things were quiet at this time of night on a Sunday. Most of the hotels were boarded up until the tourist season began. Finding a room was difficult on your own when you looked like a teenager, especially in a town that wasn't expecting guests. In a big city, you could always find a place that took cash upfront and didn't ask any questions. In a place like this, people asked lots of questions. She was lucky she had stumbled over dinner and shelter in one go, last night.

The old fisherman had looked at her like she was a dream. "Are ye an angel?" he asked in a hoarse voice. "Come te take me awa'?"

Lola had approached him, glowing. "Would you like that? I will give you the peace you crave."

Entranced, he barely made a sound as she bit into him. His face still held that look of wistful wonder when she was done. When she slipped his corpse into the briny water over the dock, his eyes seemed to follow her as he sank, colour leeching from him as he disappeared.

The alcohol in his blood had made her dizzy. With luck, if his body was found, it would be assumed he had tumbled over the edge and drowned.

Now, the idea of such an inconsequential death made her chest tighten. She had never considered the life or end of her meals before, and now it made her skin crawl. She shook out her arms until the feeling passed. The only lit window along Main Street drew her in, and she approached to distract herself from her disturbing thoughts.

Over the shop door hung a metal sign: *The Pain Perdu, Patisserie and Café*. And in the window were glorious cakes and confections: éclairs, croissants au chocolat, millefeuilles, sugared beignets. Everything was magazine-perfect, dripping with chocolate and crystalline fruit. Lola found herself pressed against the glass, taking it all in like a child in front of the Christmas toy display.

The draw was puzzling. She couldn't eat this food. Yet this place spoke of comfort to her. The door opened, and warm chocolate-laden air wafted out into the night sky. Memories half-remembered floated through her mind as she inhaled.

A low chuckle broke her reverie. Lola's eyes snapped open. A woman stood in the doorway, watching her with obvious amusement.

Lola eyed the woman warily. She hated when people saw her with her guard down.

The woman had long dark hair in a plait hanging over her

shoulder and a cherubic face, with rosy cheeks. Her arms were crossed over a flour-dusted apron.

"Hey, hon, I'm closing up shop soon," the woman called. "Why don't you come on in and get yourself something."

Lola backed away. "I was just looking."

A flicker passed through the woman's eyes. "Come warm up. I insist. It's on the house."

She turned back into the patisserie without waiting, giving Lola the chance to walk away. That's what she should do, but some impulse had her following the woman into the warm fragrant air. Lola paused over the threshold, dizzy with it.

"Have a seat at the counter," the woman said. Her voice was husky, like someone who laughed too much, drank too much, lived too much. "What can I get you?"

The countertop display contained even more delights: cookies, cakes, fruit pies. Lola's fingertips played over the glass. "Just a black coffee."

The woman looked her up and down with a raised eyebrow. "You sure about that? You look like you could use some meat on your bones."

"It's all I want."

The woman disappeared into the back. Alone, Lola took in greedy gulps of the air, trying to find the memories that passed just out of reach. She pressed her palms down on the countertop, hard. It was as though something had unleashed inside her chest and was unfurling, causing her to unravel. Was it the curse of the island?

The baker returned to the counter and stopped, taking in her expression. Her face creased with concern. "Are you alright?"

"I'm fine."

"Well, hon, if you don't mind me saying, you look hungry." She held a plate stacked high with sweet baked bread, which she set in front of Lola. Maple and cinnamon mingled irresistibly, and Lola closed her eyes in pleasure.

"It's my specialty, French toast. In French, it's called—"

"*Pain perdu*," Lola finished in her mother tongue.

The woman gave a low whistle. "Beautiful accent," she said. "Where are you from?"

Lola paused for a long moment, unsure if she wanted to answer. "Paris," she finally said. "Originally."

"The City of Lights." The baker's eyes lit up. "I trained to be a *patissier* there. Loved every minute of it. How lucky you are to have grown up there. What arrondissement did you live in?"

"Hmm." Lola didn't want to delve further into her past with this woman. Especially since she didn't know it. "I left when I was a child. I barely remember it."

"Well, I would never forget it. The history, the beauty, the food. Mmm, the men." Her eyes fluttered closed, then popped open. "Sorry, I get carried away when I think about it."

Lola held in a laugh. She shouldn't be connecting with the locals, but the woman's lusty love of life was impossible to ignore. "All of Paris is designed to make the blood race. Including her men."

The baker shot Lola a cagey look. "Very elegantly said. You speak like my grandmother. She was French as well."

Lola raised one shoulder, an insouciant moue on her lips. The woman chuckled again.

"Ah yes, the Gallic shrug. You truly are French. I'm Faye Ducharme, by the way. I own this place, but I'm from away, like you."

"From away?"

"If you're not local, you're from away, and the locals will all make sure you remember it."

"How long until you become local?"

"Depends on the person. I've been here for more than a decade, but I'm still from away. Could be a few more years. Could be several generations. Some people will always be from away."

The tinkling bell announced a new customer, and Faye glanced to the front door before tapping on the counter beside the French toast. "*Maintenant, tu manges.*" Faye used the informal French, as many Canadians did. "There's more if you'd like some."

Lola watched the front door out of the corner of her eye to see who had entered. A sturdy-looking man with deep brown skin hustled into the café, huffing under his heavy coat.

"At least one place in this damn town is still open," the man said, his voice harsh and low. "I arrived here an hour ago, and everything shuts down at some hick-early hour."

"I was about to close, actually." Faye's tone was cool.

As he took in Faye, his sour expression shifted to something else Lola couldn't quite determine. "Please, miss, I'm begging you. A cup of coffee and a crust of bread. There's nothing in my cupboard but the mice that came with it, and I don't want to eat them tonight."

Faye gazed at him for an extra moment, letting him sweat, before softening. "I think I can do you better than a crust of bread." She looked him up and down. "A baguette, with prosciutto?"

The man's features softened. "Yes. Far better than what I expected."

"Let's see if we can't raise your expectations a little higher." At this, Faye laughed, a low enticing sound that shivered over Lola's skin, like a weak supernatural ripple. She glanced over her shoulder, eyes narrowed on the baker. Did the magic of the island permeate everything and all its people, or did Faye possess her own form of bewitchment?

The man raised an eyebrow and sat at the table, warm brown eyes following Faye like a puppy dog. "Actually, I looked up your shop before I came. I heard you have the best chocolate croissants in the province."

"Compliments will get you everywhere." Faye looked back over her shoulder. "I'll see what I can dig up." She swayed to the back on high heels. She had clearly inherited some of her French grandmother's feminine wiles. Faye held court in her café like an enchantress.

Once she was out of sight, the man's sharp eyes travelled over the café, landing on her. Lola stared at her plate, shoulders hunched. She did not want to stir up interest, especially not from someone as observant as he seemed to be.

After his gaze had passed her by, Lola noticed a newspaper behind the counter and snatched it up. The *Duchesne Daily*. Laying it open in front of her, with a cup of hot coffee in her hand, gave her a shiver of pleasure she didn't quite understand, as though she was exactly where she was supposed to be. She read of the weekly comings and goings on the island, including a full weather report and ferry schedule. She eavesdropped as Faye returned to the other customer with a large sandwich, croissant, and a steaming cup of coffee.

"You're a sight for sore eyes," he said, and Lola rolled her eyes at the cliché. Faye didn't seem to mind, though, and stayed with him, hand on her hip.

"You said you've only just arrived in town. Are you here for business or pleasure?"

"Business, although I had hoped there would be more pleasure involved." Some of the levity dropped from his voice. "I'm with the RCMP. I transferred from Ontario."

"RCMP, is it? I'm surprised; I wouldn't have guessed."

"Why not?" His tone was prickly, as though he was used to defending himself.

She snorted. "Because you crawled into my shop like a bedraggled vagrant, begging for food. I would expect our new captain to be slightly more presentable."

"I'm as presentable as they come, with a proper meal in me."

Faye's lips curled into a half-smile. "I'll keep that in mind." Lola fought to keep in a laugh.

"How did you know I was the new captain?"

"Well, I certainly know now, don't I? Besides, our last captain retired a few months ago."

"Huh. Small town, hey? I guess everyone knows everything around here."

"It's going to seem awfully small to you, after the big city."

"That was the point. Something quiet…"

"Provincial?" Faye's tone had bite.

"Peaceful. I worked in organized crime before, and it damn near killed me. Literally. I was looking for a tranquil life from here on out. Only…things didn't work out that way. I got called in early."

"This doesn't have to do with the body found by the wharf this morning, does it?"

The new RCMP started, his chair scraping against the tiled floor. "How the hell do you know about that?"

"I heard it was Anthony Graves," Faye continued. "Everyone knows he was a drunk. He hired himself out to the fishermen when they needed a hand. I assumed he finally drank himself into his grave."

There was a pause, then the policeman laughed. "Shit. Small town indeed."

Lola went utterly still. *Merde.* She had messed up, and for once the currents hadn't been working in her favour. His body should have washed out to the Atlantic. By the time he was found, she'd hoped the creatures of the sea would have made it unlikely for the cause of death to be determined.

Now, there would be a murder investigation on the man. And she was squatting in his shack. *Merde* again.

"Was there something more to it?" Faye leaned over slightly further than necessary and topped up his coffee.

"Er. I can't discuss the details…"

"Of course you can't." Faye's tone was soothing. "What did you say your name was?"

"Captain Theodore Greyson. Everyone calls me Greyson."

Lola slipped out of the door of the café. Neither of them looked up to see her go, although she got the sense Captain Greyson was aware of everything that happened around him. She would have to be very careful from here on out.

Four

The mist was thick and soupy the next afternoon as Lola made her way to the treasure tree. Creating mist through her affinity with water was the most reliable way she could travel in the daytime, without risking the sunlight. Fortunately, Duchesne Island seemed like it enjoyed a great deal of natural fog. She needed only ask the water hovering in the air to gather around her, and it obeyed with little effort.

She could have made the hour-long journey up the trail in mere minutes, using her demonic speed, but today she relished the hike. The air was fresh and cool over her skin, even as anticipation buzzed through her. She was going to see Gael soon, the tasty morsel who had fallen into her hands so easily.

When she arrived, he stood under the oak tree, leaning on a shovel. He peered into the swirls of fog, looking lost.

"I'm here!" Lola called, and his head shot toward the sound of her voice, taking a moment to distinguish her from the mist. A slow smile crept over his face before he could wipe it clean to a neutral expression.

"Oh, hey, you came. That's cool." He picked at the tag on his shovel.

"You didn't think I would come?" She carried a heavily rusted shovel over her shoulder, taken from an unlocked shed in town.

He laughed then, and she liked the rich sound of it. "A part of me still thinks I imagined you yesterday. I definitely didn't think you would come."

"Why not? What girl wouldn't jump at the chance to dig for treasure with you?"

"I would guess about every girl in school, and probably some who aren't even in school. You don't have to be in school to not want to hang out with me."

Lola paused, taking him in. "I don't believe you. Are all the girls you know blind?"

Gael gave a small smile but shrugged. "I'm...well...this nerdy kid who everyone's known since forever."

"Nerdy. You mean intelligent? Please, that clearly isn't it."

Gael looked uncomfortable. "I don't exactly fit in. I'm not... the same as everyone else."

"I don't understand."

"This island, it's not exactly a diverse place, you know? Like, stuck in another era. My mum's Bolivian, and we stick out. The other kids pick up on that."

Lola stared. "Oh. That I do understand."

Gael shook his head. "Now I don't believe you. When have you ever not fit in?"

Lola turned away from him, chin tilted up. "You don't know everything about me."

"True. I don't know anything about you." Gael's gaze travelled over her face before he hoisted his shovel. It looked like his smile came easy, even after everything he'd been through. "Let's get digging."

"After you." Lola gestured at the dirt with a wide sweep of her arm. "This is your hunt, your treasure, after all."

He nodded as though bracing himself, then thrust his shovel into the earth and overturned it. They both paused as if something special was going to happen. But it was only dirt, and he kept on going, so she stepped over to help him.

"How wide will we go?" he asked.

"Six foot by six foot should be good," Lola said, gesturing to the outline she could see in her head.

They dug in then. Lola savoured the moment, one where all things were going well. They were rare in any treasure hunt, and especially in one that meant her life or death.

The soil here was loose and sandy, easy to dig. It had obviously been dug out before, which would speed things up.

"You know what you're doing," Gael said, watching as Lola casually scooped earth again and again.

"I've done this a time or two before." She paused to lean against her shovel, fluttering her eyelashes at him.

"Are you a professional treasure hunter, or is this just a hobby?"

"I guess you could say it's the family business."

"You travel around with your family and dig for treasure? That's so cool."

Lola straightened and pretended to wipe sweat from her brow. "My family..." She trailed off, looking away to feign sadness. "They're not actually with me anymore. I'm alone." She let the words seep into the silence. "But this is the only thing I know how to do."

"God, Lola, I'm so sorry. I shouldn't have pressed."

She shook her head, and to her horror, a strange pressure closed her throat. What was this horrible feeling? The thought of her crew, the only family she had ever known, turning on her, was opening a gaping hole in her chest. She found her grief wasn't feigned. She cleared her throat. "It's okay. I know you have troubles of your own. I don't want to burden you with mine. We can each only hold a certain amount of trauma, right?"

Gael came to her side and put an arm around her shoulder. His scent surrounded her, shaking her out of the inconvenient feelings lashing over her. "Like you said, maybe it's easier to share with a stranger."

He really had no idea what he was doing, doling out kindness as though there would always be more to spend. His T-shirt crept up, exposing a thin band of tan skin over his beltline. He was building up a sweat; Lola was so close she could very nearly taste the salt. Underneath that, there would be the tang of coppery blood. This young man was distracting in so many ways.

She stepped out of the circle of his arms before she did something she couldn't take back. "I know a little bit about the Duchesne Island treasure," she said, to focus them both on something else. "All treasure hunters know about it, but you probably know so much more than I do. The shaft your great-great-whatever found was well constructed, right? A deep tunnel through the clay, going straight into the earth, filled with loose soil. Boys with shovels were able to make easy work of it."

"Easy, sure, if moving tons of earth is easy for you." Gael mopped at his brow with his t-shirt. Lola wished he would stop doing that; it was too easy to lean into him, to breathe in his scent, and she was worried she couldn't maintain her self-control. Already, the desire to sink her teeth into the soft V where his neck met his shoulder was crushing. Her fangs started to push at her gums, demanding to be unleashed.

She straightened, blinking, trying to regain mastery over herself. "Only they found sturdy wooden platforms they had to break through."

"That's right, every ten feet or so. They knew there must be something good buried down there."

"Yes, a chest full of treasure."

"And a giant stone with carvings on it."

"Carvings?" Lola knew this part of the story, too, but wanted to get Gael's take.

"A big rock, almost like a boulder, had been smoothed on one side, with carvings marked on it. No one ever figured out the markings."

"What do they look like?"

"Weird dots and lines."

Cold interest curled inside Lola. She licked her lips as her mouth went dry. Like the markings on her map of Duchesne. "Like constellations?"

Gael looked up, as though trying to remember something, and gave a slow nod. "Yes, I think you're right. Nobody's been able to figure out what it says. Some said it just marked the treasure. But other people thought it was a warning."

"Warning of what?"

"*The curse of Duchesne!*" Gael put on a dramatic accent, enjoying telling his family's tale. "Some figure it warns whoever disturbs the treasure will be doomed."

"Why?"

"A lot of accidents happened. One of the boys fell and broke both legs in the hole. And all of the discoverers of the treasure died early deaths. My great-great-whatever was the only one to have a family, and he died shortly after that."

His face darkened, and Lola couldn't read his expression. "What happened to him?"

Gael shrugged. "Nobody knows for sure. He left his wife and baby at home and went out to sea one morning. It was clear blue when he left, but a storm blew in. No one ever saw him again, and his boat was never found either."

Lola paused. "Do you think maybe he just...left?"

There was a strained silence. Gael had stopped digging and was squinting at the sky. He had certainly considered it. "I don't know," he said finally. "It would be sad if he had died at sea, but I think I prefer that story to one where he left his wife and kids all alone."

Lola did not comment on how the story had changed ever so slightly. There was more there, and it was not the time to push.

Besides, it was refreshing to be around someone who would actively think the best of others. Anyone on her crew would have automatically assumed the old man had skedaddled.

Gael stood over his shovel, panting. They'd been working for some time. He would need a break, so Lola leaned back and pretended to sag with fatigue.

"Do you mind stopping for a break?" she asked.

Relief flashed over his face. "If that's what you'd like." He braced himself at the lip and hoisted himself out. "I can't believe how far we've dug. This is insane. It's nearly six feet deep!"

"We've dug a grave." Lola accepted his hand up out of the hole.

"Whoa, you gave me shivers."

Lola gave a light laugh. "Sorry, I couldn't help myself. It's so easy to dig this soil," she reinforced, hoping he hadn't noticed how much of the earth she had moved herself. If she had been alone, unconstrained, she could have done much, much more. "It is getting deep. We'll need other supplies, I think. Buckets."

"Yes, we can rig a pulley system. We can use the tree branch used by the pirates, once upon a time."

She accepted the bottle of water and pretended to take a sip. She didn't sweat and didn't need the replenishment. Now, if it were coffee, she would happily take the stuff. Caffeine bubbled and fizzed in the veins, giving life to the blood she stole. She delicately wiped her lip before continuing. "I love all this talk of graves and pirates and curses."

Gael sat on a root. "It's not only the treasure that was cursed. This whole island is cursed, according to legend." Gael spread his hands out. "These oaks are protected. We could have made a fortune in the timber industry, but nobody wants to disturb the curse."

Lola arched her eyebrow. "I'm surprised nobody risked it."

"Some have," Gael admitted. "Even when I was a young boy, a developer tried to clear some of this land. I remember my da was so excited about the prospect of getting out of the fishing business.

But then everything went wrong. Machines broke, there were sabotages, bad things kept happening until finally, the developer called it quits, completely broke. Da was devastated."

Lola stared into the dark forest, listening to the call of the birds. Where was his da now? But she didn't ask the question.

"I am happy the trees are untouched. They are special." Lola placed a careful hand on the treasure oak. This one, in particular, called to her. Again she felt that slow heartbeat. It hid something precious, of that she was sure. Perhaps it led the way to unlimited power. Or her death. She stared at the knotty bark, which seemed to peer back at her, inscrutable.

"You sound like Diego. He loves it out here. He used to take his tent and set up camp in the middle of the forest. It drove my mum halfway crazy, worrying about him, but he's fearless." Gael drooped, his lips twisting for a moment.

"How old is he?" Lola asked quietly.

"Twelve now. Twelve years old."

She slipped her hand into his, her fingers entwining with his. "He sounds like a tough one."

Gael's smile was lopsided. "When he's back home, I'll take him camping out here whenever he wants. It's a bit spooky, to be honest. Like you're in another world." He gazed into the sombre trees, swirling with mist. "It makes me think about a poem by Robert Frost, the woods being dark and deep."

"*The woods are lovely, dark and deep / but I have promises to keep / And miles to go before I sleep,*" Lola recited, her smile dimpling. "I love that one."

Gael gave a bashful laugh. "Me too. The forest is like that; it holds secrets. The trees are supposed to be sacred."

Lola let her gaze linger on his face, his lips, wondering what it would be like if she pressed hers against his. She couldn't help it; she wanted him. It wasn't feigned in any way. Maybe she could use this to her advantage. She could control him, and enjoy herself as well. She had learned that from Beau, after all, from their tumultuous decades together.

She moved in closer, her knee grazing his. Gael stared at their legs where they touched. "I have to say, I find it odd other girls haven't noticed you."

"Maybe you're seeing me wrong."

"I don't think so." She wanted to run her fingers over his arms, ropy with muscles and tinged with sweat.

She was close enough to count the rings of gold around his irises. "I see you fine." She inhaled the cinnamon scent of his skin and glanced at his lips. She needed to stay in control. Could she indulge in him, without taking too much? She trailed her hand up his arm.

"Whoa, you're so cold." He took her hand and ran his thumb along her palm. Delicious shivers travelled down her arm.

"It must be the weather." Her faded heartbeat picked up as he smiled slowly.

"That must be it."

She held her breath as he reached out. His hand trembled, as though unsure of what he was doing, but he smoothed a hand over her hair and tugged on a curl. Her nerves frayed.

She should pull back, reassess the situation before she got too far out of control. But her deeper urges betrayed her once again. She leaned forward, her lips a breath away from his. A spray of goosebumps rippled over her body.

Underneath her, the tree's pulse matched her own, as living warmth pooled heavy inside of her.

She let out a gasp at the heat, unheard of for a vampire. The want, the hunger, flared into something darker, and Lola jerked back, staring at his pulse pounding in his throat. She wanted all of him. And if she let herself, she was going to destroy him.

Her gums vibrated, canines elongating, and she ripped herself out of his arms. She brought her hand up to her mouth, staring at him in horror.

"What is it?" Gael asked. He ran his hand through his hair, eyebrows scrunching together.

Trembling with her need, she shook her head, furious at herself, and stumbled away. "I really should be getting home," she said, lisping through her fangs. "It's late."

Gael stood and took a step after her. She held out a hand to keep him at a distance.

"Can I see you again? Tomorrow?"

She gave a shaky nod and fled. She could only pray he wouldn't follow her.

After several minutes of hard running, she had put the oak forest between her and Gael. She slowed to a trot, clenching and opening her fists, fighting the urge to feed, trying to leash her runaway thoughts. She had wanted him, the sweet boy who knew of curses.

She wanted his blood, but there was something more. *He* made her think there might be more to have, which left her crouching on the forest floor, hands dug deep into her hair. What was that? In all her long undead life, she had never felt *that* before. A longing for something she never had.

Lola wrapped her arms around herself. For a moment back there, she had felt warm. Whatever had gotten into her, it had to stop. Her desire to feed from him was far more intense than it had a right to be. If she got her fangs into him, she didn't know if she would ever be able to stop.

FIVE

Restless, Lola hunted wildlife through the night and was still unable to settle. She was unsure if it was her encounter with Gael, or the energy of the island that seemed to prickle over her skin, but instead of resting she paced the fisherman's shack. The walls were covered with bright-coloured buoys and nets that reeked of the sea. Lola did everything she could to avoid touching the walls. Black mould crept up around the sink, and the shower was so fetid she could taste it.

She wanted to open a window, allow the clean ocean breeze to come and freshen the air, but she couldn't touch anything. Since Anthony Grave's death had been deemed suspicious, an open investigation meant the police had already done a thorough search. Led by the newly minted Captain Greyson, they turned the shack inside out, while Lola watched from underneath the dock. The captain, who seemed to see everything, was going to be inconvenient. And she couldn't trust he wouldn't come back. That meant she'd have to stay on her toes, her grab bag always at the ready. It also meant she couldn't clean the shack.

But its location suited her purposes nicely, so Lola was reluctant to move. And feeding on someone else was out of the question, for the moment.

Lola squinted at the light outside, waiting for nightfall. She wouldn't pull the mist in from the ocean until necessary. She needed to rest, but was still spinning from Gael yesterday, the heady *feelings* that swirled through her, as unwanted as sunshine. If she continued to lose control, as she nearly had, she wasn't sure what was going to happen on this dig.

Should she stop what she was doing? The thought was nonsensical. Things were going according to plan. She had followed through on her strategy: enlist the help of a local. Get him to do what she wanted.

It was true she felt a pull toward him. There was a substance to him rarely found in one his age. But she couldn't let her sympathy get in the way of what needed to be done. She snorted, incensed for even thinking this way. What was he to her, anyway? He would help her, and she would get what she wanted. There was no problem here. If she didn't find the Well of Soul treasure, if it didn't live up to the legends and provide her with the power to protect herself, Beau would eventually find her. And that would be the end.

It was long past midday, and Gael would be waiting for her; she was sure of it. She had given him a reason to dig. He would continue on his own without her, so they might as well work together.

But as she had discovered last night, she couldn't engage in any kind of flirtation with him. She didn't trust herself around him. But she didn't need to follow through on her desire. Gael was invested in the treasure. She didn't need to seduce him. She gave her shirt a tug, zipped to her neckline. No nonsense.

On a deep breath, she stirred the water along the shoreline with her mind's eye. The mist rose up as though waiting for her command. The cloud grew until it enveloped her, and she eyed it with distrust. Water manipulation had never been so easy, and she couldn't explain why.

When she arrived at the dig site, the hole was deeper, a pulley hanging on the overhead branch. It was rudimentary but workable.

Gael's head popped out from the hole, brightening when he saw her. Lola's heart gave a twist of longing. Keep things professional, she chided herself. *Mon dieu*, she saw him and perked up like a lustful bunny. She needed to control herself. His death would be very inconvenient to her hunt.

Gael climbed from the hole, using a weathered rope ladder attached to a nearby root. He approached her cautiously, like a wild animal.

"I didn't know if you would come. I thought I might have done something to scare you off."

She held back a mad laugh at how easily he read her and straightened her shoulders. "Do I look like the type to scare easily?"

"Not at all. But you ran away quick enough last night." He stood in front of her. "I'm sorry if I did something..." He hesitated, then reached out and pushed her hair behind her ear with devastating gentleness, his thumb grazing the upper circle of her ear.

Her knees shivered. His pulse pounded in his throat and sweat beaded at his neck. She licked her lips. She had gorged herself on deer the night before, but it was nothing compared to human blood. He would be delicious, she was sure of it. If he got any closer, she was going to hurt him or devour him, probably both. So much for controlling herself. She had set out to seduce him, and now she was spinning out. She leaned into his heat. "Gael..."

"There you are," a bright voice called out from the forest.

Both Lola and Gael whirled as a slight redheaded girl crashed into the clearing.

"I'm surprised I found you at all. This is some freaky mist, it's so effing thick, but I remembered how you hang out at the treasure tree when you're being weird, so I figured this is where you'd be hiding..."

She nearly bulldozed right into them, heading towards the edge of the hole. Gael lunged to grab her arm before she tumbled in.

"The hell?" The girl brushed him off, taking in the scene: the hole, the ladder, the rusty bucket dangling above. But her sky-blue eyes fixated on Lola. Her fair, freckled skin splotched into red patches.

"Oh, wow. Um, I didn't expect you to be with someone." She pulled her gaze from Lola and glowered at Gael from under coppery brows.

"Nix, hey." Gael rubbed the back of his neck. "This is Lola. Um, I met her the other day. Lola, this is Arabella Nix."

"*Enchantée*, Arabella." Lola stepped forward and held out her hand to the girl, who stared at it a long moment before taking it.

More colour flooded Nix's cheeks until she was bright as a tomato. "Just Nix, actually. Only my Mum calls me Arabella, and then only if I'm in trouble."

"Just Nix, then." Lola smiled, and the girl stepped back, rubbing her arms.

She turned to Gael. "What are you doing here? I thought we were going to the wharf, but you ran out of class."

Gael's eyes widened. "I completely forgot! Shit, I don't know what to say. Sorry, Nix. I've been distracted."

"I can see that." Nix shot a pointed look at Lola, then looked away, pressing her lips together in a hard line.

She wasn't a girl to hide her emotions. Nix was short and boyish, with a flaming mane of long red curls she scraped back into an elastic. She didn't play it up, but she had the most enviable head of hair Lola had ever seen.

"We were supposed to watch the lobster boats come in," Gael

explained to Lola. "Today, we celebrate the fishermen and have an unofficial-official lobster festival."

"It's tradition," Nix told Lola sternly, as though this was her fault.

"We buy fish pies, and...we do it every year." Gael scratched his arm, staring at the ground.

"It sounds amazing," Lola said. After a strained pause, she continued. "Do you want to go?"

Gael shuffled his feet as Nix glared. "It's too late to catch the boats," she said. "We'll have to wait until next year." She let out a huff, crossing her arms.

Gael peeked at her. "There's still all the festival stuff going on. We don't have to miss all of it."

"That stuff doesn't get started until later anyways." She turned her glare to the hole. "What's this?"

"I ran into Lola here, who knows a bit about the island's history, and the treasure, and we got talking...we thought we'd see what we could find."

"Nobody's allowed to dig here," Nix said. "That's island law."

"Nobody but me. It's in the deeds."

"But you *hate* treasure hunters," Nix continued, with a nasty look at Lola. "All those times I've heard you going on about money-hungry bastards—"

"That's enough, Nix." Gael's ears turned scarlet, and he scratched at the back of his head.

"I'm more interested in the history than the money," Lola said. "Wouldn't it be incredible to be part of a treasure find like this? The legends say there must be more to the Duchesne treasure. And it's right here. I don't think we should miss out on an opportunity like this."

"Nix, it could help," Gael said under his breath. The way Nix softened, Lola could tell she knew of his family's troubles. "I mean, my family could use a bit of good luck. Why not see if we could find something, even a few spare coins? It would pay the bills."

Nix took a reluctant step to the edge of the hole. She whistled as she looked down. "You've already gone so far." Her sharp gaze pierced Gael. "How long has this been going on?"

"We started yesterday," Gael said, a placating hand on her shoulder. "The dirt is ridiculously easy to dig."

"It's already been dug before," Lola said. "It moves quickly."

Nix turned narrowed eyes on her. "And you're what? Some kind of professional? You don't look any older than us."

Lola chose her words carefully. "I'm... looking for an adventure." She gave Nix a crooked smile, aiming to disarm her.

"And you are Lola...?"

"Monteux," Lola supplied for her.

"Monteux," Nix repeated, pouting her lips as she imitated Lola's accent. "And, what, you're like, French?"

"Yes, actually."

The girl in her baggy jeans and prickly attitude might prove to be an opportunity. A buffer, at least, between Lola and Gael. She wasn't likely to succumb to any of her desires with this spiky girl standing in between them.

"Would you like to join us?" Lola asked.

Gael looked like he might argue, but Lola shot him a beaming smile. "Things will go quicker. We'll be counting your riches in a week."

Nix stared into the hole. "Do you really think there's something to find down there?"

She was on the edge. Lola stepped next to her, gazing into the dark loamy earth as well. "Only one way to find out," she whispered.

Nix smiled then, one that transformed her sharp face into fae beauty. "Okay, then. Should I get a shovel?"

They took turns digging and hoisting the bucket full of earth up to throw to the side. Despite her initial suspicion, Nix was hard-working, and they progressed swiftly. Two hours later, both

Gael and Nix dripped with sweat, and Lola pretended she was exhausted as well, running her sleeve over her neck.

"Should we take a break?" she asked.

Nix climbed to the top of the ladder and collapsed against a root, wiping at her sopping forehead. "All this for a few coins that probably don't exist?"

"That's the attitude." Gael handed her a bottle of water from his backpack. Lola waved off the one he held out for her.

"Kidding." Nix drank deeply, gasping at the end. She wiped her mouth with the back of her hand. "But I feel like we're going to need better equipment if we're going to actually get anywhere. I know my island history. Wasn't the original hole more than seventy feet deep? I don't know if a bucket is going to get us there anytime soon."

"The boys who discovered this site wouldn't have had much more than that," Lola pointed out.

"I guess." Nix's brows pulled tight. "But real treasure hunters have real equipment, don't they? We're total amateurs here. At least a metal detector would come in handy to find loose coins. A couple of guys sweep the beaches with theirs, right? Maybe we could borrow one."

Lola stared into the depths like the well might reveal its secrets. She knew from experience that humans with massive machines could easily destroy a delicate dig. The fastest way was not always the best. "Maybe we're supposed to do it like this."

"It's not like I can afford anything else," Gael said. "A bucket is pretty much my financial investment here."

"If you say so. I'm not exactly flush either." Nix gave an elaborate roll of the shoulders. "But if you ask me, we've done enough for today. We deserve a treat. Let's show the new girl around." She wiggled her eyebrows at Gael. "Lost Souls? The party should have started by now."

Gael groaned. "We don't have to go to Lost Souls. Every time is exactly the same."

"This time, it will be different." Nix leapt to her feet, bouncing on her toes. "This time, Lola will be with us."

"What's Lost Souls?" Lola asked, hesitant to get further involved.

"It's a bar in town. Technically it's a restaurant because minors are allowed. But everyone goes there. Sometimes there's live music." Nix grabbed Gael's arm and pulled him to his feet. She hesitated, then held out a hand to Lola as well. Her hand lingered a moment longer than necessary, and then Nix pulled it away as though burned. She covered this with a too-bright smile. "Come on, you'll like it. Or maybe not, but it's the only place worth going to this time of year."

Gael turned the full weight of his soulful gaze on her. "Come on, Lola, it will be fun."

Merde, but she loved the way her name sounded on his lips. She should leave them in peace. A proper vampire would never consider mingling with the edibles.

And yet, that was a part of the problem. As she worked alongside Gael and Nix, she felt more and more like she was one of them. She felt almost as though she was a teenage girl.

But that couldn't be right. Vampires weren't even able to feel. Since she'd arrived on Duchesne, everything inside of her had been blown off course. She would tell them no, then spend the night hunting deer and drinking from their still-warm bodies.

"Is it a part of this festival?" she asked instead.

Nix and Gael looked at each other and shrugged. "Pretty much," Gael said. "Everyone goes out tonight. Some kids at school have fake IDs so they can buy beer, which is kind of hilarious since everyone knows everyone else, but nobody's looking very hard on festival night."

Lola couldn't hide her incredulity. "This is what you do? You go to a bar and drink beer?" Gael and Nix were so fresh and clean she could make soap out of them.

Nix laughed. "God, no! My mother would kill me if she caught me drinking. Definitely not worth it. We go and drink coffee and make fun of the live acts. They're usually awful, until the summer when the real bands come to play to the tourist crowds."

"It's lame and the music is terrible." Gael's lips lifted in a half-smile. "But it will be different with you."

Nix glanced over her shoulder at him, her smile fading before turning back to Lola. "Yeah. Save us from our boring little lives."

"You're not boring. Not many people would jump into a hole to dig for gold, no matter what they say."

Gael grabbed his shovel. "Awesome. Let's go."

"I'm not sure I should." Words came back to her, spoken by Jacquotte, her former boss: *Sometimes, I think she just wants to be a normal girl.* Her chest felt like it was crushed in a vice when she remembered those overheard words. It was the reason Jacquotte signed Lola's death warrant.

She couldn't pretend she was human. She'd never survive. Or she'd slip up and destroy these fragile edibles.

Gael reached out to firmly take her hand before she could pull away. His warmth steadied her. "Who's it going to hurt?"

Everyone. You. "Okay."

SIX

Gael and Nix walked ahead in comfortable camaraderie. Gael glanced back to Lola and smiled, white teeth shining in the gathering darkness, his hair falling over his forehead. Lola's heart gave a lazy thump of approval.

She shook her head at her reaction to him. All she was trying to do was gain the locals' trust. It was convenient for her to be out with them. But even she didn't believe herself. She wanted very badly to go to Port Despardoux's unofficial-official lobster festival.

"My house is over here," Gael said as they breached the edge of the forest. The mist thinned, as though contained by the branches of the trees. A sliver of moonlight illuminated the path ahead of them. "Lola, you can leave your shovel at my shed. With the crowd that hangs out at Lost Souls, this probably constitutes a weapon."

"Thanks. I didn't really want to show up with a mud-covered shovel."

"Mud covered is right." Nix brushed at her jeans with a grimace. "Mum will kill me if she sees me."

"Your mum will kill you for about everything you do," Gael said. "I'm surprised you're still alive."

"Isn't that the truth."

Lola followed their repartee with interest. Gael, tall and dark, and Nix, tiny and fiery, were as mismatched as any two people could be. Lola jogged to catch up with them. "How did you two meet?"

"We've always known each other. We're islanders."

"I mean, how did you become friends?"

"Oh, that." Nix laughed but flushed, looking away. "We were twelve. I don't remember."

"Yes, you do." Gael watched Nix from the corner of his eye. "Ethan had grabbed my book, and he and his little gang were pushing me around. And Nix stormed up and started yelling in his face, calling him a miserable little pissant."

"Miserable piss-ant?" Lola tried this out.

Gael started to laugh. "Shocking language, back then. And Ethan wouldn't give it up, so Nix went in all elbows and wild red hair. And none of the other guys knew what to do because they're not supposed to hit a girl. And Ethan came up with a shiner, and Nix came up with the book, and we've been friends ever since."

Nix glared at Lola as though daring her to make fun.

Lola nodded. "Nicely done."

Nix shrugged, then punched Gael on the shoulder. "Anyone would have done it."

"Anyone would *not* have done it," Gael said.

"And guess what he was reading? *Great Expectations.* What twelve-year-old reads *Great Expectations*?"

A rush of blood heated Gael's cheeks.

One who wants more out of life. Lola didn't speak the thought out loud. "An intelligent one, no doubt," she said. She caught Gael's glance flicker back to her.

"Yeah, I guess," Nix said. "Still, it's no wonder he needed me so badly. He was a lot smaller back then. We were about the same size. Then he went and shot up about a foot."

"She's still got my back, though." Gael wrapped an arm around Nix's shoulder, gazing at her with devotion. Lola felt a sudden possessiveness, wanting to protect both of them. She wasn't sure why that was; she should be thinking about eating them.

"Here we are," Gael said as they sauntered down a steep incline toward a stone cottage, covered in moss and set in the hill as though it had grown right from the ground. Flowering vines overtook it all the way to the thatched roof and potent fragrance floated towards them on the night air. It might have looked like something out of a fairy tale, with the proper care and attention. But part of the wall was crumbling, and the windows were darkened, as though no one had lived there for a long time. Empty as it was, if it belonged in any children's stories, it would be the Brothers Grimm's.

"This is your house?" Lola asked.

"For what it's worth." Gael kicked at the old stones of the shed. "I'm on my own right now, and I haven't had time to do much upkeep."

"I love it."

He snorted. "Why?"

"It's cosy and ancient and holds so much history," she said. "If these stones could speak, and all that."

"If you want a speaking stone, check out Gael's fireplace," Nix called. She was prying open the deadbolt on the shed as though she'd done it before. "One of them has a message for you."

Lola glanced at Gael, questioning.

"You know the rock I told you about, the one with the etchings? Old great-great-whatever Smith had it made into the chimney. It's right over the mantle. You can see the etchings."

"The etchings nobody has ever deciphered?" Lola's fingers tingled. She was very good at deciphering ancient text. Could it offer clues as to the nature of the Well of Souls treasure?

Gael seemed to sense her eagerness. "You can come in and see it."

Before Lola jumped on the invitation, Nix threw out a deprecating hand. "That dusty old stone isn't going anywhere. Let's get into town before the festival is over."

Lola felt a surge of antipathy for the girl. Who was she to get in the way of what Lola wanted? But she swallowed down a snarl. "Okay, sure."

"Some other time, then," Gael said.

"When does your mum get back?" Nix asked Gael.

"Should be back by the end of the week."

Nix's eyebrows knitted together. "How's Diego?"

His jaw tightened. "His treatments are hard on him." There were shadows in his eyes, and Nix didn't seem to want to dig any deeper.

"So, you like history?" Nix asked Lola, clearly wanting to change the subject.

"It's fascinating." Lola kept her tone light, hoping to distract Gael. "All treasure can be found if you peer into the past. It's a matter of knowing where to look. For example, the chimney of an ancient cottage, where a mysterious message is inscribed."

"You think you could figure it out?" Nix's voice dripped with scepticism. "Other people, like educated old people, have failed to interpret it. Looks like alien writing to me."

"You'd be surprised what a fresh pair of eyes can see," Lola said.

Nix arched her eyebrows.

Lola hadn't won this girl over yet. "No more talk about musty old history. I want to see this bar you've been talking up."

"Have we talked it up?" Gael laughed. "We definitely didn't mean to. You're going to be so disappointed."

In contrast to what Lola had seen of Port Despardoux up until now, the streets near the wharf swarmed with people. The heavy fog had dissipated, and families were out enjoying the evening air. Children screeched in excitement at being out so late. Many were on bicycles, nudging their way through the crowd. It seemed as though the entire population of the town was out for their unofficial lobster festival.

"It's an entirely different place," Lola said. The smell of humanity threatened to overwhelm her senses. She dug her nails into her palms, the pain steadying. As she took in the faces around them, she could see expressions of glee, curiosity, irritation. She'd never really noticed the emotions of people around her. For the first time, she felt a corresponding pang of feeling inside her chest. This was unheard of. Humans were edibles, nothing beyond a source of convenience or food. She couldn't feel the way they felt.

"We take lobsters very seriously here," Nix was saying.

Lola shook her head, trying to focus. "I can see that. I thought..."

"What?" Gael asked.

Lola put her hands over her face. "I'm going to sound lame, but I read a guidebook about the island. And I thought your lobster festival was a few weeks away?"

Gael laughed. "You are from away. That's for tourists; it pulls in good money and starts the season. But this is for us."

Booths lined the edge of the wharf. From each, vendors tried to outsell one another with lobster rolls, fish and chips, and donairs. The scent of grease and fish mingled heavy in the air.

One of the booths bore the same painted sign as the patisserie, *The Pain Perdu*. She spotted Faye's face through the crowd, flushed pink from the heat.

Lola wondered how friendly the friendly baker had gotten with the new detective in town and smiled at the thought. Barely three days in town, and she already felt involved.

"Lost Souls, Pain Perdu...everything here is lost," she murmured. Gael heard her.

"It's because of the legend. Or one of them, anyway. Duchesne has lots of legends."

"Which one?"

"The island is surrounded by heavy reefs and hidden rocks, and the currents are tricky. Hundreds of ships were wrecked here, thousands of lives lost. It got a reputation, *le port des âmes perdu*. The Port of Lost Souls. Eventually, it dropped the souls and was bastardized by the English to Port Despardoux."

Nix elbowed him. "You sound like a tourism brochure."

"The Port of Lost Souls." Lola gazed out to sea, a calm shimmery blue tonight. What secrets hid under her tranquil face? Lola felt the water pull inside of her, as though she could lose herself to it, like all those ships and souls.

"Don't forget about the pirates, tour guide," Nix added, poking Gael's side. She perked up, talking about the island's bloody history.

"Right. The island was also a pirate haven for centuries."

"All those surrounding rocks must make it difficult to get in and out," Lola said, remembering the shoals they came through to arrive at Duchesne. "Must be a good place to hide goods."

"Exactly. Even as late as the past century, bootleggers taking Canadian whiskey to the speakeasies in the States during Prohibition would hide out here."

"Rumour has it smugglers still operate along the coast," Nix said. "There's likely so much still hidden on the island, if you're stupid enough to look for it."

"The proverbial jackpot," Lola whispered. She was absolutely stupid enough to look for it.

"If you're around this summer, you won't be the only treasure hunter, believe me," Nix said. "There's always shiploads of them coming over. Keeps my da busy."

"What does he do?"

"He's the guardian of the island." When Nix looked over her shoulder, blue eyes sharp and mischievous, Lola got the sense of a misplaced pixie.

"I'm sorry, the guardian?"

Gael gave Nix a gentle shove. "She's being melodramatic. He's the lighthouse keeper. Lights the way for the ships coming in, so they don't bash in their bows like the old schooners."

Nix gave a spritely laugh. "The Nixes have always been the

lighthouse keepers, going back way into the mists of time. It's our family business."

A man in the crowd shouted a chant. It seemed part Gaelic, part French, and people paused to listen. At a particular moment, they all raised their arms up and clapped twice, shouting. Even Gael and Nix shouted at the top of their lungs.

Lola froze, confounded, as everyone laughed, waving at others in the crowd. The chant was a tradition. Everyone belonged to this community but her, and she felt like an intruder.

People were looking her over, trying to place her. This was a local festival and she was obviously "from away." There was curiosity, even animosity in some of their gazes that caused her skin to shrink.

Her body reacted before she could even think about it. Her demonic power rose up in face of a threat, and she snarled at a woman looking her up and down with interest. The woman glanced up at Lola's face and blanched, backing away from her. It took all of Lola's discipline not to lunge after her.

Lola had to control herself before she caused a massacre. She pinched the skin of her hand, pain reminding her who she was, and she slowly mastered her instincts. The experience left her panting, and Gael and Nix were nowhere to be found. Lola dashed through a break in the press of people.

"Hey, you!" a voice called. Lola whirled in alarm before relaxing. She had come to the side of The Pain Perdu's stand and found a familiar face.

"How are you, hon?" Faye asked. "You ran out of the café so fast last night I didn't even get your name."

"Sorry about that." Lola backed away, then was jostled forward. Faye caught her, kindness in her eyes. "I'm Lola."

"Nice to meet you, Lola. Hang on." Faye handed someone a pastry, wrapped in striped paper napkins and dripping grease. She turned back to Lola. "Sorry about that. We're mad right now."

"What are you serving?"

"I have here my Duchesnen hand pies. I'm quite known for them." Her tone was happily boastful and she let out a deep belly laugh.

"What's an Duchesnen hand pie?"

"It's an island thing. Fish and potato, smothered with gravy and wrapped up in fried dough. Would you like one?"

"No, thank you."

"Hmm. Not much of an eater, are you? I bet I could change your mind if you hung around long enough."

Lola smiled. "I believe you." The crowd began their chant again, the local's way of showing they belonged to one another. Faye didn't join in. "Are you not one for chanting?"

Faye let out a full-throated laugh. "I'm not against it, but it's not my chant. Remember, I'm from away as well."

"Does it bother you to be an outsider?"

Faye shrugged. "I belong in my own way."

Lola looked over the sea of faces. "I couldn't ever imagine belonging here." The people were so close, too tight, so *human*.

"Give it time," Faye said. "This island; it gets its hooks into you. Crowd's thinning." She nodded toward the street, where fewer people pushed against the stand. Somehow, Lola had a fish pie in her hand as well.

"Thank you," she said quietly.

Faye smiled briefly, already focused on her next customer.

Lola wandered the street, bemused by Faye's gentle spell. Finally, she spotted Gael's head above the crowd. She raised her fish-pie arm and waved.

Gael and Nix wiggled through the masses to get to her side. "What happened to you? You disappeared." Gael asked.

"I got caught up in the crowd," Lola said.

"Ah, you got one of Faye's pies?" Nix said, disappointment crinkling her face. "They're the best, but the line was unreal. How'd you manage that?"

"Lucky, I guess." Gael and Nix held pies in their hands, too, wrapped in a different colour paper. Gael had two, and she flashed him a surprised smile.

He leaned down to be heard over the roar of the crowd. "Glad we found you," he said, his mouth against her hair. "We're going inside to find a table."

They stood in front of a large wooden shack at the edge of the water, little more than an unpainted barn. Large rolling doors opened to the elements, and a tangle of white lights twinkled overhead. Boisterous music came from inside, fighting with the voices of the crowd. Seawater lapped at the beams underneath the patio.

The place was rollicking with lights and music and people laughing, talking, singing, fighting. Energy swirled around them, spiralling off into the starlit sky.

As they entered, the heat hit Lola, along with the scent of stale beer and warm blood. Gael took her arm. "Welcome to Lost Souls."

SEVEN

Lola kept her head down as they eased through the crowd. The percussion of heartbeats pressed in on every side. She concentrated on keeping her fangs in check as she was inundated with a crush of humanity. *Dieu merci* she had fed the night before because this veritable feast laid out for her was one she could not touch.

Every walk of life gathered here. Weathered fishermen rubbed elbows with heavily pierced young locals. Children with their parents, bouncing at the thrill of staying up late, sat next to twenty-somethings just starting their evening. Good-natured arguments rose in the air among people who had known each other for a long time.

Several of the older men called out to Gael, and he raised his hand to them. He spread his easy smile to everyone. Nix's hair, bright like a penny, made her easy to follow as she moved between the people she had likely known since infancy.

Lola was jostled, and Gael moved in next to her, using his broad frame to give her more room. "You okay?"

"I'm fine," she shouted over the din. "Crowds aren't really my thing."

"Over here!" Nix called. Jammed to the side of the room was a small sticky table. She was in the process of haggling with another group over an extra chair so they could all sit.

"Sorry, I didn't know you had a problem with crowds," Gael said as they wiggled over to the table, where Nix placed a third chair with satisfaction.

"It's fine. It's just been a long time since I've been around so many people. I wasn't expecting this in a small town."

"It starts to get crowded when everyone gets together. We're not a shy group."

"I noticed."

The décor could best be described as shabby fisherman chic, with less emphasis on the chic. The wooden walls were painted a faded red, showcasing posters of vintage beer ads and former bands that had performed there. Baskets of peanuts were placed on each table and the shells littered the floor. The ceiling was strung with netting – thankfully not as pungent as that in the Grave shack – and bare bulbs that cast dim yellow light.

The music started up. The live act was "Drunken Danny." A man, presumably Danny, sawed on a fiddle, making one chord out of four, by Lola's count.

"You were right. The music *is* terrible," she said to the other two. "But this place is a gem."

It was the right thing to say; Gael and Nix glowed.

A waitress hurried to their table, pulling a pencil from her frazzled bun. She ran an eye over the fish pies they still held and sighed. "What'll it be?"

Lola ordered a black coffee. Nix asked for a complicated caffeinated drink-dessert, which pushed the waitress into total impatience. At the last second, Gael ordered a hot chocolate, abashed at Nix's teasing.

"I can't drink coffee this late!"

"Are you sure you don't want a cup of warm milk?" Nix dug a finger into his ribs, making him yelp with laughter.

"I'm sorry, would you like a bit of coffee with that sugar of yours?" he shot back. It was clearly an old fight, and Lola's chest twisted ever so slightly that she wasn't a part of it.

After they'd received their drink orders, Nix turned bright, inquisitive eyes on Lola. "So, where were you before coming to Duchesne?"

"I was in the Caribbean." Best to stick to the truth as much as possible.

"I've always wanted to go there," Gael said. "What's it like?"

"It was warm, and the sea life was unbelievable," Lola said. She left out the part where her crew had declared her life forfeit and she had fled over the side of their yacht in the middle of the night.

"And what were you doing there?" Nix's gaze tracked her with intensity.

Lola chose her words carefully. "Looking for a shipwreck."

"Wow, that's *so* weird. Who were you doing this with?"

Lola narrowed her eyes, unwilling to share this part. "My family," she settled on. Her crew, her clan, the vampires who had made her, were as close to family as she had ever known. Her stomach filled with acid at the thought.

"I thought your parents were gone?" Gael said.

Lola shrugged. "It's complicated."

"So, you came to the island, by yourself, after searching for a shipwreck in the Caribbean. And you randomly stumbled across Gael and convinced him to dig for treasure?"

Lola squirmed under Nix's scrutiny. Gael kicked Nix under the table. "Stop giving her the third degree."

"I want to get to know her. No harm in that."

Lola eyed her, tilting her head to the side. Few people were as genuinely bold as she was. Then Nix went rigid. "Assholes incoming," she said out of the corner of her mouth.

Gael glanced up, then hunched in on himself. Lola followed his gaze, tensing. Should she be worried?

Making their way to their table was a swaggering group of

teens. The boys were tall and athletic; the girls were heavily made up. They bore themselves with a confidence Lola understood immediately. Her entire vampire life had centred around a strict pecking order, one in which she always found herself at the bottom. Like Beau, like Jacquotte, these teens were the alphas of their world.

A girl stepped up to the table. She wore a mauve sleeveless polo shirt with a matching pleated skirt. Her carefully highlighted blonde hair and designer bag screamed 'Queen Bee.'

"Look who's here tonight." Her voice was sugary sweet. "I didn't realize it was discount night."

"Funny, Violet." Gael didn't make eye contact, and his energy dimmed. Nix seemed wound up, eyes shining, her fingers gripping the table until her knuckles whitened.

"I'm sorry, didn't get that amigo," a boy at the back said, to mean titters of laughter. "Maybe you should go back to your shack and learn English."

"Very clever." Nix's cheeks flushed nearly purple. "You guys are so brilliant with your witty insults."

"Nobody asked you, Hix," another girl said, her voice lingering in a hiss. "I'm surprised you can afford anything off the menu. Or are you hitting on the waitress to see if she'll give you some scraps for free? She looks like your type."

Nix looked ready to jump out of her chair, but Gael put a hand on her arm, shaking his head. "They're not worth it," he said in an undertone.

"Who's this?" The tallest and most muscular of the group nodded at Lola. When he spoke, the others hushed in respectful silence, leaning forward. Lola had been around gangs long enough to know this one was the leader, getting others to follow through charm, or intimidation, or both.

She sensed the threat as he leered over her shoulder. Predators were all the same. She slowly took him in, good-looking in a blond, clean-cut way.

He gently pulled one of Lola's curls. "You're new." Lola stiffened at the intimacy. There was yeasty beer on his breath and absolute disregard for others' wants in his actions. "I'm Ethan. Maybe you should hang with us sometime."

She met his eyes dead-on. "Don't touch me again," she said.

Taken aback, he paused before a slow smile spread over his face. "You're feisty," he said, then knocked his hip against their table hard enough to rock their drinks. Lola's coffee spilled into her lap.

She jumped to her feet as the stinging liquid soaked to her skin. "How dare you!"

"Oops," he said, smile still in place. "Maybe you need help getting out of those dirty clothes. I could give you a hand."

One of the boys giggled. Violet, the queen bee, shot him a murderous look. "Ethan." Her voice was tight, like a warning.

Lola got into this Ethan's face. It took every ounce of her control to keep her fangs from slipping out and ripping into him. Her entire undead life, she had been forced to take this behaviour from everyone around her. But she would be damned if she would let this swaggering child bring her down. She'd been kicked far too many times. "And what would you know about helping me?" Lola smirked, looking him up and down. "You look a little limp to me." Her hiss was loud enough to be heard by the group.

In the shocked silence, somebody snickered. Violet flickered a smirk before shifting to outrage. Nix stared at Lola, eyes wide and bright.

Ripples of fury rolled off the blond boy. He held a finger in her face. "That was a mistake."

Lola inspected her nails, as though they were far more important than the boy gaping at her. "I'm fairly certain it was accurate."

His eyes bulged. It must have been quite some time since anyone talked back to him. Would he physically attack her? Lola shifted her stance. She wasn't the cringing runt of the crew she once was, and she didn't want to run from fights anymore. Delight lit up inside her at the very freedom of it and she prayed he would make the first move.

Violet watched him as he hyperventilated, facing off with a girl nearly half his size. She slipped her hand into his.

"Come on, Ethan," she said. She brushed against his arm, getting his attention. "Let's go. I don't want to waste my time with these dorks."

Ethan refused to move, and Lola grinned like a dare. She could see the waitress coming behind him, as well as a few fathers from nearby tables watching to see what would happen next. The tension in the room ratcheted.

Ethan snorted with contempt. "You're right, Vi. You losers are not worth my time."

Lola's eyes rounded. "Oh, my, it must be frustrating to be so *impotent*." She knew she was baiting him. Of course, getting into a brawl with the locals was hardly keeping a low profile, but she was having too much fun to stop.

One of the boys in the group broke the mounting pressure. Tall and thin, he hadn't reacted to the back and forth. But now he spoke, his tone drawling as though entirely unaware of the drama around him. "I heard you're digging at the treasure tree," he said to Gael.

Gael's head shot up, and he narrowed his eyes. "What's it to you, Walt?"

Walt shrugged, jamming his hands into his pockets. He seemed independent of the rest of the group, uncaring of what they were doing. "What're you looking for?"

"None of your business."

Ethan had caught onto what Walt was saying. An ugly smile spread over his face. "I bet you're scrabbling through the dirt for change," he said. The group burst out laughing, relieved to get back to everyday pettiness. "If you're looking for money, you can start scrubbing my toilets. Oh, wait, your mother already does that."

Gael flushed deep red, and both Lola and Nix reached out on instinct to hold him back. But Gael shook his head in disgust and looked away. Ethan burst into a horsey laugh. Violet tugged at his arm, giving him a private smile, and he allowed her to lead him away. The others followed him eagerly, and the blood-thirsty tension filtered from the air.

Walt was last to go, shooting Gael a questioning look before leaving.

The waitress was finally able to approach the table. "You kids shouldn't come here starting fights," she said under her breath, tossing a wet rag on the table and sloshing the coffee around over the top.

"Us? We didn't start this stupid thing, they did!" Nix pointed at the group leaving the bar.

"You know what I mean."

"Yeah, I do. The rich kids get away with everything, and the poor kids are left to clean up after them."

The waitress slapped down the bill. "We've all gotta make a living. You want to stay here, don't make any more trouble." She stomped away.

The three of them stared at their mugs before Nix let out a snort of laughter. "Nothing. Absolutely nothing in the world will top you calling Ethan impotent."

Gael was watching her. She couldn't read his expression. "You didn't help our social life much."

Lola's stomach sank. "I didn't mean to make things more difficult for you. I lost my temper."

"Brilliantly lost your temper!" Nix crowed.

"It was awesome." Gael grinned finally. "Completely worth it."

"Good." Lola picked up her coffee mug. "Although maybe he won't want everyone talking about what I said. He seems pretty fragile."

Nix snorted so hard sugar coffee came out of her nose. People at surrounding tables shot her dirty looks as she gasped with pain and laughter. Gael chuckled, pounding on her back.

Once recovered, Nix held up her drink. She grinned ear to ear, whipped cream smeared across her face. "To Lola."

She held out her drink, as did Gael. "To Lola."

Lola lifted her ceramic cup, empty as it was, and clinked against theirs. They drank their warm, sweet drinks while Drunken Danny caterwauled on stage. A heady sense of giddiness overtook her.

She could almost believe she was one of them: a light-hearted kid on an adventure. Free to tease one another and make grand plans that would go nowhere. Perhaps, this one time, it would be okay to pretend.

EIGHT

It was close to sunset, and the mists were pulled in close around Lola. She trudged to the dig site, lethargic from being awake day after day without feeding properly.

"Oy! There she is!" Nix popped out of the pit as Lola approached. Two beat-up bikes rested against a tree root, surrounded by piles of dirt.

"I lost track of time," Lola said.

Nix pulled herself over the edge of the hole. "This is what I don't get. You're not in school, and you don't work, so what did you lose track of time doing?" She shook her head at Gael, who climbed out of the hole behind her. "Something doesn't make sense here."

Lola's limbs went cold. Had the girl figured her out? Would she need to take care of a situation? It was bewildering to find she had no desire to harm these locals.

Nix shot her a cheeky grin as she grabbed a water bottle. "Lola must be an international spy." The tightness in Lola's chest loosened. "I mean, you got the accent and this whole Bond girl look." She swept her hand in an arc that took in Lola's body-skimming black outfit and high ponytail. "You're on a mission, right? I can't figure out what it is. Unless it's to take down high school douchebags." She cackled as she descended the ladder again. "Not that I mind!"

"Ignore Nix; she's had too much caffeine." Gael braced himself, pulling the bucket out of the hole. "Like, eight mochaccinos, it's obscene. But...where were you? I kinda expected you here earlier."

"I was exploring the island," she said. "I was on the opposite shore when I realized what time it was, and I had to walk back."

"That's intense. It's like fifteen kilometres. Are you sure you're not an international spy?"

Lola forced a laugh. "Would an international spy be walking? I'd have a hovercraft, at least."

Gael was pulling up buckets of dirt, so Lola grabbed his shovel and descended into the pit. Alone together, Nix was quieter than usual, digging steadily.

"I thought you were pretty cool last night," Nix said finally. "I wish I could stand up to people like that, but I get all tongue-tied when I'm mad." She paused as if confessing a horrible secret. "Sometimes I cry. I hate it so much."

Lola hid her smile and nodded. "It was easier for me because I don't live here. I didn't have to deal with the fallout." She paused. "Did you have any trouble today? I mean, at school. You must have seen them, right?"

"It wasn't too bad, actually. Samantha pushed past me a few times, but she does that every time she sees me, so it's not like anything changed. I think you were right. Ethan didn't want the story repeated. It was well done." She sounded impressed with Lola's gall.

Though Lola could have ripped apart any of these humans without breaking a sweat, Nix's words inflated her more than any kill had in a long time. "I'd be happy to do it again."

"For the record, I'd pay good money to see it."

They worked in stilted silence for some time, deferential to each other as they moved, widening the shaft so two people could dig at the same time. Lola got the sense that Nix was going out of her way to not touch her – that she was uncomfortable with her presence.

They had been at it for half an hour when voices floated above them. They glanced at each other.

"Is Gael talking to himself again?" Nix asked.

"Does he do that often?"

"Ha! No. Well, not all the time. He's always been a bit of a dreamer. I wouldn't bet against him wandering the forest and quoting Frost out loud."

Lola couldn't hold back her snort of laughter. Nix rounded on her, eyes large with laughter. "Did he quote Frost to you? He did, didn't he? God, what a dork. He's so predictable." Nix shook her head. "No poetry today. I think somebody's up there."

Alarmed, Lola dropped her shovel and hustled up the ladder. She was wary of newcomers at the dig site. The smallest interruption could throw their hunt off course. She peeked over the edge, to see Gael arguing with a tall boy.

"What the hell are you doing here, Gael?"

Lola recognized the newcomer and his bored drawl. "So much for 'no point in digging up the past.' You told me the treasure was off-limits. What's changed now?"

"What's it to you?" Gael's shoulders were tight. "You're the one who left the past behind him."

"We talked about doing this dig for years. You were always the one to hold us back. I thought if you ever did start, I would…" Walt trailed off, shoving his hands into his pockets.

"Who is it?" hissed Nix, dangling under Lola's feet.

"It's Walt," Lola hissed back. "From last night."

"Walt!" Nix did not keep her voice down. "Get out of my way. I have a few choice words for that spoiled bourgee."

The two young men stopped as Nix scrambled out from the pit and stormed over to Walt.

"You have a lot of nerve showing up here!" Her face was scrunched, hair flying out of her ponytail in every direction. "Wasn't last night enough? Can't you leave him alone?"

"I'm talking to Gael." Walt's face was stony in the face of her fury. "I was pretty sure you had everything taken care of last night." Walt's gaze flickered to Lola, curious.

Lola tried to make sense of their dynamic. Who was Walt to them?

He raised an eyebrow. "That was spectacularly funny. Nobody speaks to Ethan that way. You should have seen him pouting for the rest of the night." He snorted in laughter, then stopped, as though he'd surprised himself.

Nix's face twisted in contempt. "I don't want to hear another word about them, especially since you're clearly one of them."

"I'm not—" Walt protested, then saw the scornful looks from Nix and Gael. He took a deep breath, and his words came out with great effort. "I mean, what if I wanted to help you? To dig?"

Nix snorted. "I say you missed the chance a long time ago."

Walt met Gael's eye for a long moment, his eyebrows bunched together and his mouth downturned. "Right. I'm being an ass." As he turned away, he blinked several times, his shoulders slumping. Gael had the identical look.

Nix huddled next to Gael after Walt left. "What the hell was that about?" she asked.

Gael twisted a rope between his fingers, then threw it away. "I don't know."

Nix's eyes blazed. "How dare he?" There was a beep from her bag. She stormed to grab her phone, then dropped it with a curse. "Holy mackerel, my mum is going to kill me! I told her I would babysit tonight. I should have been home an hour ago. I have to go." She stopped mid-panic attack and turned back to Gael. "Is this okay?"

"Yes, go," Gael said, laughing now at his friend's antics. "I don't want your mum to kill you. Say hi to her from me!" he yelled after Nix's retreating back. She had already taken off on her beat-up bike, her penny-bright hair the last thing they could make out in the gathering darkness.

Gael nodded after her. "Nix is the eldest of six. She's basically always babysitting. She complains about it lots, but she loves it."

"That's a lot of siblings," Lola murmured. "I couldn't imagine." She glanced at Gael, the downturn to his mouth. Was he thinking of his brother? But his eyes were clear when he looked up.

"Do you have any? Siblings, I mean?"

Lola startled at the question. "Me?" She thought of Jacquotte's crew, of the endless days and nights they would spend below deck or camping out inside caves. They would hunt together, sharing the spoils of their finds, both edibles and treasures. They were tough and it was a life unlike any other, but there had been a time when she felt like they were her siblings.

And they would kill her if they found her. The thought was like driving a knife straight through her chest and she clutched her throat. She didn't want to think of the good times. Or the bad times.

"Lola, I'm sorry. I shouldn't have asked." Gael covered the distance between them and wrapped his arms around her, pressing her into his chest.

Lola allowed herself to be held, finding comfort in his warmth, in his strong arms around her. She closed her eyes as her thoughts tumbled against each other. She wondered, maybe for the first time, if perhaps she had a family before she had been created. It stood to reason. Creatures like her did not have memories of prior to their rebirth. The life that came before was wiped clean; the people they had once been no longer existed. But they must have come from somewhere.

Her first memory was waking up as a vampire. Jacquotte stood over her, her face hard as if carved from obsidian. Her eyes glowed amber, and even as she choked on the blood in her throat, Lola knew she would follow this goddess to the ends of the earth. She struggled up, surrounded by blood and bodies piled around her. It was hazy, but she remembered a train in the distance, in the middle of a valley. In France, she had discovered later.

Jacquotte created vampires and groomed them to become a part of her crew. Together they tracked down the treasures hiding in the darkest places on Earth, whether they be ancient or modern. Long memories and invulnerable bodies made them naturals for the work. They sold their finds to fuel a glamourous immortal life. Their life swung between months of research, hiking, digging or climbing to unearth precious jewels or long-lost art; then months more of feasting, living like royalty of old. For decades, she had never wanted anything more than an approving nod from Jacquotte.

She had always tried to keep up with the crew, no matter what it cost her. Though she didn't always enjoy their company, they were all she knew. She understood that was true of family. She didn't know any other way to be.

Lola steeled herself. None of this mattered; these memories were a distraction. She needed to get centred; otherwise, she would be an easy victim when the crew came after her. Nothing mattered other than finding the treasure at the end of the Well of Souls.

She brushed Gael off. Her cheeks were dry. Demonic as she was, she couldn't cry. The very idea was foreign to her.

"You just surprised me. I hadn't thought about them in a long time." She wiggled, ridding herself of these inconvenient heart pains. Both of them stood staring at the pit, neither inclined to dig anymore.

"Do you want to go get a bite to eat?" Gael asked.

His words gave her vivid imagery of sinking her fangs into him and she looked up in alarm. "No! I'm not hungry."

"Okay." He put up his hands against her vehemence. "I feel like this scene is over, but maybe we could do something?"

She heard the note of hope in his voice. "Like what?" she asked, wary of being alone with him.

"I can show you the boulder with the etchings. In my chimney?"

"Oh, yes." That distraction was exactly what she needed. Surely she could keep her hands and teeth to herself when there were ancient messages to study. "I'd love to see it."

NINE

They gathered the equipment, Lola carrying the shovels while Gael walked his bike along the path. "I missed something back there," Lola said. "With Walt, I mean."

Gael sighed, staring at the handles of his bike. "Walt and I used to be best friends; he was always over at my house. It was a long time ago. We loved *Star Wars*." His chin dipped and he gave a shy smile. "We played all the time. He let me be Han Solo."

"I know him." Lola nodded. "The handsome one."

Gael laughed. "That's right. Anyways, we started junior high school, and that's when Walt decided I was beneath him. He's really rich, you know. He lives in this mansion in town. His mom's the mayor and his dad is this bigshot businessman." His laugh held a bitter edge. "And my mum is the cleaning lady. He didn't want to associate with a poor nerd anymore. So he dropped me and started hanging out with Ethan and Violet and them."

"He dropped you?"

"Stopped answering my calls. Ignoring me in the hallways at school. And I couldn't accept it, I just kept trying. A sucker for punishment, I guess. It wasn't until Ethan knocked me over one day, and I looked up to see Walt laughing along with everyone else. He'd never done that before. That's when I finally got it."

"That was cruel of him. You shouldn't feel ashamed about wanting to keep a friend, but he doesn't deserve you."

Gael shrugged. "Well, as you say, *c'est la vie.*"

She smiled at his French. "Why do you think he came today?"

"No idea. I haven't spoken to him in years – not by choice, at least. I mean, he doesn't actually say much to anyone anymore."

"He had something to say today."

"About the dig. We used to talk about it all the time when we were kids, how we'd be these great treasure hunters. But it was only a dream then. He has no right to come asking for it now." He shook his head. "Enough of him. What do you like, Lola? Besides treasure hunting, of course, which is one hell of a hobby."

Lola blinked. "What do you mean?"

"Favourite movie? Music? What do you do in your spare time?"

Lola hummed as she scrambled for an answer. *Hunt to kill* didn't seem appropriate. "I like...old movies."

"Old movies like the classics?"

"Yes, back before they put special effects in. It seemed more real, somehow."

She studied films, watching the actors' faces as they impersonated someone else. They, too, faked human emotion, and she copied their mannerisms. "Anything with Audrey Hepburn. Her grace was unparalleled."

"I can see that. You look a little like her."

Lola dimpled at the thought. "When she entered a room, people stopped and stared. She was magnetic."

"You talk as though you've met her."

Lola's eyes flew open. She was getting lost in memories. "Of course I haven't!"

"Well, obviously." Gael gave her a funny look, but left it. They had arrived near the edge of the forest, where the trail levelled out.

"Do you want to get on, sit on the handles?" Gael nodded his head at the bike. "I can strap the shovels to my backpack. We'd get there a lot quicker."

"I haven't done that in years," Lola said. Decades. She hesitated, but remembered, a long time ago, enjoying it. "I'm in."

Gael held the bike steady as Lola perched in front. "Ready?" At her nod, he pushed off, pedalling furiously to get momentum. Within seconds they breezed down the path. Lola's hair whipped behind her, the wind rushing past.

Gael's warmth was comforting against her back, and she could smell the spike of his sweat. She closed her eyes and let her arms drift out to the sides, as though she flew through the air.

Her laugh bubbled from deep inside of her: pure delight. Gael crowed in joy as they careened down the path and out into the fields beyond. The skies were lit by starlight, the wind burned her cheeks, and Lola never wanted it to stop.

All too soon, Gael braked, and Lola held on as they bumped to a stop. She leapt off, light on her feet, and faced him. His eyes shone with the wind and something brighter.

"You hardly ever laugh, you know," Gael said. "You have a really nice laugh; I like hearing it."

Lola's brain fizzled, and she could think of nothing to say. She turned to his gate, which was rickety and badly needed repainting.

As though reading her thoughts, Gael ran his hand over the wood. "Things have been a little hard for us lately," he said. He gave a one-shoulder shrug, a sign he didn't want to get into it. "Things have gotten a little run down."

Up close, the stone cottage was humble but well made, and the creeping ivy was covered with a shower of spring flowers. It needed work and was forlorn without lights or smoke curling from the chimney, but Lola knew good bones when she saw them. "Your home is perfect. It's intimate and folksy."

Gael snorted. "Intimate and folksy? Those are fancy words for small and ramshackle."

"Ramshackle is a fancy word, too, and it's not true." Lola gazed at the darkened windows. "Your mother still isn't home?"

Gael looked at his watch. "My mum's coming home later this evening. Diego's treatments on the mainland are done, and he's been transferred to the hospital in Port Despardoux. He's weak and needs round-the-clock care." Gael's mouth twisted as he opened the door to the yawning dark beyond. "I'll visit him tomorrow. But my mum's going to try to get here for dinner, rest while he's resting." He nodded his head. "Come on in."

Lola stepped over the threshold. Gael turned on the light in the front entryway and led her through the tiny kitchen, flipping switches as he went.

It was clean, although some places had been missed: a table that hadn't been wiped down and a pile of folded clothes on the chair. In the corner of their living room, a Lego playset gathered dust.

Lola eyed Gael. Did he keep the house tidy so his mother didn't have to bring her work home with her? She stopped in front of the Legos, scattered as though a child had dropped them mid-play. Diego. Maybe the last thing he had played with before he went to the hospital, and Gael didn't have the heart to put them away. Her chest ached as she watched him bustling in the kitchen.

"It's behind you," he said as he brought food out of the fridge. "The stone? It's set into the fireplace."

She had forgotten for a moment why she was there. She muttered a curse, telling herself to focus, and turned to the chimney, as ancient as the rest of the walls. Set prominently in the centre was a jet-black rock, smooth enough to reflect light.

The etchings were three lines of incomprehensible marks carved deep into the stone. Her skin prickled. It was just as she had expected. The markings matched the ones on the ancient map of Duchesne: dot and lines like constellations, only the stars belonged to some other universe.

"This is very cool, Gael. Thank you for sharing it with me."

"Any time. You know, the local museum is always on us to donate it. It's pretty old and a part of the island's history. Mum always refuses. I think it's because the entire house would probably collapse without it." Gael frowned at the stone.

It wasn't *pretty* old; it was archaic. Lola brought her hand near. The stone hummed with a strange energy, vibrating in a way that set her teeth on edge. She was both drawn to it and repulsed.

A sizzling hiss went up from the kitchen, and the luscious smell of melting butter floated through the house.

"I'm starting dinner," Gael said at her questioning look. "Mum will be exhausted when she gets in. It's the least I can do."

Again, that nagging ache inside her chest. Lola rubbed the spot absently, wishing it would stop.

"What do you make of it?" He gestured to the rock with a kitchen knife. "It's not much more than an oversized paperweight, really, but it's cool nobody has figured out what it means. There's still a mystery left."

"It's fascinating. Could I take a rubbing of it? I'd like to study it more."

"You want to try your hand at solving it? I'll warn you, experts have puzzled over it for years, but no one's ever figured out what language it is." Gael chuckled. "I think because the treasure had been found, there wasn't much interest. It probably says: *Here's your treasure.*"

Lola lips curved up. "Or it could say: *You'll find so much more if you keep on going.* It's a mystery, like you said. And there's something about it, like I know it somehow."

"Like it's at the tip of your tongue. Or if you just crossed your eyes in the right way, it would suddenly become clear." Gael came to stand next to her, arms crossed as he contemplated the etchings. "I understand. I have some paper and pencil here." He rummaged through a cupboard until he came up with the tools. "Here you are."

Lola hesitated. "Do you think you could do it? It's a little high for me." She didn't want to touch the stone, frightened something dramatic would happen if she did. If she burst into flames in the middle of his living room, it would be difficult to explain.

"Okay, shorty." Gael reached with ease to rub the pencil over the paper, taking in the grooves of the message. His shirt slipped up, and once again, Lola fixated on that strip of visible flesh. It would be warm if she put her hand to it, and hard with muscle.

He caught her gaze as he finished, and his eyes darkened. He ran a thumb over her arm, and she bit her lip at the line of fire that followed. She looked to his lips. He would be soft and delicious.

Gael's hand drifted to her hip, fist bunching in the fabric of her shirt before tugging her in closer. She stretched to meet him, her breasts grazing against his chest. She leaned forward, brushing her lips over his.

His hand slipped around to cup her neck, and his lips moved gently over hers. He was warm and tasted sweet and held her with excruciating gentleness. A spray of goosebumps rippled over her skin.

Lights flickered in the window, and Lola pulled back with a gasp. Gael froze as a car pulled in front of the house, then he let out a rueful laugh, squeezing Lola's hip gently before releasing her.

"Mum's home." He stepped away, handing her the rubbing. "I know you said you weren't hungry, but want to stay for dinner anyway? She'd like to meet you."

"*Hola, mi amore,*" came a tender voice from the front door. "Can you believe it, the rabbits have been at the garden again? *Pequeñas bestias!* I had been counting on those vegetables."

A surge of panic flared through Lola. She had no right to be in this house. "I should go."

"At least come and say hi," Gael said over his shoulder. "Here, Mamá, let me take that for you. Come and meet my friend Lola."

Burdened as he was by the bags in his arms, he didn't see Lola slip around him in a burst of speed and sprint down the garden path as though her undead life depended on it, etching clutched in her hand.

Lola slowed once she reached the town square and slumped down on a bench. She had no idea what spurred her to run away like that. She should have smiled graciously and met his mother, made polite excuses and gone on her way.

But she panicked. She couldn't contemplate meeting Gael's suffering mother, knowing she was using her son, her family's legacy, for her own ends.

Lola groaned and rubbed at her chest. It *hurt*, like shards of glass digging through her skin from the inside. This was happening more and more since arriving on Duchesne, these feelings. They were horrible.

And then there was the stone. She'd felt its presence, like a third person in the room. She wondered if Gael felt it too. Then she wondered if Gael would forgive her for running away as she did.

She gripped her hair, tugging it away from her face. She was lucky her crew couldn't see her now. They had always picked on her weaknesses, but this vulnerability was new, terrifying. Emptiness yawned inside of her, and she didn't know how to outrun it.

Whatever was going on with her, sulking on a bench wasn't helping. Lola shook out her limbs and prowled the empty streets of Port Despardoux. No town festivities tonight. A few pedestrians hurried when passing her by, as though driven to get away from her restless energy.

The lights were still on at The Pain Perdu. Lola lingered at the front display. Maybe coffee in a warm café would make all of it go away. She entered the patisserie, announced by the tinkling bell. A few patrons sat scattered around the tables.

"Lola!" Faye greeted her with a warm smile. "I've been thinking about you. You've stayed away too long. Come have a seat."

Cautiously, Lola approached the counter, perching on the

chair. Faye was already pouring her coffee in a delicate cup with a saucer. "Black, right?" She placed a paper next to the coffee. "There you go, hon. Let me know if you want a top-up." Her guileless eyes were filled with such kindness Lola ducked her head. She was struck by sudden shyness, to have someone fuss over her.

Faye bustled to another table, and Lola pulled out the rubbing she had taken from Gael, spreading it over the newspaper. She traced her fingers over the constellations. Lola knew many languages. She had learned to be useful for the crew. Weaker than the others, at least she could be their linguist, translating documents from ancient civilizations. She understood the basis of most human languages ever spoken and how alphabets were constructed and phrases laid out. But this was new. She would wager a fortune in solid gold the message was not human.

She stared at the markings until they shimmered under her gaze.

With a grunt of frustration, Lola folded the paper with care and slipped it into her pocket. When she caught her eye, Faye beamed at her. Lola had enough presence of mind to smile back. She clutched the cup, letting the warmth soothe her.

With deliberate motions, she opened the newspaper. The newest edition of the *Duchesne Daily*, printed today. The front page splashed a headline about the murder of Anthony Graves, a local fisherman. His body had been found tangled in seaweed off the wharf. His death was deemed suspicious, and the investigation was ongoing. The new RCMP captain, Theodore Greyson, had a few terse quotes in the article, but most of what he said screamed "no comment."

The reporter, Richard Dawgsby, was also credited as the paper's editor and relished the ghoulish details. He spoke of rituals and potential cults, more interested in digging up the island's gruesome history. *Was Anthony Graves yet another victim of the Duchesne curse?* the article wondered.

Her stomach dropped. The fisherman's body still bore wounds that suggested rituals. Or demons.

Lola picked up her coffee too quickly, cursing as liquid sloshed over the edge. She drained the cup, pulling out enough cash to pay for it. She needed to be careful with her money, but she didn't want to take advantage of the baker. It never served to be in anyone's debt.

Her blood buzzed with caffeine and the need to satisfy her hunger.

Faye glanced up as Lola stood. "See you tomorrow," she said as Lola headed to the door. Her tone was firm, more command than invitation. Lola gave a jerky nod.

The pit in her stomach sank even further. She felt as though a trap laid around her had cinched tighter. She needed to keep her eyes open, even as she desperately needed to eat.

TEN

After a night's hunting and a day of rest, Lola stalked out of the shack into the evening air, determined to get this treasure hunt back under her control. A bizarre rift had opened inside her, making her feel like a human. It was a weakness, and she would force it shut because she could not fall apart. Finding the Well of Souls was her chance at survival, to gain enough power so she would never have to run again.

Even as she made her way to the dig site, she knew the others weren't there. There were no telltale sounds of digging, no teasing or laughing. The bucket had been cast to the side, and she kicked at it. It looked like an abandoned dig. Once the momentum was lost, it was hard to get going again.

Lola glared at the tree placidly standing guard above.

"This is your fault, isn't it?" Its leaves rustled at her. She should just get to digging on her own. She didn't need them. She was certainly better off without the confusion of humans, the distraction of their good smells and playful banter. She wanted no part in it.

"*Merde*!" Lola threw her hands up and turned back to the

path. She could run as fast as Gael could carry her on his bike, but it was far less fun. She passed Gael's cottage, empty and lifeless. Gael wasn't there, and his mother was likely at her other son's side in the hospital.

She continued into Port Despardoux. It was a sultry evening, with starlight twinkling over the still bay. Warm spring air cast itself over the island, and the buzz and hum of humanity rose from Lost Souls. Something was happening there, and with any luck, Gael and Nix would be a part of it.

This time, she was prepared for the tumult of humanity. It wasn't as busy as the unofficial-official lobster festival, and she could take in the scents and abundance of blood surrounding her.

The atmosphere was different tonight, mellow, less frantic shouting and sawing fiddles. The band hadn't started to play yet, but even their warm-up proved they were of a higher calibre. A woman sat at the edge of the stage, strumming the guitar. It sent ripples of sensation over Lola's skin.

The crowd thinned on the ocean-facing patio, where the air was crisp as it rolled in from the Atlantic. That's where she found Gael and Nix. They sat in the corner, faces lit by the string of coloured patio lights on the railing. Both of them stared out to sea while Nix's thin fingers picked at the label on a Coke bottle.

Lola cleared her throat. "Hello." Neither showed any enthusiasm to see her.

"Look who it is," Nix said after an awkward pause. "Finished whatever it is mysterious strangers do during the day, and now you want us to come work for you?"

Lola hovered, then sat without an invitation. "I'm sorry, I'm a little bit...I'm not sure how to say it. Distracted? I went to the dig site. I'd hoped to see you there, but not because..." she trailed off, not entirely sure why she was there.

She could dig much faster without them. But she had been disappointed not to see them – digging with them was fun. It was best not to think too hard about that. "Listen, I'm not great at being—"

"What? Reliable?"

"The thing is, Lola," Gael said. He still hadn't looked at her. "We did go. And it's obvious we need better equipment. We're not going to get anywhere on our own, a bunch of kids. And once again, you weren't there. It kinda seems like maybe you're done with us."

"I wanted to see you."

"You ran out on me yesterday," Gael said, finally meeting her eyes. "Mum took my temperature; she thought I was hallucinating. Which is what I thought when I first saw you."

Delicately, Lola reached out and pressed her fingers to his wrist, feeling the uptake of his pulse. Nix glared from under the coppery eyebrows. "See? There I am. No hallucination."

He swallowed and pulled away. "That doesn't explain why you couldn't stick around to say hi."

"I'm not great with parents," Lola said. "Mothers especially have a hard time with me."

Nix snorted into her Coke. Gael assessed her with his gold-rimmed eyes. "Maybe it's because you, like, run away without a word. That was really weird."

"Point taken."

"It was like you got what you wanted and took off." His intense gaze was peeling back a part of her.

The band had started to play, beautiful ethereal strings coming in over a deep bass thrumming. They played a dreamy version of Cyndi Lauper's 'Girls Just Wanna Have Fun.' The lead singer's voice was light and smooth like honey as she crooned, "I wanna be the one to walk in the sun."

Lola's head spun, as though she was falling through empty space.

Then her gaze connected with Gael, and the world straightened. "I haven't got what I wanted," she whispered.

Gael blinked, and his face softened. "And what is it you want?" A hint of a smile tugged at his lips.

"Adventure, of course," she whispered.

Nix snorted again, more forcefully, and the intensity was broken. But a chord of amity remained, and the mood was less strained.

"Listen, I get it; I've been a flake, and I'm sorry for it. I will be at the dig site when you finish school tomorrow, and I will work so hard you won't even know we missed the day. We'll be up to our elbows in pirate gold by this time next week." She gave them both a winning smile, making sure it showed in her eyes.

It was working; they were going to cave. Nix shrugged, pouring her Coke into a glass. Gael started to say something, then froze.

"I'm pretty sure you scabs aren't allowed here anymore," a voice sneered behind her. Lola turned slowly to face the crowd of teenagers surrounding them, led by Ethan.

Her adrenaline spiked as she took in the gang. Wildness sparked in their eyes, a ferocity that spoke of violence and the nastiness that hid behind a group. Her demonic powers kicked in on instinct. The fuggy scent of anticipation and ill-intent swirled around them. This was more dangerous than her friends might guess.

"We're not bothering anyone," Gael said in a measured voice.

Ethan leaned over the table. She sensed heartbeats pick up, and bodies stilled as everyone waited to see what would happen. "Here's the thing, amigo." His voice was vicious. "I think you and your ugly little friend take up entirely too much space by existing. So, when I say this place is off-limits, it's because I don't want to have to look at either of you slugs any more than I have to."

Gael's face was now a dusty rose, while Nix's eyes, narrowed to slits, glittered with fury.

Ethan brushed against Lola. She could smell him, the shower he had taken earlier and something much darker, muskier. He was aroused by his power. He got off on making others feel small, and here, backed by his sycophants, he was untouchable.

Or so he thought. She faced him straight on, imagining he was every demon who had dismissed her for being too weak. Her stolen blood pounded in her veins, ready for anything.

"Now you, I don't understand," Ethan said. "You're obviously high-quality and I would assume Gael here is paying you, except he doesn't have any money. Why would you hang out with these losers? I feel like you could do better." He reached out as though to touch her face.

Both Gael and Nix were on their feet, shouting. "Get away from her!" Gael yelled.

Unmoving, Lola stared him down. "I'm pretty sure I made myself clear. Touch me and you'll regret it." Every part of her was lit up, and she desperately wanted him to push her again so she could give in to her instincts. She would rip this spoiled child apart.

Nix elbowed her way between them and shoved Ethan.

"Leave her alone!" All hundred pounds of her stood guard in front of Lola, trembling with fury. Her hair had snapped its elastic and curls floated around her face.

"Oh my God, Arabella, stop being such a loser!" Violet, the queen bee blonde, grabbed Nix's drink and moved to throw it on her. Quicker than anyone could track, Lola grabbed it from her hand and poured it over her blonde head.

Violet gasped and burbled as the sticky brown liquid dripped down her face, smearing her makeup into a clownish mask.

"You bitch!" she hissed as some of the boys started to laugh. They pushed in closer, the mob building to its breaking point. Several servers were making their way toward them. Things might still fizzle out, unless someone threw oil over this fire.

Gael now stood in front of Nix and Lola. "Leave them alone, Ethan. What's your problem?"

"That little bitch is my problem." Ethan's face sneered in anger. "You show up with a psycho, there's going to be trouble. Somebody needs to teach her a lesson."

"She's none of your business."

"Protecting your girl, is that it? I'm surprised; I didn't think you had the balls for it."

Lola couldn't hold back her huff of disgust. She curled her lip at Ethan over Gael's shoulder. "Is this because I implied you were impotent? You're not really convincing me otherwise."

He pointed at her. "One day, I'm going to find you alone and make you regret that."

Lola snorted. "What are you going to do? Flail around limply?"

"Shut up, slut!"

Gael grabbed Ethan and shoved. Ethan stumbled into the group of boys, who in turn fell against other diners who had been monitoring the altercation. People shouted, and several men stood up to stop it.

Ethan righted himself and threw a wild punch that would have knocked into the side of Gael's head. But Walt came flying out of nowhere and knocked Ethan down. They both crashed to the floor, and a woman screamed.

The restaurant manager came pushing through bodies, yelling at everyone to calm down. More of the teens started to scuffle against some of the men trying to get them to leave, and it looked like a full brawl was in the making.

Her bloodlust up and pounding in her ears, Lola made for Ethan. He spotted her, eyes widening in fury. He grabbed her arm and pulled her in, his other hand reaching for her chest.

In a blink, she grabbed his arm and flipped him onto his back, riding him down to land on top of him, one knee at his throat. With a rush of wild, predatory joy, her fangs slipped down, and she lunged for his neck.

Ethan's face went white, and he shrieked, struggling to get away from her.

Lola halted herself mid-bite. She couldn't feed off him in the middle of a crowd. Surely somebody would notice.

With more effort than she had put into anything before, she forced her teeth back to normal and rolled off him.

"What...the hell are you?" He scrambled away from her, heaving, transformed by fear. Gone was the swaggering teen. He held out his arms blindly for the others to help him up.

The patio had emptied as people fled into the main bar.

Blue and red lights flashed on the road. A voice over a megaphone ordered everyone to stop what they were doing. The mob dispersed, most of the gang scuttling away.

Captain Greyson stormed over to what was left of the group. Lola, Gael and Nix stood in the middle while Violet held on to Ethan, who was screaming at Lola.

"She attacked me! She's some kind of monster!"

Despite her hair and makeup being a sticky disaster, Violet stared at Lola, more curious than angry. "What did you do?"

Lola tried for nonchalant and rolled her eyes. "It's no big deal. I know jiu-jitsu, and I knocked him over to protect myself. He's completely fine."

Walt stood nearby, his perfect hair mussed, and snickered. Violet stabbed him with a sharp look but didn't say anything.

"No, she's a monster, a thing!"

Violet patted Ethan's hand. "Okay, let's get you home."

"What is going on here?" Greyson shouted.

The manager was behind him, eyes bulging as he looked over the patio.

"It was them." Ethan pointed at the small group in the middle.

Nix held up her hands in innocence while Lola turned wide eyes to the police. He narrowed his eyes, taking her in, and she wondered how long it would take him to place her from the patisserie.

Not long at all. "You were at Faye's."

"That's right, officer. My name is Lola Monteux, and we did not start this." She gestured to her friends. "We were just having a drink. Out of nowhere, a gang of more than ten people confronted us. That girl tried to pour a drink on one of us."

Greyson looked to Violet. "*She* tried to pour a drink on you."

"Yes. She missed."

There was a beat. Nix pressed her lips together as though trying not to laugh as Violet choked in indignation.

Greyson stared at Lola. "What happened to him?" He indicated Ethan, who was trembling. He shook his head emphatically, unwilling to say more.

Lola sniffed. "He went to punch my friend. Only Walt here knocked him aside. He went to attack again, and I made sure he stayed down. He's not hurt."

There was more shouting, and Greyson put his arms up and told them all to shut it. "Everyone settle up. There are people actually trying to enjoy their evening here." He pointed at the teenagers lingering on the scene. "All of you out in the parking lot. I'm taking names."

As they gathered on the asphalt, lit by the flashing police lights, one of the teens sneered at Greyson, "Who are you, anyway?"

"I'm the one who can throw you in a holding cell if you piss me off."

The teen was clearly not impressed. "And where are you from? The *hood*?"

"What the – man, I'm from Mississauga. You know what, it doesn't matter. You're first; I want your name. Don't put up a fuss, and you can get away with a warning."

Greyson took names, and the gang skulked away in little groups. Violet put her arm around Ethan, trying to lead him away. Ethan threw her off, and she teetered back on her wedge sandals before regaining her balance. With a quick glance over her shoulder, she followed him.

Soon only Gael, Nix and Lola were left.

The manager bustled over, sweating in his fury. "I should ban you from ever coming in here again."

Gael bristled, and Lola understood. The manager had waited until the influential kids were gone before throwing around threats. Gael and Nix were easy scapegoats.

Once again, Walt came to the rescue. Quiet and unobtrusive, he was waiting at the side of the patio. "Mr. Anderson," he said, intercepting the manager and putting his hand out to shake his.

"Is that Walt Seaborne?" The manager squinted at Walt's diffident face, clearly fighting the urge to scream at him, too. The son of the mayor had some sway, though, and the manager thought better of it. "I didn't see you there, son."

But the music started again, and diners returned to their evening, voices raised as they discussed the excitement, calling out for more rounds. The manager might have a better night than he expected. He let out a long breath, cooling down.

"My mother has been discussing hosting one of her fundraisers here. Said she'd enjoy working with you." Distaste passed over Walt's face as he placated the red-faced man, who reluctantly allowed himself to be led back into the restaurant. Their voices faded away and Gael watched them go.

"Now, you three seem to be at the heart of this." Greyson pointed to Lola, Gael and Nix.

"We were victims here," Lola said. "Anyone would have seen a large group approaching us. They were the aggressors."

Greyson stared at her, marking something on his notepad. "Lola Monteux. You are awfully cool under pressure. Faye likes you."

"Faye is very kind."

He let out a long breath, considering. "I think that's the end of this. Listen, you kids get home and try not to get into any more trouble."

They nodded, slipping away before he changed his mind. Lola

heard him from down the block, muttering about this "dumbass backwards town."

She bit her lip to cover her smile. She had not made up her mind about Captain Theodore Greyson yet, but she might like him.

Eleven

Lola had been working at the dig site for hours, despite it being the middle of the day. The entire area was shrouded in mist, thick enough to wade through. It accumulated in her hair, beading like sweat. Her hair was mussed, and her clothes were streaked with mud, but she had made substantial progress to the next platform. She was pleased; at this rate, they would reach the original treasure site within a couple of weeks.

Gael and Nix were late. Maybe they weren't coming. Lola obviously stirred up trouble, and they probably decided she wasn't worth the risk.

She jammed her shovel into the earth up to the shaft. It shouldn't matter to her. It didn't.

Unless something terrible had happened. So many horrible things could happen to frail human bodies all the time. She couldn't think about Nix being hurt. Or Gael...what if something happened to him?

Or his brother. Perhaps Diego had taken a turn for the worse, and they were at the hospital.

The walls of the hole seemed to press in around her. She put her hand against the wall, digging her fingers into the clay. She never had trouble being underground when on a hunt. Humans hid their secrets in the dirt; they always had, and so she had spent much of her undead life in holes and tunnels. But now, her thoughts were so scattered, she found herself surprised to be surrounded by earth.

The crushing panic pressed in on her, pushing on her ribs as she stifled a scream. She shouldn't feel like this. She should just dig, just get to the bottom and find the treasure. This whole endeavour had been about survival. But somehow, it had become something much deeper than she ever imagined.

She scrambled out of the hole, determined to find her friends. It wasn't until she heard Nix's snorting laughter and Gael's joking reply travelling ahead of them on the forest path that she calmed down. Out of the hole, under the protective branches of the oak tree, she finally felt the pressure ease. A wild thought flew through her head that everything would be all right now they were here.

Her eyes popped open. Her friends. That's what she thought of them. Gael and Nix were her friends, and she cared about them.

"*Merde*," she whispered. She had no idea what to do with this information. She'd never had a friend before. Beau had been the closest thing she'd had to one, and she could hardly call what lay between them friendly. Wild and passionate, yes. But there had been no kindness, no camaraderie. He was more than a century older than her in vampire terms, but he was also a nineteen-year-old, reckless with her as with everything. He was as stuck in his immortal life as she was, never ageing, never gaining wisdom. They fought and they made up over decades, but never once had she imagined he harboured tender feelings for her.

A vampire didn't require kindness in their life. Besides, no matter how she cared for her friends, she wouldn't get to keep them.

She was staring wide-eyed, trying to come to terms with the flood of emotions, when Gael and Nix arrived, climbing over the massive root. Both were sucking on massive slushies.

Nix bounded to Lola. Her mouth was blue and she smelled of sugar. "There you are! You're filthy, you know?" She squeezed Lola's hand to let her know everything was okay, and Lola clenched her fist afterwards, still feeling the pressure on her skin.

Gael put a friendly arm around her, pulling her into a half-hug. Humans threw their affection around effortlessly. Lola wished for more even as she was wrapped in Gael's spicy scent. He offered her a sip of his slushie, and she sipped from his straw. The sweetness made her cough, the lemony taste fizzing over her tongue.

"Sorry we're late. I picked up a shift at the docks after school."

"That's good, isn't it?"

He shrugged, trying to smile, but his shoulders were strained as though something weighed on them.

"He had to miss baseball tryouts," Nix said, lowering her voice though they were both right next to her. "They were today, but he didn't want to miss a shift that came his way."

Lola remembered the cluster of pockmarks in the treasure oak. "You're a pitcher," she said. "And a good one."

Gael shrugged. "I'm fine enough. I had thought if I could make the A team, then I might be able to attract the attention of some scouts for schools. Like for a scholarship. They'll even come from the States if you're showing enough talent. But I guess I won't know now."

"I'm sorry." Her voice was heavy, loaded with the sadness she felt for him. She genuinely wanted him to have something normal in his life, a baseball team and a chance for a scholarship, to go to school somewhere beyond a haunted island.

"No worries on that account." Nix put a brusque arm around Gael, possessive and proud. "He doesn't need it; he's going to be drowning in scholarships anyways. Our boy here scores all the top marks. There won't be a university in the country that isn't begging for him to go there. He'll be fighting them off."

"I do okay."

"He does better than okay. He's the only reason I haven't flunked out of English class yet. Nobody needs all that crap they make you read in school. Nobody cares about a bunch of fusty old books. Except you," she said to Gael as he opened his mouth to protest.

"Were you waiting for Gael to finish his shift?" Lola asked her.

Nix gaped at her. "Are you stunned? Of course I wasn't sitting around watching a bunch of men toss fish around. What a waste of time. I had field hockey practice. Our season's starting up."

"That sounds like fun." Belonging to a team, racing around the field with the simple goal of putting the ball into a net, Lola could see Nix in her element.

"It is." Nix broke into a broad smile and looked approximately twelve years old. "Only, we're absolutely terrible. It kinda makes it more fun, to be honest. But look at you!" Nix whistled at the hole. "You must have been working on this all day!"

"I wanted to make up for everything."

"Cool, don't worry about it. Especially not after you took on Ethan last night. Lots of people were talking about it this time, about how he's scared of you. You're a local legend, and nobody at school has even met you."

Relief that Nix wasn't upset about last night washed over her. Lola would never forget how the tiny girl placed herself in front of her to protect her, not knowing it wasn't necessary. Courage like that could not be bought.

"You've made this year so much better," Nix said as she descended the ladder with a shovel.

Gael watched Nix in glowing affection. Lola felt a sharp pang of jealousy, wishing someone had ever looked at her like that, then shook it off. They had come back; that had to be enough.

"Was it really okay at school?" she asked. "Last night got out of hand. I hope nobody hassled you because of it."

"Things were calm, actually. That new RCMP seems like more of a hard ass than old Captain Peterson from before, and I think it shook some of the kids up. Only…" he paused, brow furrowing.

"What?"

"Ethan was asking questions about you, trying to figure out where you came from. He was trying to be subtle, but he's not really smart enough for that."

Lola snorted, but the creases on Gael's forehead didn't ease. "I think he's got it in for you. You need to be careful."

"I'll be fine." Lola tried to hide her smile, as elation filled her. Gael cared about her.

"You don't understand. I don't know how stable he is. I wouldn't put it past him to try to, like, actually hurt you. He's a bit of a psychopath, to be honest."

She laughed outright at his concern. "I promise I'll be careful."

He took her in with those warm brown eyes. Lola could melt into a pool at his feet when he looked at her like that.

The sound of a motor, muffled by the mist, startled them. Surrounded by earth and fog and the ancient tree, it was as if they had gone back in time. The rev of a modern engine intruded on the illusion.

"What the hell?" Both Gael and Lola turned as lights illuminated the mist, and an ATV pulling a small trailer puttered down the path near the treasure tree. It stopped with a jolt at the foot of the roots.

"Walt?" Gael asked. Nix climbed from the hole, and she stared open-mouthed as the tall boy climbed out of the ATV. He jammed his hands into his pockets and stared back at them, chin lifted and jaw tight. His face was white, as though he was facing his executioner.

"Get out of here," Nix said, eyes flaming.

Walt jerked at her anger but stood his ground. "Before you say anything, I had no idea what was going to happen last night."

Gael was still mute with confusion, so Lola stepped in. "You made that clear when you tackled Ethan."

"That's all fine and good, but what are you doing here?" Nix's arms were crossed tight over her chest.

"I thought I could help." Walt cleared his throat, then turned to the trailer. He stumbled over a root and a slight tremor shook his hand. Lola raised an eyebrow as she took this in. This boy who acted as though everything was beneath him cared very much about what was about to happen. What was this treasure to him?

He removed the tarp from the trailer. Neatly packed within were shovels, helmets, lanterns and collapsible metal ladders, all new and shiny. The ladders could be bracketed against the side of the pit, making their descent and ascent easier and safer. In one corner sat a motorized winch. They could rig their pulley system to that so they wouldn't have to waste time removing earth by hand. Lola itched to sort out the tools, most of them the highest quality; it appeared the rich boy knew something about treasure hunting.

"Listen, I've found some equipment you might need. A dig like this is going to need more than a rope ladder." He passed a dismissive look over the hole in the ground.

"We don't need you, Walt." But Gael's shoulders slumped, and he sounded tired rather than angry.

"Debatable. Maybe you don't want me around, but I can be a big help. It would speed things up."

Nix's eyes glittered. "And you happened to have all of this lying around?"

"Some of it." Walt scuffed his foot in the dirt. "I've done some research on digs over the years, in case..." His face creased with tension. "I mean, I always thought that maybe we could..."

"You thought you could just come back and be a part of this, even though it's obvious you don't give a shit about me."

There was a long silence, and Walt's pale face flushed magenta. "It's not like that." His voice caught in his throat.

"Cause it seems like you're only interested in me when there's treasure involved. I'm not an idiot. I'm not going to be used like that."

"I don't care about the treasure. It's not like I need it."

Nix snorted, and Walt dragged his hands through his hair. "Sorry, that was a shit thing to say. It's just, I can help you. And I want a chance…" He floundered, muttering low under his breath "… to make things right." Lola wasn't sure anyone but her heard him.

While the other two stared at him in astounded silence, Lola began to understand Walt. Didn't she want the same thing? To belong to these two humans, so warm and bursting with humanity it flooded the air around them. All the wealth and power on the island didn't seem to compare to what they could offer. Walt was a part of the popular crowd, and didn't it say everything that he had spent so much time thinking about how he could befriend Gael again.

Besides, if Gael sent him away, he would take all his shiny toys with him.

"C'mon," she said to Gael in an undertone. "You said yesterday we needed better equipment, and here it is."

Nix looked mutinous, on the point of refusing, but Gael stepped forward. "You want a chance? You'll have to prove yourself." Walt glanced up, finally meeting Gael's gaze, but Gael frowned. "This can't change the past," he said. "And we are not friends. But if you want to help on the dig, we can give it a trial."

"That's all I ask," Walt said.

"You actually have to work, though," Nix said. "No hiring less fortunate people to do the digging for you."

Walt held up his hand. "Nobody will work harder."

"And we're digging for Gael," she said, her blue eyes narrowing to slits. "You don't get a single coin out of this."

"I think we can make this work," Lola stepped in. She ran greedy eyes over the equipment. She could get so much more work done during the nights on her own. She put a consoling hand on Gael's arm, and his eyes flicked to her, softening at her encouraging smile.

"Yeah. Maybe it could work."

"Let's get to it." Walt rolled up the sleeves of his shirt and slipped off his deck shoes in favour of a pair of steel-toed boots he had brought.

They spent the next few hours setting up the equipment, Lola ensuring everything worked properly. Walt held a ladder in place as Nix scrambled down, forcing the brackets into the pit wall to keep them in place. Lola would go over them later to reinforce them. Walt was right; these would make a difference. The frayed rope ladder wasn't going to hold up for much longer.

"So, what does this mean?" Nix called to Walt. "Are we allowed to talk to each other in school now?"

Walt gazed at her intently. "Yeah. That'd be...I'd like that."

A bemused look spread over Gael's face, but he didn't seem unhappy. "You guys are going to be friendly? This is a sure sign of the coming apocalypse."

"I can hear you, you know." Nix didn't look up, but a pleased smile spread across her face.

After the sun had set and they shook out their sore muscles, they gathered at the edge of the pit. Walt leaned on his shovel. "So, tomorrow?"

"I can be here in the afternoon," Lola said.

Nix nodded. "I have to help at my mum's shop tomorrow anyway, but I'm sure I can wiggle out of it by mid-afternoon. Try for that?"

Walt tried to hide his smile, as though he'd learned it was something to be ashamed of. Lola felt a pang for him. Walt didn't need a chance so much as a real friend.

Gael shouldered his shovel. "Let's find some buried treasure."

Twelve

"I found something!"

Nix's voice floated from the pit. Lola and Walt, operating the winch, looked to one another, then peered over the edge. They had worked incessantly for the past week and a half, in between dock unloadings and field hockey practices, school clubs and babysitting jobs. Lola worked every night through to the early morning hours. At this point, the shaft was vertiginously deep, five twelve-foot ladders bracketed down the side of the wall, lit by hanging lanterns along the way. Gael and Nix were shadows in the glooming dark.

"Are you sure it's not another root?" Lola called from the lip of the pit. Gael's laughter floated up. Last week, Nix was convinced she had found something important. She dug her heels in and heaved, only to have the soil release a tree root, sending her onto her backside and showering her with earth. When she opened her eyes, they shone with surprise behind a mask of dust. Lola had laughed so hard she had to sit down.

"Haha," Nix said now. "No, this is different, it's hard and..." Her shocked gasp caused Lola to still.

"What is it?" she finally called when the two remained silent.

"It's a...a body." Nix sounded shaky.

"An animal?"

"It's not an animal, Lola." Gael's voice was deep and serious. Lola jumped into the pit, the ladder gliding through her hands as she slid down.

When she arrived at the bottom, Nix gripped a human skull in outstretched arms, held out like an offering. Her gaze was riveted on the gaping eye sockets, her lip curling back as though she couldn't believe what she held. The bone was greyish-brown, and most of the teeth were missing.

It had obviously been in the hole for a very long time. Lola's skin rippled when she saw the back of the skull caved in, as if it had been crushed by a shovel. Signs of foul play. Was it sacrifice, or part of a protective spell? Her eyes lit up. A human sacrifice was a sign of something precious. Or the work of a madman. Either way, it made things interesting. "We're on the right track," she said.

Gael's eyes were dark and hooded. "That person was murdered."

"Did you find anything else?" Lola asked.

"Not yet," Nix said, coming out of her reverie, shaking her head. "It was here, at the side. The rest of the body might be inside the earth."

"*When* is this body from?" Gael asked. "I've heard all the stories. Bad things happened when my great-great-whatever dug here. Do you think he had anything to do with it?"

Lola shook her head and reached for the skull. Nix nearly threw it at her, rubbing her hand vigorously on her jeans.

"This wasn't from when your great-great-whatever dug here," Lola said, feeling the rough surface of the bones. "This is many centuries old." She looked at them. "I think this is from the original dig. The first people to hide the treasure in the Well of Souls. They left more than the treasure down here."

Her voice echoed around the earth walls.

"But why?" Gael asked.

"Pirates would often kill a man and leave his body behind after burying a treasure. They were superstitious; they thought the ghost of the dead man would haunt the site and scare others away."

Gael's gaze flickered between Lola and the skull. "How do you know that?"

She let out a puff of laughter, trying to diffuse the dread that had settled inside the hole. Their adventure digging for pirate treasure had just turned darker, but she didn't want them to get skittish. "I've been doing this a long time. I know a few things about buried treasure, and bodies aren't uncommon."

"Ridiculous," Nix said, but her voice was hollow. Her eyes gleamed in the dim light, gaze locked on the skull.

Gael looked as though he wanted to take the skull from her, but then dropped his hands, shoving them in his pockets instead. "So, what do we do? Do we, like, tell people about this?"

Lola chewed her lip. Telling the authorities about human remains would bring the police, then probably archaeologists. Interest in the Well of Souls would explode. Their dig would be over. Not only that, but there would be a flashing red light signalling to the world that something was going on here. Jacquotte would pay attention. Lola shivered. Someone would come looking for her.

Ever since she had overheard those words spoken on Jacquotte's yacht, she'd known she was running on stolen time. *She's weak and becoming a problem. Something will have to be done.* Lola had been waiting for the command for some time. She was weaker than the rest of Jacquotte's crew, though she tried to make up for it in speed and her research. But it didn't seem to matter what she did; everything about her seemed to irritate her leader.

Even worse than Jacquotte's dismissal of her was the easy reply that came: *Consider it done.* Words spoken by Beau. Demon or not, he had been the closest thing to a friend she'd had, and he agreed to track her down. There was only one way out of Jacquotte's crew: annihilation.

So no, they could not let anyone know what was happening on Duchesne Island.

Lola shook her head. "No, we don't tell anyone about this. We put the skull back where we found it and try not to disturb the rest."

"But..." Something flashed across Gael's face. Disappointment in her? "We can't leave this. You're supposed to—"

"Gael, we tell someone about this, and it's over. The dig, the possibility of finding anything. Is that what you want?"

"Obviously not." Emotions played over his face, one after the other, struggling between what was right and what he wanted. "But still, it's a corpse."

"This corpse has been here for centuries. The murderer is long dead. There is nothing we can do. It's best if we pretend this didn't happen. Tell nobody."

Gael and Nix both finally nodded. Something dark seemed to ripple between them, and neither would meet her gaze.

Lola crouched and carefully fitted the skull back into the hole where it had been found. At that angle, it was easy to pretend it was nothing more than a rock. As she gently pushed, she murmured a few words under her breath, a blessing for the departed.

Gael and Nix both slumped over their shovels, so she attempted a smile. "Let's take a break."

They climbed silently. Walt waited for them at the top. "What happened?"

Nobody said anything, so Lola put her arms around each of them, getting them to sit on a root. "There was a body, Walt. A skeleton, from a long time ago."

"What?" Walt spun to stare into the hole as though he could see it himself.

"We can't tell anyone about it. It would kill the dig, and this search would be over."

Walt turned back to them, his gaze intent. "We can't let that happen."

"Then we're understood. We never found anything."

"It was so creepy," Nix shivered. She dug a crumpled napkin out of her bag and scrubbed at her hands, as though to rid them of grave dirt. Then she took out a box of granola bars and handed them around. She bit deeply into one speckled with chocolate chips. The sugar revived her. "I've never seen a corpse before, not for real."

"Want to go to Lost Souls?" Lola asked Gael. She enjoyed their nights there. They would often go after digging. The manager scowled at them but looked the other way when Walt was with them. She could sip her coffee and stare at the sea and surround herself with all that life. Tonight, she wanted to wipe the pensive look off Gael's face.

He wasn't listening to her, though. She nudged him and his head shot up. "What?"

"Lost Souls? Tonight?"

"Oh, I can't. I promised my mum I would sit with Diego at the hospital. He sleeps most of the time, but it's nice for him to have someone there if he does wake up, and she's working tonight."

"How is he doing?" Lola asked quietly.

Gael shrugged, staring at the hole. "Not good. I should get there soon, actually. I'm going to take off."

He didn't offer her a ride on his bike like he usually did. The highlight of her day, if she was honest about it. Instead, he left the clearing without a glance back.

Nix and Walt mumbled goodbyes and shuffled to their bikes as well. A dark cloud descended over the dig site.

Lola slammed her shovel to the ground harder than necessary and headed into town. She spotted the lights at The Pain Perdu with relief. A coffee and a paper would soothe her, as would Faye's bustling kindness as she bossed her customers around while wringing every last ounce of gossip out of them. It had become her habit to visit the café after they finished digging for the night. When she entered, Faye would greet her and pour her coffee without asking.

Lola never said much and paid with cash, but she knew the baker kept a careful eye on her. She didn't pry, either, as she did with everyone else, content to let her be. In these quiet evenings, Lola found rare tranquillity.

Tonight, though, she couldn't settle in that warmth. Spreading the paper in front of her offered no pleasure. It even gave her a frisson of anxiety, as though she had somewhere else to be. The coffee sat bitter on her tongue.

Was it finding the skull? Lola was hardly new to death, and the corpse did not affect her the way it did the others. But she wasn't immune to the way Gael looked at her when she asked him to go against his deeply ingrained sense of what was right.

He, of course, had no idea how monstrous she really was. There was no way forward for them, there never had been. Gael was only a distraction, after all.

She stared unseeing at the words spilling together in front of her, listening to the conversations surrounding her. To her left were three teenage girls, giggling over videos on their phones. They kept on trying new filters and posing for selfies. A couple was arguing about the landscaper they had hired to finish their yard. Dull. And Captain Theodore Greyson was tucked into a corner at the back, watching everyone, no doubt. Lola stilled, listening as Faye approached him with a stack of French toast dripping in syrup.

"Pleasant day today?" she asked him.

"Hardly," Greyson responded, his voice gruff. "This place is living up to its gruesome reputation." Lola's ears pricked at his comment.

"What happened?" Faye's voice dropped.

"I can't talk about it, Faye, you know that."

"Is it Anthony Graves?" Faye's voice was a whisper, enticing, demanding Greyson give up his information.

"No, it's..." Greyson shook his head, then let out a rueful laugh. "What the hell, you probably know more than I do. You'd be better at my job than I am."

"So very true." She was smug with triumph.

Greyson leaned in. "Another body, found in the woods on the other side of the island."

Lola froze. Another body? That couldn't possibly be. She hadn't fed from another human since that first. She didn't want to bring suspicion down on her. But now... She couldn't help it; she turned and stared at Greyson. His face showed the wear from his work.

"Another murder?" Faye repeated in a whisper. "Oh my god. Is there...a serial killer on the island?"

"I couldn't really say." Greyson's eyes narrowed, and he looked straight at Lola as he noticed her attention. She whipped back around, staring intently at the paper, cursing to herself. She needed to know what the police knew, and whether they had a suspect in mind.

Greyson must know she was new to Duchesne by now, that she belonged to nobody. Would he suspect her, the orphaned misfit, of being involved in the bloody crimes tallying up on the island? Never mind that he was only half right. If this truly was a murder, then there was another killer on the island, besides herself. Lola didn't like those numbers.

Shaken, she slipped out of the café. Her throat was tight, like a noose closed in on her. She needed to find the treasure before everything fell apart. She would get to work, push herself to her demonic limits, to get to the bottom of the Well of Souls.

With the town closed up and everyone in bed, it seemed as though she was the only creature awake. Her footsteps on the cobblestoned road were muffled by the heaviness of the night air.

All was silent, otherwise.

Lola slowed. The silence was unnatural. The night was a bustling time for life and death; she should hear nocturnal creatures hunting. She strained to sense what had her on edge, but she couldn't pinpoint it. She felt on display, a spectacle for unseen eyes.

Giving her shoulders a shake, she marched into the forest over the hill. The trees were still, not even a breeze whispering through the new leaves. The moonlight shone bright, the shadows of branches making strange symbols on the beaten dirt path. Lola paused for a surreal moment, wondering if the trees were trying to tell her something.

The faintest rustle sounded behind her. Her demonic powers kicked in, her senses sharpening. A peppery cologne wafted to her under the forest smells, and the underlying musk of old blood. The scent conjured long nights on starlit beaches, and her stomach bottomed out. She knew who stalked her.

She resisted the urge to flee in blind panic and instead continued along the path at a steady pace to where the trail curved. Without warning, she bounded to the side, coming around the side of an oak. There she huddled against the trunk, waiting for her predator to reveal itself.

He came into view, creeping silently along the path, eyes alert in the trees now he had lost his prey.

Seeing his face was like a gut punch. Dread and desire filled her belly at the sight of him, a familiar combination. His dark hair peaked sharply over finely drawn features, exactly as the first time she had seen him, many decades ago. Long before she had learned how cruel he could be.

Beau had found her. There was no place she could hide since he'd agreed to end her immortal life, not even a cursed island. She was going to die, here and now.

As he passed her hiding place, her thoughts whirled frantically. She could run and hide, but what good would that do? He'd proven to her, again and again, he could find her anywhere. No matter how many times she walked away from him, he always found her. She shouldn't be this surprised he was here.

She had to face him, but she was defenceless. She had thought, on Duchesne, she was the wolf among lambs, but it turned out she was prey.

Stealthy and silent, she leapt behind him, crouching. Beau spun, startled, landing in an attack position, fangs bared. They froze, staring at each other.

What way would he lunge? She tensed, preparing for the attack that would end her.

Beau broke first, laughing. He slowly stood, straightening out his dark coat, and his curved fangs slid back into place. His eyes didn't leave Lola.

"Mercy, I always forget how fast you are," he drawled. "You seem so fragile. And then you move and I don't even see it. The mouse must always be faster when playing with the cats, isn't that right, love?"

"Don't call me that." Lola's heart slammed in her throat, taking in his perfect face, the familiar sneer. His cheeks were flushed and pink, and he could have passed for human if it wasn't for the glow of his eyes. He'd fed on human blood, and recently. Lola had just solved Cpt. Greyson's case, though he likely wouldn't thank her for the information.

"Come now, chérie, it doesn't have to be like this. Hear me out."

"Hear you out nothing," Lola said, her voice throaty. "You're nothing to me."

Beau's mouth curved into a cruel smile. "Liar. I'm everything to you."

Arrogant bastard. "How did you find me?"

He smirked. "I have my ways."

"This stalker thing is so boring, Beau." Lola kept her voice steady, though her insides were turning to liquid from terror. She couldn't read him, didn't know why he wasn't attacking. Instead, he was settling in for a chat. As though it was expected he would track her around the planet. "Did Jacquotte…"

"She doesn't know half as much as she thinks she does," Beau snarled. Lola flinched, remembering his temper. "She had no idea where you disappeared to. But I did. I've got you all figured out, chérie."

Lola closed her eyes for an instant. "Did you tell her?"

"I thought this could be our little secret."

Lola edged away. She didn't want to share anything with him ever again.

This was dangerous, so very dangerous, and it put her friends at risk. He would find a way to use them against her. Beau was excellent at reading people. It meant he nearly always got what he wanted. It also made him a remarkable sadist, as he knew where the pain point was.

Beau's contempt showed plainly on his pointed face. "You're looking a little rough. Not your best." He paced a circle around her. Lola turned, wary, never letting him get behind her. His eyes were heavy-lidded. "But, then again, you haven't been a good time in a long time, have you?"

He paused to take her in. His gaze travelling over her body had her back up like nails scratching down a board. She growled deep in her throat.

"That's more like it," he said in approval. "How about it, darling? Once more for old time's sake?"

Lola glanced over her shoulder for escape routes. Her heel caught at a root, and she stumbled, bracing for the attack.

It didn't come. Beau crossed his arms over his chest. "What do you think you're doing here?" He drawled out his vowels. "You're not feeding on them, that much is clear. Pretending to be human, is it? You're so predictable; it's embarrassing." He snorted, shaking his head sadly like a parent telling their child Santa Claus doesn't exist. "This is a phase when you think being human might actually be desirable. We all go through it. You'll cringe about this later. I've half a mind to let you play this out to the end. Because do you know what you'll do, in the end?" He stepped close. His eyes gleamed dark red as his voice dropped to a poisonous whisper. "You'll kill them all. Then, you'll set aside this childish fantasy forever."

"I won't." Lola lifted her chin, hating that she sounded like a child.

"What's the plan, then? You find the treasure and pretend to be a teenage girl forever?"

"I don't..."

"Have you forgotten why you're here? It's not to make friends with the edibles. It's not even for the fortune. You are here for one reason only: the power." He lunged forward, and Lola stumbled back, cringing as he laughed. "I didn't know you had it in you, to risk the curse to go after the Well of Souls. I'm proud of you, chérie. Think of what we could accomplish together."

His voice was low and seductive. Lola blinked, shaking the tremors of want he invoked in her. "I don't need you."

He smirked. "You're not as strong as you think. How much longer can you pull the mist in around you? It's impressive, but you can't go on like this. I'm surprised how far you've gone without feeding." His eyes flicked over her face, her neck. "Your stubbornness is compelling."

"Just go," Lola whispered.

"Jacquotte doesn't think you have it in you to be great. She thinks you're too weak, too sentimental. But I've seen you hunt; I've seen your speed. You rid yourself of your mercy, and you will be glorious."

"No."

Beau's smile was wicked. "I'm prepared to wait, darling. You can have this. It won't last forever. How much longer can you convince your pets you're something you're not?"

He took a step back and disappeared into the fog.

"I'll be waiting. When they turn on you, I'll be here. Then, you and I will make history together." His voice coiled around her, coming from everywhere. Like her affinity for the water, Beau could move and shape the wind at his command. Now it blew hard, dissipating the mist. He disappeared with it.

All that was left was his mocking laugh, echoing off the trunks of the ancient oaks.

THIRTEEN

A day and a night had passed without sign of Beau, though Lola had no idea how long that would last. She paced rather than walked, her head swivelling at the slightest sound. Because Beau knew about the dig and he knew about her friends. He told her he'd stay out of their way for the time being, but she trusted him as far as Nix could throw him. He would get bored and he would come after her, like he always did.

When digging with the others, she preferred to be at forest level to watch for trouble. Her worst nightmare was climbing out of the hole to find them lying on the ground, throats ripped out, staring at her with unseeing eyes. She couldn't get the image out of her head.

Staying above ground cost her, though. Before Beau arrived on the island, she could flood the island with fog. It was easier; it didn't take any nuance. Now, as the sun grew brighter, she kept the mist thick around herself and the dig site, letting the sun shine on the rest of the island, keeping Beau at a distance.

Her head pounded from the strain, but if it kept Beau away from them, it was worth it.

A squirrel chattered behind her, and Lola whirled.

"Are you okay?" Gael asked. "You're jumpy."

"It's nothing." Lola's eyes swept the perimeter of the dig site.

"It's not nothing. You're on red alert. Did something happen?" His warm brown eyes were full of concern.

"No, I..." She squinted against the light of the sun, filtering through the leaves of the forest and the haze of her mist. It was ferocious out there, and she should be underground. "Maybe we should call off the dig."

Gael nearly dropped his shovel. "What are you talking about? We've come so far. There's something down there, I can feel it." He paused. "For real, what's gotten into you?"

She finally met his gaze. "Do you ever get the feeling something is too good to last? And you keep on looking for the moment it all falls apart so you can point to it and say – I knew it was too good to last?"

Gael's shoulders relaxed. "I know exactly what you mean. This whole thing has been pretty crazy. But when it's over, we'll move on to the next crazy thing."

Lola's spirits sank. There would be no more adventures for them after this, not together. This dig would end, and they would go on with their normal human lives. And she would move on, too. It was what she had wanted.

"What are you lazy asses doing?" Nix clambered out of the hole, covered in dirt. "I didn't know sitting around was an option." Walt came out after her, just as filthy but looking more relaxed than Lola had ever seen him.

Gael grinned. "We'll relieve you."

Lola squinted at the misty forest. The sun was high in the sky, and Beau should be squatting in some dark corner. Still, as she descended into the pit, she allowed the mist to dissipate so Nix and Walt stood in sunshine, protecting them.

As they reached the bottom, Gael lifted Lola down the last few feet. Her shirt slipped up, and his hand grazed her bared waist. Shivers rippled across her skin.

She licked her lips, scrambling to think about anything other than how close he was. How delicious he smelled. How much she wanted to press her mouth to the V of his t-shirt.

As they worked, Lola enjoyed the steadiness of his presence. His scent surrounded her, making her light-headed. Occasionally their arms brushed one another, and he would breathe in sharply. She could smell his desire; knew he was as affected as she was. The chemistry between them was building to a breaking point.

She feinted a stumble, steadying herself on his arm, feeling solid muscle under her palm. Gael glanced at her as though he knew precisely the game she was playing.

"Hang on," he murmured, reaching for her hair. He teased at a curl, every tug excruciating. "You've got something stuck in here."

"I probably have a whole forest stuck in there," she laughed, taking his hand in hers. She didn't want to let go, and they stood there, fingers twining together. His lips were smiling, inviting.

Her eyes fell to the exposed line of his throat. She could see the beads of sweat that clung there in high definition, could see the beat of his pulse under the tender skin. She gasped as her fangs slid out, driven by her desire and overwhelming need. She couldn't do this. She didn't have the willpower to flirt with this desire. If she touched him, she was sure she'd crush him.

She whirled away, wanting to scream in frustration. Instead, she flexed her fists, focusing on calming her racing pulse, on retracting her fangs before he saw. "We should take a break."

Confusion played over his face, but then he let it go. His smile still came easy, though she was sure he was as frustrated as her. "How do you dig all day and never be affected by it? I'm sweating like a pig over here, and you're cool like ice cream." He reached out as though he wanted to smooth his thumb over her face, but he didn't touch her.

"Maybe it's being so far down here, in the earth."

He frowned, and a stab of panic ran through her. He was getting too close; he would soon discover what she was, and he would hate her. And she didn't want him to stop looking at her like she was somebody worth seeing.

"Gael?" Her voice was little more than a whisper.

"Yeah?"

"What is it you like about me?"

His laugh was loud and genuine, bouncing around the earth. "Are you serious?" He took in the look on her face and stilled. "You are…. Okay, you're beautiful and mysterious, which helps. But that's not it, not all. There's this thing you do when you're talking to people. You tilt your head, and you really concentrate, like they are the only person who matters, and I know you care what they have to say. Not many people do that. I like that about you."

It was a nice reply, observant and real, but Lola felt as though he had thrust a dagger through her chest. She analyzed people when they spoke because she was copying their movements, their mannerisms. She was trying to figure out how to pass as a human. It had nothing to do about caring.

She pressed her lips together. "We should go up," she said.

She started to climb the ladder, pausing when Gael didn't follow. "It's not cold down here," he said. "You think it would be, but it's warm. And dark. Like…" He broke off.

"Like what?"

"It's stupid. Nix would laugh her ass off if she heard me say this, but it's like a womb. A place to be reborn."

His words flickered through Lola like lightning. They were truth, absolute truth, whether he knew it or not. She pressed her hand to the earth, feeling its pulsing warmth. They were nearing a place of creation.

But was it a place that should be disturbed? Doubt ran through her, but she shook it off. She needed this. It was her only chance.

"Don't tell Nix I said that."

"Don't tell me what?" Nix's shadow appeared at the top of the hole. "Gael, stop being creepy!"

Gael laughed, not noticing Lola's dread.

"I'm tired, and it's getting dark," Nix said. "This weird mist just crept in again."

Lola climbed out into the fog she'd made, still shaken. The last thing she wanted to do was hurt Gael. Beau had promised that she would. It was so selfish for her to continue this dig with them.

"My god, you're filthy." Nix reached over to brush dirt off Lola's shirt. Her hand lingered on Lola's arm, and Lola could sense her tension. Nix's eyes were burning into hers, and her pupils were dilated.

Realization struck. Lola caught Nix's hand, holding her gaze. "Nix." Her voice was sympathetic, nearly an apology.

Nix's hand stilled in Lola's, then she whipped around to tidy the dig site, her cheeks flaming red.

"Lost Souls?" Walt asked Gael, as he locked the equipment in the trailer he had brought on the first day.

"Sounds good," Gael said, his eyes only for Lola. "Ride with me?" It had become their routine, but she wasn't sure she should be that close to him. Her bloodlust pulsed under her skin. Her gaze darted around the forest.

"I think maybe we should all just go home," she said. Safe and sound.

"Come on, Lola." Gael reached for her, and she danced away from his touch. His hand hovered before clenching into a fist.

"Let her go." Nix scowled as she brushed dirt off her hands. "If she doesn't want to be with us, fine."

"I'm just tired. And hungry." She'd been under strain for too long. Forget Beau. As the need grew inside of her, they wouldn't be safe around *her* for much longer. She paced, keeping the urge to feed at bay.

Nix let out a disdainful snort. "You? Eat something? That's a laugh."

Gael shushed her, but Nix exploded, all fiery hair and flashing eyes. "Are we never going to talk about this? The girl clearly has an eating disorder."

The group went still. Lola stared at Nix, then pulled out a cigarette. She avoided smoking in front of Gael, but tonight she hoped the sparkle of nicotine would soothe her nerves.

"Lola, Nix didn't mean anything by it," Gael said.

"You agreed with me yesterday!"

"You two talk about me? While you're sitting over your books in school?" Lola let out a thin stream of smoke, looking at them coolly, not even sure why this rankled her so much.

"Look, it's nobody's business," Gael said, hands out as if to calm the situation. "But if you needed help…"

Lola closed her eyes and let out a bitter laugh. "*If* I needed help? You have me all figured out, don't you?"

"I meant it seems like things are hard for you, and you don't have to go through this alone."

He was so confident, ready to take on the world for her. Lola wanted him so badly, it shuddered through her. "I can't talk about it."

Gael's face shuttered. "Right."

"I need to go."

But Nix, temper up, wasn't done with her yet. "Yeah, you should probably go throw up that sip of water you nearly had."

"That's enough, Nix." Gael turned, partly putting himself in front of Lola as though to protect her from the onslaught.

"What's your problem?" Lola's temper was starting to spark as well. This was becoming dangerous. She needed to leave, yet she was rooted where she stood.

"You're my problem. I think you're going to pocket all the treasure we find. Get us to dig for you, then swipe it once we find it. You'll disappear and we'll never see you again."

It was true enough to sting. A steady whine of pain built behind her eyes and she pressed her fingers against her forehead. "So, I'm a thief. Anything else?"

Nix waved a hand over Lola. "This whole pin-up thing is a little sexually aggressive. You play these little games and it's obvious you're desperate for male attention."

Lola laughed out loud, without mirth. "Are you calling me a slut?"

Nix sniffed. "I didn't have to."

"You're out of line, Nix!" Gael yelled. "What's gotten into you?"

"Whatever. As if you could ever see anything wrong with her, the way she has you twisted around her little finger." She stopped, then whirled on Gael, tears of anger bright in her eyes. "Can't you see how she's using you?"

"Are you jealous of her?" Gael stuttered, taken aback by his friend's rant.

"Of a slut like her? Hardly."

Lola's temper pushed straight through her, leaving behind cold fury. She laughed again, puffing on the cigarette. She slowly paced around Gael to face Nix. "Oh, she's jealous all right." Lola's voice was low and mean. "But it's not *me* she's jealous of, isn't that right? In fact, it's *you* she's jealous of."

"Jealous of me? Because of..." Gael trailed off in utter confusion, watching the two girls face off.

"Did you wish it was you down there with me, Nix? Want me to press myself against you? I've seen the way you look at me when we're alone."

"What are you talking about?" Nix's voice spat fury, though her eyes were overly bright. She had a wild look, like an animal searching for escape.

Lola's heart sank, anger fading as soon as she spoke. *Merde*, what had she done? Words spoken could not be erased. She backpedalled. "There's nothing wrong with that—"

Nix's tears spilled over. On a sob, she whirled away.

"Nix, wait!" Gael caught her arm, but she ripped free of him.

Launching herself onto her bike, she tore away from the clearing, a copper streak between the trees.

Gael spun on Lola. "What the hell just happened?"

Lola looked away, not wanting to face his anger, though she deserved it. "I thought we were sharing personal observations."

"But...Nix? I didn't know."

"No?" Lola cocked her head. "I thought you must have known. At first, I thought she was in love with you. But soon it became pretty obvious. To me, at least."

"You shouldn't have."

"Told the truth? Sapphic leanings are nothing to be ashamed of."

"Lola, we're not all cool and French about these things. This is a big deal in a small town like this. Nix could be really hurt."

She deflated, now nothing more than a bitter core. "I didn't mean to hurt her. I spoke in anger." She pressed her fingers against her temples, banging with insistent pain. "*Merde*, what a mess I've made of things. Does it change how you see her?" Lola prayed she hadn't ruined their friendship.

He stared into the sky. "Nix is Nix. This doesn't change a thing."

Lola slumped in relief. "She still has you."

"Yes, she'll always have me. But I wish she had had the chance to tell me herself." He turned to Lola. "You took that away from her. She didn't get the chance to tell the people she cared about in her own time."

Her chest squeezed uncomfortably. "I handled things poorly."

"You think?" Gael's look was hard. Lola couldn't meet his eye. Losing his regard was physically painful. She could have laughed if she weren't so damn confused. *I'm not even a person!* she wanted to shout. How could she know how to do these things?

Walt had been leaning on a root, silent during the entire fight, but now he spoke up. "Nix? A lesbian?"

Gael whirled. "Don't you dare tell anyone. You know how they can get."

Walt shrugged. "Who would I tell?"

"I don't know, all your amazing popular friends you felt were much more important than me for all these years."

"Gael, about that..."

"I don't want to hear it. I'm going to find her." He strode to his bike.

"I'll come with you," Walt offered.

"Leave it." Gael stormed away, grabbing his bike to catch up with Nix.

Lola and Walt stared at each other, the two left behind. Walt's eyebrows were bunched together, as though trying to figure out a complex math problem.

"I never meant to hurt him," he said suddenly.

"I know." Lola took another drag of her cigarette. She understood Walt the best. She suspected under all his bored rich kid image he struggled to connect with others. He stood outside looking in on true friendship and wondering why it was so easy for others. Just like her. "And yet, that's exactly what we do sometimes."

"Are you going home?" The plea in his voice tore at Lola. What had happened to her, that she felt the suffering of others so clearly?

She let out a slow stream of smoke. The pressure built under her gums. If he stayed near her any longer, he would start to look like a tasty snack. "You need to go home, Walt. It's the safest place for you."

As his tall frame crumpled, Lola crumpled too. Three people now, three friends maybe, she'd managed to let down within a few minutes. Excellent night's work. But she needed to hunt, and Walt needed to be somewhere else.

She watched as he slouched to his bike and disappeared into the forest, then threw away her cigarette with a huff of derision.

She needed to replenish her blood, to get control of this cataract of emotion seeping out of her. She was sick of it. The hunt was calling, and she had reached the edge of her control.

The wind blew the scent of a nearby animal to her, and she growled, low in her throat. Her fangs slipped over her lips, and silent as a lynx she prowled into the forest, away from Walt and the others.

Fourteen

A massive storm blew over Duchesne, coming in from the east in billowing thunderheads. Lola peeked out of her window at it, her fingers running over the newly plucked wildflowers she'd put in a cup. She thrummed with weird energy, the storm matching her mood exactly. *Did I make you?*

Normally she could direct currents and nudge mist to a certain place, but an entire storm system would have been far beyond her abilities. Since arriving on Duchesne, it was as though her senses had opened to the natural world around her and played off of her state of mind.

She shivered as a pounding took up in the air, like a drumbeat in her veins. There was nothing natural about it. It pulled at her, calling her out.

She had eaten her fill of wildlife the night before, which left her not hungry, exactly, but still craving her true sustenance. Her hands twisted into claws. She couldn't have that. She would not give in.

The first week after Anthony Graves had been found, she'd been careful not to disturb the contents of his home, but the Port Despardoux police service seemed disinterested in a dead man's shack. Now, she opened one of the dresser drawers, pulling out a sweater far too large for her. She hadn't planned on wearing a dead man's clothes, but her clothes were crusty with filth from digging and she was running out of options. The place had been condemned; nobody would miss a sweater.

She slathered cream over her skin, rough and flaking off. Though she was eating enough to survive, without human blood her body couldn't regenerate as well as it should. Everything was going to fall apart. She couldn't just wait while she either wasted away or succumbed to her demonic needs.

Though it was mid-afternoon, there was no need to protect herself from the sun. The growing tempest cast billowing cloud cover over the island.

A boom of thunder sounded in the sky as she hiked through the ancient trees. The static energy spurred her forward at inhuman speeds.

When she arrived at the treasure oak, she gazed at it, part in wonder, part in irritation. This tree was playing tricks on her, without a doubt. She didn't know if it was otherworldly, but there was far more to it than an ordinary tree, ancient or not. Was it the tree itself putting out the call, summoning her to this place? Lola placed her hand against the trunk, feeling the same pulse pounding under her skin. It was warm. "What do you want?"

On another crack of thunder, the sky unleashed, and rain poured down on her. The crown of leaves overhead offered little protection against it, and droplets lashed her face, cooling her turmoil. She had the feeling the tree was sentient, watching her. Waiting for something.

"So be it," she whispered. She slipped into the treasure hole and descended into the earth. Being closed in by the earth was comforting, as though she was being cradled.

She worked with single-minded devotion, with every layer of mud lifted feeling as if she was getting closer. Hours later, she had moved masses of earth. She slowed, noticing the rising water around her boots. She cursed as she splashed through the growing puddles. The pit would flood if the rain didn't stop.

She stared up at the progress she had made, raindrops trickling over her face. According to the documents she had studied about the Well of Souls, the original treasure chest had been found at seventy feet down, a mark she had just passed. From here, they were in uncharted territory.

"Lola?" a voice called from above.

She craned her neck. Gael's head was little more than a smudge.

"I'm here! I'll come up!"

"No, I'll come down."

It took several minutes. He carried a shovel on his shoulder.

He jumped the last few feet, landing right in front of her. In the confined space, there wasn't much room to back up. Lola was trapped, Gael entirely too near. He crossed his arms as he looked down at her, and she remembered the things he had said the day before. Everything she had said. Her heart pounded and she wondered if she could somehow flee this entire situation.

His head tilted as he took her in. "You've dug more than we've done in days. You've been here awhile?"

Lola gave a tentative smile. "I wasn't sure if anyone was going to come."

"I'm here now."

"And Nix?" She hesitated, trying to read his closed face. "Did you speak to her?"

His stony expression eased and he shook his head. Water caught in his black hair, causing it to cling to his neck. "I didn't see her until this morning. She point-blank refused to even look at me. That girl knows how to hold a grudge."

Lola ducked her head. "I wish I could take it back."

"It's going to work out; she just needs some space. I can give her that. I'm not going anywhere."

Her tension eased a fraction. Gael and Nix were dedicated to each other. He bore such confidence they would weather the storm. She had never known such devotion; she certainly hadn't earned it.

She cleared her throat. "About what Nix said... I'm not looking to hurt you." She wished she could tell him that Nix was wrong, but the girl had figured out her game and she didn't want to lie. She couldn't confess, either. She blinked water out of her eyes. "I wasn't expecting you. I don't quite understand it, but there is something about you that makes me *complètement folle*. Completely crazy."

Gael was quiet before he reached out and pushed her hair back over her ear. "I know the feeling." His fingers brushed over her cheek and her knees went shaky. "Lola, I'm just not sure exactly why you're here."

The way his gold-tinged eyes were looking at her, she wanted to reveal everything, up to and including her non-existent soul. Instead, she whispered, "What do we do now?"

He gave a lopsided smile. "We can dig. We're good at that." He held out a headlamp. "You always forget yours."

"*Merci.*" Lola took it, unable to explain she didn't need it.

In their cocoon, it was as if they were the only people who existed, working shoulder to shoulder, outside of time. She never wanted this moment to end.

Gael threw himself into the work, digging with more intensity than ever. When his shovel hit something with a thunk, he let out a yell of triumph.

The look he gave her matched the shock wave that shuddered through her. *This* was what made everything worthwhile. The discovery, when the hunt pays off. She would chase that high to the ends of the earth.

"It sounded like wood," she said, kneeling to peel away the mud with her hands.

"Another treasure chest?"

She glanced at the walls. "If my research is correct, the original treasure was found a few feet above here." She pointed to a line she had marked herself for reference. "We've dug further than they did."

"Is your research correct?"

A smile played over her lips. "If they had kept on going, they might have found something else."

"My god, Lola, this is actually happening." Gael covered his eyes with his hands.

"Let's clear it off."

But as they scraped mud from the wood, they couldn't find an edge that would suggest a chest.

Lola sat back on her knees, wiping hair from her face and spreading mud across her cheek. "It's another wooden platform, like the ones your great-great-whatever had to break through." She pulled up clumps of matted fibre pushed in around the wood. "These are logs; they go right into the side of the shaft."

"But what does that mean?"

Her eyes gleamed with excitement. "It means whoever first buried the treasure went deeper. The treasure chest found by your great-great-whatever *was* a red herring."

Gael thrust his shovel into the wooden platform blade first, barely making an indentation. "Damn, this wood is thick. It's going to take us forever." He wiped rain out of his eyes. "Maybe Walt has a chainsaw."

The excitement of the hunt had Lola's demonic energy buzzing. "Hang on," she said, turning her back to him so he couldn't see. There was no way she could wait for the others to arrive to break through the platform. "I think some of the wood over here is rotten. I'll see if I can..."

Lola plunged her shovel with all her force between the shaft wall and the platform. It bit in deep, and she used the shovel as a lever to crack the wood.

The logs finally broke, splintering in a geyser of mud. Lola fell back into Gael, and they crashed to the ground.

Sputtering, Lola struggled to right herself. She was on top of Gael, one arm hooked under his shoulder. His lazy grin reappeared.

"Well done." His voice was husky. She felt his unbearable warmth under her body, and lust thrummed through her, electrified by the discovery.

Heedless of every stern warning she had given herself about this, she closed the distance between them, kissing him.

Gael groaned, his hands gripping her hips, holding her against him. Her hands tangled into his hair as her tongue slipped along his lips, greedy for him.

His mouth trailed over to graze at the side of her jaw. "We did it," he whispered, his breath warm at her ear.

The log platform beneath her shifted, and she felt a thrill of panic. Both of them froze, wrapped around each other. "Do you hear that?" Lola asked. "Like an echo?"

Gael's eyes widened as the floor shifted again. They scrambled up, Gael kneeling next to the hole as he peered down.

"Lola, there's nothing underneath."

"*Incroyable.*" Lola shifted to kneel next to him, shifting mud out of the way to peer over the edge of the platform. Instead of more earth, the log platform held them over a cavern. It sounded enormous and empty, echoing with dripping water. "The shaft drove straight to an underground cavern. But why? What's down here?"

"Here, let me." They shifted, and Gael removed his headlamp to aim it into the abyss.

The light was swallowed in darkness. They couldn't see the bottom or the sides of the space. The acoustics of the stone walls echoed strangely, and it was difficult to pin where the running water was.

"This changes everything," she said, speaking as rapidly as the thoughts popped up. "We're going to need new equipment. We need to know how deep the cavern is and where it goes."

"Goes?" Gael echoed. "There are caverns and caves that honeycomb the whole island. It could go anywhere."

Lola bounced on her toes as her mind flashed through all the different scenarios. Where was the Well of Souls treasure? And what exactly was it? Everything about this dig told her it was going to be the find of a lifetime.

"I wonder if a cave survey of this area has been made. Have these caverns ever been mapped? We can't tell anyone about this."

Gael watched her wide-eyed. "Keep it a secret?"

"If this gets out, there will be a wild dash to find the treasure. People from all over the world will hear about this." Jacquotte would hear about this.

"But the land's protected..."

"Do you think a piece of paper saying no one can dig here is going to stop them at this point? It might have not been worth it on a rumour, but we've proven there is more to the Well of Souls. We've already done the hard work. They will be down here so fast, scrambling to take what is rightfully yours; you won't be able to fight them off. No, we can't tell anybody."

"What about Nix?"

"Of course Nix. And Walt, if you trust him."

Gael thought about this for a long moment, then nodded. "I do."

"Good. His deep pockets are going to come in handy now." She let loose a giddy laugh. If she found this treasure, according to the legends she'd never have to worry about Beau or Jacquotte ever again. "Gael, this is huge!"

He stepped toward her. An ominous crack stopped him midstride.

"No!" Lola screamed.

The wood around the hole collapsed, giving under Gael's weight faster than she imagined possible.

She lunged for him, but it was too late. He disappeared, sucked into the yawning hole.

Her heart stopped as she threw herself along the platform, still trying to reach for him even as she heard his scream echoing through the cavern. An abrupt splash ended his cry.

"Gael!" The edge of the hole crumbled further, and Lola half fell through. With her fingertips, she held on.

"Gael?" Her voice was choked with terror. The rest of the platform held, and she leaned further in, one hand gripping the wall. "Where are you?" Her voice was a frantic shriek.

A stifled groan drifted from deep below.

"Gael!" She couldn't dive into the cave without a way of getting him out. Lola flew up the ladder to the surface, barely touching the steps as she vaulted to the top and grabbed the old rope ladder.

She slid down back to the hole. Knotting the rope ladder to the metal one bracketed into the wall, she let it fall into the emptiness.

"I'm coming." She lowered herself into the cavern. The wooden platform creaked but held. Swaying, she descended into the dark. She kept her headlamp off, knowing it would wreck her night vision.

A few rungs down, something sparkled at the edge of her vision. She twirled toward it and froze. It wasn't all darkness here, as she expected.

She blinked, trying to make sense of the light. As it grew in strength, she could make out the rough wall. A jagged entrance to a tunnel was set high on a ledge along the cavern wall. Light spilled out, twinkling like fireflies at dusk.

But it was more than light. It called to her, a siren's song demanding to be answered. Something beyond that tunnel waited for her, wanting to be found.

The treasure of the Well of Souls. Immeasurable power was within her reach. Her head emptied of all thought, save for the need to get there.

Mesmerized, Lola jumped to the floor of the cavern, the rope dangled within arm's reach. She could climb the wall. It would be easy. The light twinkled. It wanted her, and Lola wanted to answer the call.

Somewhere deep inside the cavern, stones rumbled together. A part of her told her there was something important she needed to do. She shook her head at the distraction, stalking to the light. Nothing would stop her pursuit of salvation.

"Lola?" Gael's voice sounded in the dark, weak and raspy.

She froze. Gael. He fell. How could she have forgotten? She was caught between warring instincts: to help the boy, or find the treasure. Jacquotte wouldn't hesitate; neither would Beau. What was an edible next to power? She strode towards the lights.

Gael grunted, trying to get up, but fell back with a cry of pain. "My leg!" he gasped. Lola paused halfway across the cavern floor. Gael was hurt. He needed her. But surely she could check out the tunnel first. In her next step, her boot came down into a puddle of water that hadn't been there before.

"Lola, something's happening!" Water entered the cavern, rising inch by inch. Gael's breathing was short and raspy.

He could die, she reminded herself. And she didn't want him to die.

She turned, forcing herself to put the glowing tunnel behind her. "Gael, where are you?" She splashed towards his voice, through water now ankle-deep. "Talk to me."

"Lola, the water..." Finally, she pinpointed his location, making out the outline of his body.

"I got you." She knelt at his side. He struggled to stand and fell back.

Lola tilted her head. The texture of the air changed; her heart caught in her throat.

The echoing drip of the cave became a wild rushing, a roar of water. It sounded as though the entire Atlantic was bearing down on them.

"*Merde.*" She gave one last longing look at the cavern. It would be underwater in minutes.

But she had less than that if she wanted to save Gael. With a cry of frustration, she turned back to him.

The water level was over her knees when she stood. Gael scrambled against the current, unable to rise.

"Hold on!" she screamed over the thunder of the water. She caught him, pulling him up against her chest, and stiffened.

Part of Gael's face was smeared with blood. He must have banged his head on a rock, leaving a jagged gash. The smell of him caused her fangs to slip out. The water lashed at their legs and Gael clung to her to keep himself upright.

He didn't know she was the most terrible danger down here.

She didn't have time to get herself under control. All noise went quiet in her head when Lola gave in to every instinct she had been fighting since she met him and bit into the flesh of his neck.

He let out a gasp of pain. She held him even tighter as he moaned in her arms. The surge of blood was beyond anything she could remember experiencing. Gael tasted of salt and cinnamon and *life*.

She could feel that life filling her, satiating her, pumping in her arteries. There had never been anything other than him. She would never stop.

"Lola?" he gasped. She came back to herself. This was Gael, the boy who knew of curses and cared for his family. He would die in her arms, here and now. She was a monster. She was unforgivable.

With a power she didn't know she possessed, Lola ripped herself away from Gael. He collapsed in her arms.

Merde, merde, merde. His head flopped to the side as he gazed at her, eyes unfocused.

"I knew you'd come," he said. He inhaled with a faint hiss, his eyes starry from the buzz of her feeding off of him. "You're glowing." They both wobbled as the current pushed against them. She could leave him here and continue down her path to the Well of Souls treasure.

"I'm happy I had a chance to know you before the end." His voice was low, barely audible.

The water was lapping at their chests now. He was very close to the edge, and she had done this to him. Something tickled deep inside of her, different from all instincts she had ever known.

She was going to save him. She would move heaven and earth to make sure this boy lived, even if it meant losing her chance to save herself.

She could be more than a monster. But if they didn't get out of there *now*, that knowledge would come to nothing.

"This isn't the end. Do you hear me? I'm going to get you out of here." She shifted Gael onto her back as the water pressed against them. "Can you hold onto me?"

"Yes," Gael said, then fell headfirst into the water, unresponsive. He slipped under the surface.

"*Merde encore.*" Lola fished him out before she lost him. He came up coughing, eyes rolling back in his head, barely conscious.

She heaved him into a fireman's hold, his broad body draped over her shoulders. *Dieu merci* for his blood pounding through her veins; it gave her new strength. Gael's life force gave her a power and a will she had never known before.

She began to climb the ladder, praying it would hold as it was whipped every which way by the water. Halfway toward the opening of the shaft, a tidal wave of water crashed into the cavern, flooding it with the might of the ocean.

Lola clung to Gael, praying the knots would hold, that Gael would stay with her.

He coughed, head dipping into the water. Lola braced herself and kept on climbing.

"Don't let go." His voice was hoarse. "Lola…"

They made it to the base of the pit. She glanced over her shoulder one last time. The glittering light from the cave brightened for an instant, reflecting on the surging water like the full moon on the ocean, before it was swallowed by a murky wave.

Lola crawled onto the remnants of the log platform, water churning at her toes. She found a better grip on the metal ladder and sagged in relief, thinking she'd made it.

The reprieve was short-lived. The water level surged to her thighs and kept on coming. She raced the waterspout to the surface, the bubbling mass splashing right below her feet.

Cresting the edge, she threw herself forward as filthy water spilled out behind her. Lola crawled away, burdened by Gael's weight on her back. Once she felt safely out of reach, she fumbled to settle Gael onto the forest floor.

He fell onto his back with a graceless thud. The force made him choke, and he turned to his side, vomiting water. Then he went still.

FIFTEEN

"Gael? Gael!"

He struggled, and his eyelids slit open. "Lola," he whispered. "Did you see it? The light..."

She cradled his head. "Yes, I saw it. You have to hold on. Stay with me, so we can explore." He nodded, but his eyes rolled back, and he lost consciousness.

"No!" Frantic, she pressed her fingers into the crook of his neck, feeling for his pulse. His heart was slow, weak, his breathing shallow. He needed a blood transfusion, immediately.

The rain lashed her, cold and stinging. It slid over Gael's face, washing away the blood of his wound. Lola let out a sob, trying to make sense of her racing thoughts. She needed a plan.

His phone. Humans always had phones with them, usually attached to their hands. She prayed he had left it above ground – it would be useless if it had been submerged.

She lunged for his bag, tucked into the roots of the treasure oak. She whimpered with relief when she found the phone in the front pocket and dialled 911. She had to scream into the phone over the roar of the wind.

"Yes! He fell and lost a lot of blood. I had to move him. No, he's unconscious. We're in the woods..." Lola let out a groan of frustration. There was no way an ambulance would be able to reach them. Humans on foot would take too long.

"We're at the edge of the woods. Along Cottage Road," she said, naming the one place she knew, Gael's home.

"The dispatch can be there in ten minutes," came the tinny voice on the other end. "Don't move him and stay on the line."

Lola hung up. She had less than ten minutes to get Gael to the edge of the woods. She cradled his head on her shoulder. His legs dangled to the ground. She steeled herself, pulling deep into her powers. She was utterly focused on her one goal.

Gritting her teeth, she sprinted, finding a rhythm across the forest floor.

"I have you," she whispered to Gael. At rest, he did not look younger, as some people did. His face took on sterner lines without his easy smile, settling into the aspect of the man he would become. She urged her legs faster. She wanted him to become that person because she wanted to meet him one day.

Leaping over roots, she pounded the trail, slipping over the mud and cursing the rain in her eyes but never once flagging. The trees rose like bars of a prison, keeping her from her goal, and the wind whipped in her face, batting her hair into her eyes. She let out a scream of frustration and thought she heard an answering laugh. Or had she only imagined it?

One foot after the other. She fixated only on the beat of her steps, and the oaks eventually thinned. Finally, the road came into sight, and she slipped to a stop. She could see the outline of Gael's cottage in the valley beyond, dark and grim in the rain.

With as much care as possible, Lola lay Gael against the edge of the nearest tree, protected by the towering branches above him. She removed her jacket and held it over him to keep the rain from his face.

It was a good thing Gael was unconscious. Lola had used extreme amounts of demonic energy to get them out of the cavern and through the forest. With Gael's blood pounding through her veins, she had never felt so powerful and was lighting up the dark forest. If she could look in a mirror, she knew she would see crystalline eyes and glowing skin, lips curled back in a snarl to expose overgrown canines. She wasn't looking to feed, though. Her instincts right now told her to protect.

But she couldn't be found like this. She closed her eyes, calming herself. She concentrated on lessening the power burning out of her, allowing her fangs to slide back into her gums. For Gael to get through, she would have to play at human. A vampire was very good at taking lives, but she didn't have the power to bring him back from the brink.

The minutes stretched, far longer than normal, she was sure. Finally, a siren sounded in the distance, muted by the rain.

Lola went to the edge of the road, waving Gael's backpack to catch the driver's eye in the downpour. The vehicle screeched to a halt, and two medics scrambled out, rain slickers pulled tight around their faces.

"He's over here!" Lola yelled into the storm, gesturing them to Gael's still form. They came with a stretcher, expertly manoeuvring him and strapping him to the gurney.

"What happened?" one of them yelled as she worked.

"He fell." She'd tried to come up with a plausible story. She couldn't tell them they were digging at the treasure site. And they would have to pull her nails out before she told anyone they had broken through to a secret underground cavern. "We were climbing trees, and he slipped. It was pretty far. He cut his neck, I think, and lost a lot of blood. He was talking until about ten minutes ago when he lost consciousness."

The medic gave her an incredulous look as she directed her partner to lift Gael. "You were climbing trees? In this weather?"

"It was just a dumb bet we had made. Look, does it really matter? He needs help. We can talk about it later." The humans worked with painful slowness, and she had to rein in her frustration.

"Are you coming?" the medic asked Lola.

"Can I?" Lola hesitated, but the medic stuck out her hand.

"You can't stay out here. This squall is nasty and is only going to get worse. I don't want to have to come back for you later."

Before she could think it through, Lola hopped into the back of the ambulance. The door shut with a heavy boom behind her. Out of the roar of the wind, everything went eerily quiet until the driver turned on the siren and careened down the uneven road.

One of the medics took readings on Gael's blood pressure. Lola tried to see what he was doing, but the other medic pulled her back. They swayed as they rounded a corner.

The medic had a tan freckled face and a no-nonsense look. "I need to know everything if we're going to help him," she said. "Tell me what happened."

"I told you, we were climbing a tree." At the sceptical look, Lola grimaced. "Look, he bet I couldn't climb as high as him into one of the big oaks, and I wanted to prove him wrong. And we kept going higher and higher, and it was dry at first, but once we got up really high, the rain was coming in through the leaves, and it was slippery, and he lost his footing. I tried to grab him, but I couldn't. It happened so fast." She couldn't meet the medic's eyes. If anything happened to Gael, it would be all her fault.

"Hmmm. And then what?"

Lola swallowed. "I climbed down as fast as I could. He said his ankle hurt, and he couldn't stand on it. He got up and was wobbly, and then I saw his neck." She stuttered to a stop, and her voice thickened. "There was so much blood."

They looked to Gael. There was no more visible blood, but he was coated with mud. "Then he fell over and wasn't making a lot of sense, and he lost consciousness. So I called you."

The medic raised an eyebrow and stared her in the eyes for

long moments. Lola could tell she didn't believe her, which notched her up in Lola's esteem. "Nothing more?"

"That's all."

A hard look flashed in the woman's eyes. "Then why do you both look as though we dragged you from the bottom of the bay?"

"It's raining."

"You smell like salt."

Lola licked her lip, tasting the sting of salt. She had been right; the water that flooded the cavern was coming in from the ocean. She shrugged. "That's weird."

The woman's stare would have cracked someone softer. "Have you kids been using anything? I need to know if he's on something."

Lola shook her head emphatically. "Absolutely not. We weren't taking anything."

"Alcohol?"

"No alcohol." Lola desperately wished for a cigarette. "I swear, we did something stupid, that's all." Her body was trembling so hard she couldn't control it.

"Here." The medic handed her a thermal blanket. "Wrap it around yourself. You're freezing and going into shock."

Lola took the blanket. It gave her something to do with her hands. She shouldn't need it. She had been on digs in the Arctic; she had travelled landscapes that would kill a human being. Now one spring storm and she was falling apart.

But she knew it wasn't the cold. Something had happened to her, deep inside that cavern. She'd fed on Gael, but she'd stopped herself. That wasn't something she had ever done before. Did it have to do with the lights, hidden way down there in the Well of Souls? The treasure was said to give power to the worthy. Had she touched on something there?

What, exactly, lay at the end of the treasure trail? She knew the end prize wasn't gold, no matter what she'd led Gael to believe. All the old legends spoke of the greatest power in existence, greater even then the sorcery that created vampires. It was so taboo among the otherworld, it was only spoken about in whispers; so powerful, all demons who set foot on this island were cursed for their immortal existence.

A demon would have to be very foolish or very mad to come here. Lola tucked the blanket around her. She had always known Beau was mad in a way she didn't understand. But the real question was whether she was too – or simply a fool?

For the moment, she was broken apart. She cared what happened to Gael, desperately, which was impossible but real. It was as if she was bleeding out, only she couldn't find the wound to make it stop.

She was weak with relief when the ambulance pulled to the edge of the hospital, and Gael's heart continued to beat. She could finally get away from the medic's suspicious gaze. The noise level picked up as they prepared to move him. Once the back doors were open, the rush of rain was deafening.

Lola jumped out the back. The medic gave her a searching look. "Don't go anywhere," she said.

"This is his." Lola took Gael's phone from her pocket and gave it to the medic, who squinted at it. "I hope it still works. You'll want to give his mother a call."

While they fussed with the gurney, Lola disappeared into the storm.

The rain streamed down her face as she sprinted for the woods. Gael was in a safe place. There was nothing more she could do for him. All she could do was hurt him.

Time changed and shifted like quicksand as she flew over the forest path; her feet barely touched the ground. It could have been minutes or hours before she stood at the base of the ancient oak. The hole gurgled and wept with mud, completely impassable.

Lola sank to her knees. "What have you done to me?" she gasped.

Beau wouldn't have hesitated. He would have left Gael in the cavern without a second thought to pursue the Well of Souls. It would have never gotten that far, though. He would have drained the young man dry the moment he found him alone, forget about developing a real attachment to an edible.

Now, Lola's decision meant she had lost her chance to find the Well of Souls.

She was weak. That was why Jacquotte wanted to be rid of her. The woman Lola had loved like a mother would have her put down like an unwanted puppy. Because she shouldn't have loved her in the first place.

She convulsed. A spark lit inside of her, burning her chest like liquid flame. It grew, demanding to be recognized. She reached for a root, then snatched her hand back. It was burning to the touch.

Gritting her teeth, she laid her hand against the rough bark again. She hissed at the pain, welcoming it. A faint halo of light glowed around the tree, a bright living green. "What are you?" she whispered. She looked down to see the glow spread onto her skin. Where it shone, her skin looked lifelike. Almost human.

She snatched her hand away and stumbled back. Crawling away from the tree, she caught the unmistakable scent of a living being, strong despite the rain. So close. Her need overwhelmed her.

Blind in her frantic desire, her fangs slipped out. She needed to feed.

She suddenly found the glowing tree repulsive. Under the crash of the storm, she turned and stalked in the forest.

Sixteen

It was nearly midnight when Lola returned to the hospital, cool as the rain.

"Miss, can I help you?" Her raised eyebrows at Lola's mud-stained clothes spoke volumes about whether or not she wanted to help Lola.

Lola raised her chin. "I want to see Gael Smith."

The nurse gave her a dubious look and click-clacked on her keyboard. "None of our patients are seeing visitors right now. Can I call someone for you?"

"I want to make sure he's okay," Lola pressed. "Can you tell me?"

"Let me check." The nurse reached for the phone. "Why don't you wait there?" She pointed to a central waiting area.

Something was wrong. This felt like a trap. She spun, ready to flee. But a familiar voice cried her name and she forced herself to stop.

Through the waiting room, Faye bustled toward her. It appeared she had thrown a long coat over her café outfit, apron still tied. Her mud-speckled high-heels were wilted from the weather.

"I...Faye?" Lola asked, stunned. "What are you doing here?"

"I came for you. To see if you needed something."

"You came...for me? But, how did you know I was here?"

"It's a small town, hon. Not much happens we don't all hear about. You get used to it."

Lola was aware of how much knowledge Faye stored about their town, but couldn't believe she would have heard about this so soon. But then the likely real reason behind Faye's knowledge stepped up behind her.

"Miss Lola Monteux?" Captain Theodore Greyson wasn't in uniform but spoke with a very official-sounding voice "We received information an injured young man had been brought to the hospital. By you. And that you then fled the scene."

"We?" Lola's eyes flicked back and forth between Faye and Greyson.

"We, as in the RCMP detachment." He gave Faye a look of pure exasperation. "Others have implicated themselves with no official capacity."

"I was eavesdropping," Faye said, glaring right back at Greyson. "I mean, he's got his radio on in the café, what was I supposed to do? I heard that you and Gael were in rough shape. I wanted to make sure you were okay."

Lola focused on Greyson. "I didn't flee anything. Gael fell out of a tree, and I called an ambulance. I came to the hospital with him."

"But you didn't stay."

"I was shaken up. I went for a walk."

Greyson's eyebrow rose as he tilted his head to the raging storm outside the windows. "In this?"

Lola stared at him like a surly teenager. She was good at this.

Greyson's glare told her he wasn't having any of it. "The medic thought something funny was going on."

"Funny?"

"Why don't you give her a rest?" Faye piped up in indignation.

"Look at the child; she's soaking and half-dead from the cold." The baker stepped in front of Greyson. "Listen, I don't mean to overstep—"

Greyson cut her off with a suppressed cough that sounded an awful lot like "bullshit."

Faye glared at him, and continued. "Anyway, when I heard, I thought you might need help. I thought...well, you might need a few things." Faye held out a cloth bag, bright with a patchwork of fabric. "I didn't have much time, but I threw together a care package. The clothes are mine, stuff I was planning to donate. They'll be too big for you, but they're dry, so I..." Faye's bustle faded and she cleared her throat. "I didn't know what you needed."

Slowly, Lola took the bag. Stretchy pants and a sweatshirt were folded neatly at the bottom, as well as a bottle-blue rain slicker. There was also a comb, a toothbrush, and some travel-sized toiletries, like shampoo and deodorant.

Lola stared at the items, something soft melting inside of her. It took a moment before she could speak. "This is very kind," she said finally.

"Don't look so surprised," Faye said with a relieved smile. "Why don't you go and wash up?"

"Don't go anywhere else." Warning edged Greyson's voice. "I need to talk to you."

Lola held his gaze. "Is Gael okay?"

Greyson glowered, but Faye kicked his boot with her delicate shoe. "Don't be cruel. She cares about her friend."

The officer held out for a long time, but finally gave in. "The kid is going to make it," he said. Lola's knees went a little shaky, but she told herself to keep it together. "He lost a lot of blood and they had to give him a transfusion, but it's taken and he'll be okay. He's awake and with his mother."

Lola's eyes shut. If she could cry, she was certain she would begin weeping. She hadn't killed him. "Thank you for letting me know." Her voice was a rasp.

Greyson stared hard at her. "We'll be able to speak with him about what happened soon. He has some interesting marks we need to discuss."

Lola's blood chilled as she thought of what it would look like. Identical marks to those found on the bodies that kept on turning up on the island. She made herself nod. "He fell along the tree; I imagine it opened all kinds of wounds. It's a miracle that he's doing so well."

She brought Faye's bag of kindness with her to the washroom, her relief evaporating. What did Gael remember? Would Gael tell the officer about the dig and the caverns? Would he tell about a monster who fed on his blood?

In the fluorescent light, Lola winced at her reflection. No makeup to soften the harsh angles of her face, no product to keep her hair from dragging down her back like a corpse.

Every part of her was streaked with mud. She looked like a creature that had crawled up from the bowels of the Earth. Which wasn't that far off.

She pulled on Faye's soft hand-me-downs in their sweet, pastel colours. The sweatshirt was fuzzy pink, and she ran her hands over the soft fabric. She untangled her hair, bringing her curls around her face to hide the unnatural sharpness of her features. When she looked in the mirror, she looked younger.

Faye and Greyson faced off with one another in the waiting room when she entered. Their gazes flicked to her sweatshirt at the same time. In loopy writing, it was written: *Bakers Make the Best Lovers.* Faye's mouth fell open in an O.

"I hadn't thought that one through. That's probably not the most appropriate."

Greyson coughed, smothering a laugh, but Lola gave her a genuine smile. "It's perfect. Thank you."

"I need to ask you some questions," Greyson said.

"Shouldn't a parent or guardian be present?" Faye placed herself in front of Lola. "She's only a girl!"

"Faye, you need to stay out of this investigation," Greyson snapped. Lola gently put a hand on her shoulder.

"It's okay," she said. "I don't mind answering questions."

Faye brought her hand to Lola's cheek. She didn't flinch at the cold. "I want to make sure someone's looking out for you."

"We weren't doing anything wrong." Lola turned to Greyson. "What do you need to know?"

"What were you doing out there in the first place?"

"We sheltered under a tree when the rain started. And then we decided to climb it."

"Why?"

"Because it was there?" Lola shrugged. "It was just for fun. But then he slipped."

"Hmm." Greyson looked her over. "How old are you?"

"Sixteen."

"Do you have any kind of identification on you?"

Lola regretted agreeing to his questions. She folded her arms over her chest. "Why does it matter?"

"Greyson." Faye growled next to him.

"If she's a minor, she might need to be taken into protective custody."

"Not at sixteen, I don't," Lola said quietly, eyes narrowing. This bothersome man was going to ruin everything.

The interior door of the waiting room opened, and everyone turned. A small woman with velvety brown skin emerged. She gave a tired smile to the doctor who accompanied her, then approached the group.

"I am looking for Lola?" She had a light accent.

Lola stepped forward. She didn't need to be told who she was. Her brown-gold eyes ringed with black lashes were identical to her son's. "Mrs. Smith?"

The smile on Gael's mother's face froze as she took in Lola, the skin tightening around her eyes. She gave a furtive look at Greyson, then said in a low voice, "I must speak with you. In private?"

Lola nodded, leaving Greyson and Faye arguing behind her. "Why don't you back off?" Faye hissed.

Lola approached the woman, uncertain. "Mrs. Smith, is your son all right?"

Gael's mother had staked out a corner away from the others. She stared into Lola with such burning intensity she could almost feel the heat. Her hand flew to a small gold cross she wore around her neck.

"What do you want with my son?" she whispered.

"What? Nothing!" Lola glanced over her shoulder to Greyson, but he was too busy in his whispered argument to notice. "I would never hurt your son. I swear it." Not anymore, anyways.

Anita didn't soften an inch. "You already have. You are *other*, aren't you? I sense it." She clasped Lola's face between trembling hands and inspected her eyes. "*Demonia*," she whispered.

Lola stared at her. How could she know? The otherworld lay underneath everything, and yet it was uncommon for humans to know about it. Instead, they liked to pretend they knew everything there was to know, blind to how much deeper the world went.

"I'm not," Lola whispered back.

Anita grabbed her chin and tilted it this way and that. She gasped. "Not quite. You are not complete. Not one, not the other. An aberration."

Lola stilled. Anita saw something beyond the demon inside of her, this thing that had thrown her existence out of order. "What is it?" If this woman could tell her, she had to know.

Anita peered intently, as though she could see inside of her. Then she blinked and shook her head. Her voice was firm, and she jabbed a finger at Lola, speaking slowly to ensure the point was well understood. "Gael is young, but I see things clearly. You cannot have him."

"I won't..." Lola trailed off. She already had.

Anita leaned in and hissed at Lola. "If you cared for him, you would leave."

"I saved his life."

Her lovely golden-brown eyes hardened. She was not a woman to be trifled with. "But first, you put him in danger, no?"

Lola drooped. His mother's request was simple and clear.

Anita's stance eased. Regret was painted over her delicate face. "Gael does not understand this. Some things we must discover for ourselves. He's asking for you."

Lola looked up slowly.

"He is still hurt, but nothing dissuades him from wanting to see you. Listen to me: I love my son very much, and I want him to be happy." She sighed all the way down to her bones. "But even more, I want him to be safe." She paused, her eyes razor-sharp. "He's in Room 108. Please, listen to me. Go in and say your good-byes. Nothing good can come from you."

Anita stared after Lola as she rose, her thumb rubbing a circle over the cross. Lola understood that Anita would be sharpening stakes this very night.

Lola paused at the door to the hospital wing. She had come to Duchesne to hide from Jacquotte and her gang, to gain the upper hand and secure her survival. But everything had spun out of her control. She was implicated in these human lives and found she cared profoundly about what would happen to them. Not only that, she had given up the chance to secure the power she sought. How had she gotten so far off track? And why was she far more worried about Gael than about herself?

Seventeen

Lola tapped at Room 108. "Gael?" she whispered, peeking around the door. An enormous foot stabilizer encased his left leg and his neck was wrapped thickly with bandages. Deep shadows stretched under his eyes, his skin sickly pale.

"You're okay," he said. His sleepy smile showed relief, echoing exactly how she felt. A deep ache panged inside of Lola's chest, and she rubbed at her sternum hard, trying to make it go away.

"You were worried about me?" She let out a half-laughing sob. She was terrified to approach him. "Gael, I was so scared." Her throat tightened. "I can't stop thinking about it. It was so very close."

"But I survived. Thanks to you." He knocked on the boot. "Not even broken. Just a nasty sprain."

Lola perched on a chair next to his bed, unable to meet his eye. "I told the medic you fell out of the tree. I wasn't sure what you wanted to tell after...what happened down there."

"Right." Gael stared at his injured leg. "About what happened down there."

Lola clenched her hands together during a long, drawn-out silence. When Gael finally began speaking, she flinched. "Everything is really hazy, so you might have to fill me in. I fell into the cavern, and you were coming down the ladder when the whole place started to flood."

Lola nodded, staring at her hands. Her perfectly lifelike hands, courtesy of his blood.

"And you came to get me. You pulled me up out of the water. I would have drowned without you there, Lola."

"Gael..." She wanted him to stop right there.

"I saw you, Lola. At least, I think I did." His hand went to the bandage around his neck. "I'm not sure if I was hallucinating, though."

Her throat went dry and she tried to swallow. Maybe it would be easier that way. Let him believe he imagined everything that happened.

"I can't imagine how much strength it would take to pull a body out of a hole like that. We were a hundred feet down."

"Not quite."

Gael's lips twisted. "I'm nearly twice your size. I know you're tough, but nobody's that tough."

Lola gazed out the window into the rain-spattered black. "People do extraordinary things when they need to. Mothers lift cars off their children. It's adrenaline."

"That's not what happened, though, is it?" Gael's voice dropped to a whisper. "You appear and disappear as if like magic; you're fast and strong, and it's true you never eat. Besides all that, you are the most beautiful girl I have ever seen in my life." He drew in a ragged breath.

Her chest felt like bursting. This went against all the rules. The laws of her crew, the laws of self-preservation, the very laws of all things natural and unnatural: *Nobody can know.* This had been drilled into her since the first day of her unlife. Humans who knew were killed. To tell would risk Gael's life, painting a giant target on his back.

And yet. She twined her fingers together. He had already seen so much, enough to put it all together. He had half the story. Knowledge could offer him some protection from what he was facing.

She couldn't believe she was doing this. She took a deep breath. "Gael, I'm a..."

"You're a vampire."

"What?" If she hadn't been sitting, she would have staggered back.

His eyes shone bright, with excitement and perhaps a touch of madness too. "You're a vampire, right?"

Lola stared at him in horror. "Gael, I...what you're saying is crazy." Still, with his blood buzzing inside of her, with him saying these words out loud, there was no going back for him. He had already passed that threshold.

He reached out and placed his hand on the bare skin of her throat. She tilted her head to the side to allow him. "So cold. What I'm saying is impossible. But it's the only thing that makes sense. Tell me I'm wrong." His golden eyes dared her to lie to his face.

She should. But instead she let out a hiss of breath. "You're not wrong."

"You drank my blood tonight?" Lola didn't respond, frozen as she was. How could they ever recover from this? "Will I become a vampire?"

Lola released a breath that sounded like a sob. "No, it doesn't work like that. I have never created a vampire. You would have to die to be remade. And it takes a powerful source of magical energy to make it happen. If you were a vampire, it would be the end of who you are as a person. I would never do that to you."

"So you just...snacked off me?"

"I fed on your life force. Gael, I'm sorry."

"I'm not." He released her, lying back in the cot to gaze at the ceiling with starry eyes. "I knew there was so much more to this world. And you've proved that to me."

"Gael, you don't understand. This is all incredibly dangerous. I could have killed you!"

"But you didn't." A smile stretched across his handsome face, and she wanted to smack it off. He wasn't treating this as seriously as he should.

"Gael, that was an anomaly. I shouldn't have been able to stop. I'm...I'm a monster. I exist without compassion or mercy. Every moment you spend near me, you risk your life."

Gael let out a quiet laugh. "Wait. You don't honestly believe that, do you?"

Was he playing with her? She lurched to her feet. "You think this is a joke? Then you're more naïve than I thought. There are things that go bump in the night you've never even dreamed of. So much of this world is evil, and if you're not able to accept that, then..." Her mind spun with the recklessness of what she had just done.

"Lola, I live on Duchesne Island. My family goes back generations, and I've heard all the stories. Also, my mum is ridiculously superstitious. I've seen things here that can't be explained, and I already know there's more out there than we'll ever know. You're just confirming the things that have been bouncing around my head for years."

Lola shook her head in disbelief. "Most people refuse to believe, even when they see proof in front of their eyes. They find ways to make the mundane out of the extraordinary."

"I'm not interested in the mundane."

"But you said you didn't believe I was a monster."

"No, I asked whether *you* believed that you were monstrous."

The inside of her mouth tasted bitter. "Of course I am."

Gael's fingers toyed at the bandage at his neck, and Lola's gaze was riveted to it. "Lola, you could have let me drown. If you're such a monster, why did you rescue me?"

"I drank your blood, Gael. There is no excuse for that. I wanted to suck you dry. I wanted to devour you."

"Why didn't you?"

"I thought about it." Lola's voice was nearly too low to hear. She couldn't look at him as he drew in a long breath.

"But you didn't. Instead, you went out of your way to ensure I survived."

"Maybe I still need you. Once I'm finished with you, I'll discard you." Her hands were trembling, clenched in fists at her side. She had no idea why she wanted to convince Gael of her soullessness. But it seemed vitally important that he know how dark she went.

A crease formed on his brow. "Is that real? You're just using me?"

"Maybe. Yes. I was at one point." Finally, she met his gaze. "Do you hate me for that?"

"Hate you?" He reached for her, stopping inches away, uncertain. Her heart ached that he might be afraid of her now, but his hands finally clasped hers. She allowed him to pull her close. "Lola, I could never hate you. You saved me." He looked at her hands, small and pale in his warm brown palms. "Are there other vampires?"

She nodded, mesmerized by their entangled fingers.

"Are they like you?"

She paused for a breath, then shook her head. "I'm different since arriving on the island. Other vampires would have killed you. I would have too, before all this. Before Duchesne. This place has done something to me."

"Can I ask you some things? About...about being a vampire? Or is that, like, rude?"

She gave a rueful smile. "I think we crossed that boundary around the time I drank your blood."

"Were you human?"

"This body belonged to a human. In that way, I suppose, all demons were human once upon a time."

"How long have you been…like this?" She got the impression he was going to say dead.

"I was created in 1942. I was made from a sixteen-year-old girl and have remained exactly the same since then."

"You're, like, eighty years older than me," he whispered.

Lola smiled at the idea of her as a doddery old lady. "Yes, and no. We don't age, and we don't develop the way a human does. All is stagnant for the undead. There is no emotion, no growth. We don't change, so we don't develop into different people. I have hunted on this Earth for a long time, and learned facts about the world, but could not apply depth to any of it. I am a reflection of this body as it was: a girl, nearly a woman. But inside, I am nothing more than a predator."

"Who were you before?"

She shook her head. "You don't understand. I have no connection to who resided in this body before. I am a soulless embodiment of demonic energy."

Gael stared at her and squeezed her hand. "I don't believe that."

When he looked at her like that, she didn't believe it either.

Gael stroked his thumb along her forearm, sending shivers of warmth over her skin. She closed the gap between them, pressing her lips very gently against his. There she found heat, and tenderness, and a promise of so much more.

She broke away, hating the space between them, but forcing herself to do it. "You're injured. I did this to you."

"A two-storey drop did this to me, Lola. You made sure I didn't die down there. Besides, I'm not *that* injured." Gael tried to pull her back, but she dodged out of the way. He was still so very pale.

"You must rest," she said. "Humans take forever to heal."

"Lola? Thanks. For telling me."

Lola's heart gave a sickening thump at what she had done. If anyone otherworldly found out he knew, his life was over. She had put him in such danger; since meeting him, that's all she had done. "You can't tell anyone. If people found out, they would probably call you crazy."

Gael raised an eyebrow. "Always with the secrets, Lola."

She let out a puff of frustration. She had to make him understand. "I'm not supposed to have told. You would be hurt if the wrong creature found out. I could be hurt."

He put a hand to his heart. "I won't tell a soul."

Her heart still pounding, she nodded.

"Thanks for saving my life."

"It's a life worth saving." She let the door drift shut behind her, then leaned against the wall. She pressed her fingers to her lips, savouring the memory of their kiss. Even when she had been with Beau, at their best, it had never felt like this. That had always been a game, a challenge to best the other. This was something different. She didn't think it was a phase at all. She was in unchartered waters now, and they were carrying her straight toward disaster.

EIGHTEEN

Lola stopped inside the shelter of the gazebo in the town square. She wore Faye's rain slicker, delighting in how the colour flashed against the stormy background.

It had been a day since Gael's fall. When she woke in the late afternoon, the first thing she did was check on him, but he slept, so now she wandered the storm-splashed streets of Port Despardoux. If she were smart, she would flee before Beau caught her. Now the dig site was flooded, there was no reason to remain. Her gamble to find the Well of Souls had failed.

Except she couldn't leave Duchesne while Beau was here. She had to stay and protect her friends.

The thought spun through her head. Somewhere along the line, her mission had changed from self-preservation to something else entirely.

A flash of copper caught at the edge of her vision. She turned to see Nix staring at her, eyes wide, then whipping around to head the other way. Lola didn't blame her; she had behaved very badly. She would let her have her space. Lola watched her penny-bright hair disappear into the fog toward the wharf.

A mocking laugh sounded, carried on the wind. Lola looked

up sharply. Beau was near. He could cause carnage in a populated area. Luckily, there were few humans out on an evening like this.

Except for a certain red-headed girl.

His laugh sounded again, beyond her now. Her heart bounded into her throat, and Lola sprinted toward Nix.

She could sense him ahead of her in the fog. It was as if he was made of air itself, appearing as a shadow outside of her reach and then gone. It was like chasing a ghost.

A fleeting cold brush against her cheek made her snarl and lash out. He toyed with her, as he would toy with Nix. He would kill them all to hurt her.

On a final rush of speed, she overtook Nix at the wharf, grabbing her arm. The wind died, as did her panic. Beau's presence retreated, and Lola let out a sigh of relief.

Fury lit Nix's face. "What the hell do you think you're doing?" She snapped off every word, yanking her arm away from Lola.

"I...wanted to apologize." Lola searched for the right words to get this girl to trust her. She needed to get her inside. "For the other day."

Nix sniffed. "As if I care what you think of me."

"I know you don't. But I wanted to..." Lola let out a huff. "Can we do this inside? It's miserable out here. Please, Nix, we can go to The Pain Perdu?"

"With you?" Nix's voice dripped with disdain.

"Please come; it's warm there. And delicious. It's my treat. Let me grovel properly."

Lola's outright pleading nearly got a smile out of Nix. "It *is* nice in there," she grumbled. "And I'm starving. I've been working at my mom's shop all day."

Keeping a watchful eye for Beau, Lola guided Nix through the damp-slicked street. Nix turned to say something, then froze. Lola spun, expecting Beau looming behind her.

Instead, a pale figure walked down the street, mist whipping around her feet. She was tall and held herself ramrod straight. Her dress hung down to her boots, but the hem didn't seem to fall in any of the puddles surrounding her. A grey shawl wrapped tight around her shoulders; her hands were encased in fingerless woollen gloves.

As she stepped under a streetlamp, her pale face was illuminated, showing unlined skin. She might have been any age but gave the impression of being ancient. Her misty blue eyes were on Lola.

"You bring danger." Her voice was both deep and whispery. It made Lola think of spirits speaking from across the veil, and she shivered.

Otherworldliness rippled off the woman. She held up her hand, slender fingers marred by massive knuckles at each joint. "Your weakness is your strength. It will be your choice in the end."

"Excuse me?" The last thing Lola needed were vague prophecies.

The woman gave a low chuckle and turned to Nix, who eyed her with distaste. "You know your fate."

Ignoring Nix's sneer, she turned and continued at her sedate pace toward a Victorian mansion at the corner of Main Street. A wraparound veranda was lit invitingly with fairy lights. Overhead was a hand-painted sign: *McInnes' Tea Shoppe*. Underneath a smaller sign read: *Psychic Readings by Appointment Only*.

"Who's that?"

"That's Mrs. McInnes." Nix's face twisted. "She's a crazy old lady who tells fortunes. The tourists love that kind of thing."

"Is she really a psychic?"

"More like a psycho," Nix snorted.

Lola turned, confused by Nix's scorn. "Did she give you a reading?"

Nix shrugged. "Years ago. Crazy stuff, but it's not like I believe it."

Or perhaps Nix didn't like what she heard. If McInnes was the real thing, she would deal in real divination. And, like life, true prophecies were rarely kind.

Witches on Duchesne Island. She shouldn't be surprised.

"Come on, let's get out of here. This place gives me the creeps." Nix skipped over a few puddles, heading up Main Street toward The Pain Perdu.

The café wasn't busy, with only two other tables occupied. Faye glanced up from the counter and gave a giant smile.

"Hi girls! Have a seat wherever; I'll be with you in a sec."

Lola relaxed in the warmth, remembering Faye's kindness the night before. She had been looking out for her since she arrived on the island. Based on the gifts she had brought her, she clearly thought Lola was some kind of homeless urchin, and she wasn't too far off the mark.

Lola wasn't going to complain. It had been a long time since she had someone in her corner.

She rummaged in her pockets, wondering how much cash she had on her. Maybe there was an extra ten in her shoe? "What kind of store does your mum own?" she asked Nix.

"A clothing store. It's mainly vintage pieces and stuff sold on consignment."

"Really?" Lola glanced up, intrigued. "I love clothes, especially vintage."

Nix gave her a funny look. "You like clothes?"

Lola would have blushed if she could. She still wore the fuzzy pink lovers sweatshirt Faye had given her. "Yes. When I have the... the resources, I like clothes."

Nix's prickliness diminished, and she gave a quick nod. "I get being poor."

"I'm not poor!" Lola said, indignant. "I just don't have any money. Right now."

"What do you think being poor is? I said I get it. My mum's shop does all right, but during the winter months, there's not a lot coming in. And my dad's the lighthouse keeper. There's no money in that. But it's a family thing. Every generation one of us Nixes watches over the lighthouse." Nix let out a heavy sigh. "I hope it's not me. It's boring. And I hate being poor." She shot Lola a look as though she would defy her.

Lola wouldn't dare. "What will you do, then?"

"I don't care, as long as it gets me off this island. I want to see everything."

"A world traveller."

"Ha! Something like that. I just need to finish up school and I'm out of here."

Faye approached the table. "Hello, girls. It's a good night to escape the weather, isn't it? Coffee for Lola, and Nix, what will you have?"

"Pain chocolat," Nix said. "And a mochaccino."

"Easily done."

Lola stopped Faye with a tentative hand. "Thank you," she said. "For yesterday. It was…" Lola didn't know what to say, but Faye gave her a squeeze on the shoulder.

"Happy to help. It was a hard day. I'm happy to see you out with friends." She grinned at Nix, and Lola felt a flush of embarrassment, thinking Nix might deny their friendship. But Nix only nodded, and Faye went to the back.

Lola cleared her throat. Some grovelling was in order. "About… the other day. When I said…well, that's why I wanted to speak with you, to apologize in person. I told private information, and I had no right. It was cruel, and I'm truly sorry."

"I wonder why it is people are so cruel, all the time," Nix said. She played with her curls, not meeting Lola's gaze.

"People are cruel when they are hurt or scared and don't know how to act or what to say. Cruelty is easy."

"Well, it shouldn't be like that."

"I'm not sure that will ever change. Sometimes all we can do is ask for forgiveness."

Nix sighed and met her eyes. She leaned forward, murmuring so only Lola would hear. "I've never spoken about it to anyone before. Being gay, I mean. It's like this thought that's been bouncing around my head for a long time, but I haven't given it the space to take form. Does that make sense?"

"It does."

"And then when you said it out loud, it sort of crystallized into this thing that was very real, and very *true*, and I couldn't deny it. I sort of freaked out."

"I forced you to face it before you were ready?" Lola fell back against her chair, her voice thinning. "I'm so sorry. I'm the worst kind of friend."

"You're not the worst friend," Nix said casually, unaware how those words kindled parts of Lola she hadn't known existed. "I was scared, but it was also good to hear it out loud. It made it real, and I've been letting it take shape. And I think I like the shape I'm taking. It feels *right*." She sat back and turned her sharp gaze on Lola. "I want to know how you knew."

Lola couldn't explain that she could smell Nix's attraction to her. "Well, maybe I had a bit of a sense about it. I've known many queer people."

She stopped when Nix held up her hand in alarm, darting nervous glances over her shoulder to see if anyone overheard them.

"Sorry, it's... this town. It's not an open-minded place. I'm already a bit of an outsider at school, and if anyone found out about it, it would just give them more ammunition." Nix stuck out her chin at Lola's look. "I'm not ashamed. I'm happy about who I am, and maybe I'm ready for my close friends to know I'm gay. But I'd like to keep it between us, for now."

"I understand." Lola shrugged. "I mean, we all have secrets, *non*?"

Nix started to laugh at her. "What?"

"You just sound so French. Sometimes you speak like people in movies, you know? Old movies, black and white."

Lola ducked her head. "I haven't spent much time with people my age."

"No, you don't act like it. I think you've had a hard life."

Lola shrugged, even as she longed to spill all her secrets to Nix.

"I need to apologize to you as well."

"No, you don't."

Nix's face flushed dark pink. "I called you a slut, Lola. That was a shitty thing to say, and I didn't mean it. We're cruel when we're scared, right? Well, you scare me sometimes, but that doesn't make it okay. You're so sophisticated and mature, and I feel like an awkward hick next to you. And you're very comfortable with your sexuality, which makes me even less comfortable with my own. You're kind of overwhelming."

Lola gave her a smile. "Thank you?"

Faye approached, deftly dropping off their order. "How's Gael?" she asked Lola as she poured coffee. "His mother said he was stable last night."

"He's good, I think. He was sleeping this afternoon, but the nurse assured me he was recovering."

"Good. Guess you won't be climbing trees any time soon." Faye gave a little laugh, then realized Nix had stopped tearing her pastry apart to stare at her.

"What's wrong with Gael?"

Faye looked between the two of them and retreated. "I've got some orders to get started. I'll let the two of you get caught up!"

"He's fine," Lola said immediately as she took in Nix's face, which had gone stark white.

"What happened?" Nix's voice was tight.

"He fell and sprained his ankle. He's been kept in the hospital for observation. But everything is okay." Lola babbled when Nix's eyes widened in alarm. "I've spoken to him."

"Oh my god," she said. "Anita must be so worried." She shook her head. "And what's this about climbing trees? That doesn't seem like you, although you're blowing my mind all over the place today." Nix eyed Lola's fuzzy pink sweater.

Lola leaned in, whispering. "Something happened."

Nix's eyes sparkled as Lola recounted everything from when

they pulled up the wooden platform. She left out the fact that she nearly drank Gael dry, or that she used vampire strength to rescue him.

"I don't want anyone to know about the cavern," Lola said. "The place will be swarming with treasure hunters within hours if word gets out. Not that it matters if it stays flooded."

"Do you think it will?"

Lola chewed her lip. "We'll have to wait to see. I've seen set-ups like this on other digs and this reminded me of it. I think we triggered something when we entered because it filled up immediately. It was too close to be a coincidence."

"You mean like a booby trap?" Nix's eyes were wide.

Lola nodded. "Someone put a lot of trouble into ensuring nobody found whatever is on the other side of that cavern. We shouldn't have survived the flood. That tells me there's something down there."

"I never knew if you were lying, but you're actually a treasure hunter."

"It's the family business."

"You don't talk about your family at all."

"No."

"Why?"

"It's a long story," Lola said. "But at the heart of it, they are terrible people. And my ex-boyfriend." It felt wrong to call Beau something so prosaic, but she supposed that's what he was. "He is...how do you say it? Toxic. He was stalking me. I needed to get away from them."

"It's hard not having anyone to watch your back."

"I'm used to it."

Nix hesitated, then her hand reached out to take Lola's. "If you're in trouble, I could have your back."

Lola would have liked to be able to cry then, to show what this gesture meant to her. Instead, she squeezed Nix's hand gently. "I'd like that."

"Good. That's settled." Nix released her and sat back. "So Gael is injured, and the hole is flooded. Are we just going to call this whole thing off, right when things are getting good?"

Lola raised an eyebrow at the girl's dauntless spirit. "I'm still game if you are."

The bell over the door rang, and Captain Greyson strode into the café, shaking water off his wool coat. He scanned the occupants of the café, his gaze settling with laser-like precision on Lola. She wanted to sink into her seat but forced a sunny smile as he approached.

"Captain, how are you this evening?"

"Less wet than yesterday. We need to talk."

"About Gael?" Lola put on wide innocent eyes.

"Among other things."

"I hear he's doing well. The nurse told me he'd be released tomorrow. Shame he'll probably be on crutches for a bit." Lola refused to be dragged into this conversation, which would include irritating questions about whether she had parents. It had been her problem for decades; someone was always wondering where her parents were.

"You dashed out of the hospital. Why is that?"

"It was late, and I needed to get home. I just wanted to see Gael and know he's okay."

"Still wearing that sweatshirt."

"You don't miss anything, do you?" Lola sounded like a jaded teen, but she winced inwardly. Nothing screamed homeless orphan like only having one shirt.

Hoping to distract him with his fuzzy feelings toward Faye, Lola held out the shirt, so the lettering *Bakers Make the Best Lovers* stood out in relief. His eyes briefly flicked to Faye, who was bending over to put éclairs on a lower display case, cleavage on full display. A subtle blush spread across his cheeks, and Lola hid a grin. *Gotcha.*

When he turned to Lola, his eyes were softer. "Listen, it's good

Faye's looking out for you." He grimaced and added, "But don't make any more trouble, okay?"

"Understood," Lola said.

Greyson harrumphed again and went to take a seat at the counter. Faye flashed him a smile.

"What was that?" Nix watched everything with open interest.

"Our good captain wants to know where my parents are."

Nix nodded slowly, narrowing her eyes at him. "We'll have to avoid him."

"Or keep a very close eye on him." Lola watched him through lowered eyelashes, then turned back to Nix. "So, when this rain has stopped we'll check out the dig site."

Nix crossed her fingers. "Let's hope for sunshine."

After Lola had counted out the amount to cover their bill, they said goodbye outside as the rain really started to pour. Lola waved goodbye to Nix, then doubled back and followed her all the way to the lighthouse, ensuring her friend made it home safely. Then she started to hunt, but this time it wasn't prey she was after.

If Beau had meant to attack Nix earlier, he must have gotten bored of his games already. That meant no one was safe from him. Lola stalked up and down the streets of Port Despardoux, swinging by the hospital and the café each time, but got no scent of him. It would be impossible to keep them all safe, all the time.

She sat in the empty gazebo of the town square, looking around at the town. What if she left now? Beau would follow her as always. She wouldn't have the Well of Souls treasure and the power that promised to keep her safe. She would spend the rest of immortality dodging him, and Jacquotte's crew; hunting by night and leaving a trail of devastation behind her.

It sounded like a nightmare. Lola didn't want that anymore. Besides, if she left, Beau could easily rip out the throats of everyone she cared about before he followed her, especially if she wasn't there to stop him. They wouldn't be made any safer; the damage had already been done. She had condemned them by entering their lives.

She twined her hands together and gripped them tightly. There was only one answer. The wind whipped fiercely around her. It would have been freezing if she felt that kind of thing.

Something would have to be done about Beau.

Nineteen

Gael was released from the hospital on Sunday night. Lola knew because she watched him and his mother leave, peering through the hospital windows after the sun had set. Gael flat-out refused to sit in a wheelchair. After a rapid-fire shouting match with his mother in Spanish, he stomped to the front entrance, his left foot heavy in a stabilizing boot.

All the next day, Lola was unable to rest, anxious to return to the dig site and consumed with her thoughts of killing Beau. The storm had passed and sun shone brightly over the island, allowing her some ease from her vigilant guard of the town.

She fussed around her shack as she came up with and discarded plans. Beau was stronger than her, older, heavier. He could best her in fighting in all ways except for speed, which didn't help her much if she wanted to engage. All she had ever been good at was running away.

She folded Faye's sweatshirt carefully and put it in her bag, not wanting to ruin it at the dig site, then rummaged through the drawers. She picked an oversized wool sweater in a greyish-brown colour that wouldn't show mud stains very much. Mud might actually improve it. Lola scowled at the thing that hung to her knees, rolling the sleeves several times.

It was late afternoon when she began to concentrate her powers, drawing mist in from the sea to protect her from the sun. It happened so easily now, her control over water coming to her like breathing. She wore the mist like a shawl and let herself out the door.

She took a detour on her way to the forest, passing near Gael's cottage. She wanted to find him but equally wanted to avoid his mother because she had no intention of facing off with her again.

Voices drifted from the cottage, and Lola paused. There were shouts and threats in Spanish. Finally, a door slammed, and Gael stomped out of the entrance, slowly making his way up the hill.

She waited for him at the gate. He smiled, as though expecting her to be there. When he reached her, he picked her up into a hug, then stumbled on his oversized boot.

"Are you okay?"

"I am now. I had to see you. I've been thinking about you non-stop."

"Should you be on your feet, though?" She looked him over. His throat sported a smaller bandage than before, but there were creases of pain around his eyes.

Gael's smile dropped. "You sound like my mum. She wants to keep me locked away inside, resting. She even picked me up from school when she should be at the hospital with Diego." He scowled.

Lola agreed with his mother. Gael looked weary and was likely in a great deal of pain. He kept an arm around her, and she propped up a good part of his weight.

He frowned. "Don't look at me like that, Lola. I had to get out of there. Especially now that Diego..." he trailed off. "I have to do something."

"What happened to Diego?"

"His last round of chemo on the mainland was really hard on

him, and we just got the results. They didn't work. He..." Gael stared at the forest, blinking hard. "He doesn't have much time left."

"Oh." There were no words of comfort for that, so she slung his arm over her shoulder and propped him up at her side. She'd carry him to the dig site if she had to. "Let's go. I told Nix I'd meet her at the oak tree to see how everything looks."

Limping up the path with his arm heavy on Lola's shoulder, his smile was warm with gratitude. "The two of you made up? Good, I hate it when people fight."

"Did she talk to you at school?"

"Yes. Back to her normal owly self."

"Excellent."

Gael stared at her, and Lola shifted under the scrutiny. "What is it?"

"I thought.... This is going to sound so stupid, but I thought vampires can't go out during the day."

She cleared her throat. She'd never had to explain to anyone before. "Legends about us have been warped and exaggerated over time."

"What's the real story?"

"Sunlight does burn us. It's awful; I got a sunburn once. Like, my skin burned off. It took weeks to heal. And I heal really fast, so you can imagine how horrible it was. I never want to experience that again." She gestured around them at the mist. It now flooded through the trees so no sunlight made it to the forest floor. "But as long as I'm not in direct light, it's okay."

"What about garlic?"

"Delicious." Lola grinned. "I have no idea who started that one."

Gael laughed. "Someone who hates bad breath. So you don't have to sleep during the day?"

"Normally I do, because of the sun thing. It's easier. Also, my vision is designed for night."

"You can see in the dark?"

"I see better in the dark," she said. "Like a cat."

Gael was giving her a weird look, but she held her head high. He wanted to know who she really was. "What?"

"It's just, you've been alive, or I mean, you've been in existence, for nearly a century. You've seen so much."

"And yet I still managed to be surprised by people."

"Did you really live in France? Before you...died?"

Lola looked down. "I don't know. I was created in France, so it stands to reason."

Gael seemed about to press when he tripped over a root, yelping in pain.

Lola glanced at his boot. "How is it?"

"I've felt better," he said through gritted teeth.

Lola stopped on the path. At this pace, it would be nightfall before they arrived. She was saved from saying anything when a beep sounded on the path behind them. Walt pulled up in his ATV.

"I thought you could use a ride," he said stiffly.

"I don't," Gael said shortly.

"Yes, that's wonderful," Lola said at the same time. She gave Gael a teasing smile. If he wanted to get to the dig site, he would have to do it this way. "Thanks, Walt." She went to the back of the vehicle, leaving the front space next to Walt open for Gael.

Nobody said anything. Finally, Gael let out a sigh and manoeuvred his foot into the seat. They bumped around the forest path, the only sound the whine of the engine. Walt cleared his throat first, staring straight ahead.

"It was easier with them," he said, as though continuing an ongoing conversation.

"Excuse me?"

"With the other kids. The shallow ones. It's easier with them."

Gael ruffled in righteous anger. "I wouldn't know. I can only imagine how being rich makes things easier."

"Not the money." Walt's voice was so quiet Lola could barely hear him over the puttering engine. She used her powers to make sure she caught every word. "It's because they don't care."

"I see," Gael spoke through gritted teeth. "It's *easier* to be with people who don't care about you."

Lola was nodding at the back. It absolutely was.

"They don't notice me, not really. I have money, yes; sometimes I throw parties, so they invite me to places too. It's... transactional."

"Fine, they're assholes. But why is that better?"

Gael's voice held the lingering pain from when he was younger.

Walt weaved the ATV between the roots. "I'm not like most other people," he said. "Sometimes I don't know what to say or how to act. At least I understand what they want."

"I know you're a little awkward," Gael said. "But that never bothered me."

"It's more than awkwardness. I think better in numbers, and I can make out patterns in things others don't see. But I don't know how to be *normal*." His voice broke in frustration. "I understand codes because everything is clear; there are rules. When dealing with people, the lines are blurry, and there aren't any rules. You can't say one thing and always get the same result. People are irrational." His shoulders hunched up to his ears. "When we were kids, you were just my friend. But when we got to junior high, you started to notice. I could tell."

Gael watched Walt, a careful expression on his face, his warm eyes crinkled in concentration. "It never mattered to me."

"It mattered to *me*. It bothered me you understood what we were supposed to say and how we were supposed to be, and I didn't. And you wanted to talk about it with me, and I didn't know how to do that either."

"And it's better with Ethan and Violet?"

"They never asked me how I was; they don't care how I'm feeling. They only want to know where the next party is. My parents being who they are helped me, I know. Nobody really cares if I talk to them or not, and I could be alone in a crowd. It was easier."

Gael stared at the passing trees. "I can't believe that was better than being with me."

"It wasn't *better*. I just didn't have to face myself." He hung his head. "I was a coward."

After several long moments, Gael gave a slow nod.

Walt cleared his throat. "I would like to still help with the dig."

"Yeah. That'd be good."

Lola struggled to hide her smile. They still wouldn't look at each other, but Gael and Walt shifted, bodies relaxed. Both were startled when she cleared her throat, as though they had forgotten she was there. "Walt, we had a breakthrough last week."

"Literally," Gael said. "We broke right through a wooden platform, which was over a cavern. I fell in. That's why this." He gestured to his leg. "But then the hole filled up with water from the bay."

"It's flooded?"

"All the way up to the top," Lola said. "But that was three days ago. There's a chance the water's receded. We'll find out what it looks like now." They bumped around a corner, and the treasure oak came into view. Nix stood at the edge of the hole, hands on her hips as she scowled into it.

"How does it look?" Lola called as they pulled to a stop. Nix glanced up for a second, taking in Gael and Walt, before returning her full attention to the pit.

"It looks a disgusting mess."

Twenty

The four of them clustered around the hole. The water had receded, leaving thick mud on the walls. "Mess is right," Gael said.

"What exactly did you find down there?" Walt asked.

"A cavern," Lola said. "But we didn't get a chance to explore. It flooded too quickly."

"Because of the storm?"

Lola shook her head. "I don't think so. It was salt water, so the intake was from the ocean. It's probably connected to the bay by a tunnel. And the flooding happened so fast, right after we went in, I suspect it was triggered."

"Triggered," Gael said, startled. "Like, a booby trap?"

"I'm not sure exactly how it worked, but yes."

"I have the equipment for cave exploration," Walt said.

"What, spelunking?" Lola asked. She could see he would enjoy the solitary beauty of the underground.

"The island is riddled with caves. It's fun to go down and see what's there."

Nix made a face. "Your kind of fun."

"Better that than trying to hit a bunch of girls in knee socks with sticks," Walt shot back.

"Field hockey is an excellent sport, requiring both strength and dexterity—"

Lola held up her hand to stop them as Gael snickered. "Have you done cave diving?"

Walt shook his head. "Only dry."

"Still, if the water recedes enough, that could help."

"Okay." Nix rubbed her hands together. "We have a wealthy spelunker and a professional treasure hunter." She glanced at Gael's boot with a grin. "You're obviously the albatross of the group."

"Hey!" Gael started laughing. "What do you bring to the group?"

"My wit and charm. I thought that was obvious." Nix snorted. "Anyways, it looks like the band is back together."

Walt and Lola both looked up at this. She caught his eye and smiled.

"Where do we go from here?" Gael asked.

"I have to get down there to see the water level," Lola said.

"That's not the best idea," Walt said. "The ladders might have loosened with the flooding."

"Attach a rope to me in case I fall." She raised her hands against their protests. "We need to test it somehow, or we give up entirely. Does anyone want that?" She met three obstinate pairs of eyes. "I have experience in this."

She nodded at Gael, hoping he would pick up it would be safest if she went first.

He raised his eyebrows. "Right, that makes sense," he said. "Lola knows how it's done."

Nix eyed her dubiously as Lola found the longest rope she could, knotting it around her chest and shoulders in a makeshift harness. "I'm hoping you won't need this, but loop it over a branch and feed the length as I go down." She placed a headlamp firmly on her head. "Be ready to catch me if I fall." She winked at Gael before she lowered herself onto the first ladder.

She gripped the rungs, white-knuckled, as she stared into the hole. The walls of the shaft were thick with mud, making the space tighter than before. She had the sudden thought that if she went down there, she would be lost inside the earth. She closed her eyes, not thinking about the crushing weight of mud smothering her.

"Here we go," Lola said and gave the ladder a jerk. It held firm, but her feet slipped on the muddy rung, and she scrambled to hold on. She readjusted her footing several times before descending into the abyss.

As she approached the bottom of the hole, the mud was thicker, squeezing the walls around her. The broken wooden platform they had found was covered, blocking the entrance of the cavern like a plug blocking a drain.

She pressed her foot into the mud. It squelched, and Lola shuddered at the sound. She didn't want to get caught by it, pulled down into the murky depths. She squared her shoulders and prodded again to see if it would move.

The thick mud gave a little, so she shoved her foot into it, trying to push through to the hole. With a sucking noise, the mud shifted, pulling through the hole. A thick, earthy smell surrounded her as the mud suctioned around her foot as though to suck her down with it. Lola wrapped her arms around the ladder, praying it would hold.

The mud plug drained out the hole, leaving the platform and entrance to the cavern visible. Water lapped underneath.

She banged her fist against the slick mud of the ladder. The entire cavern was flooded. Whoever wished to keep the treasure hidden had done an excellent job. Reaching the tunnel was impossible.

The ascent took much longer than going down, weighed down as she was by mud and gloom. When she emerged, she was coated with filth.

"It's hopeless," she said, slumping onto the ground.

There was a stunned silence. She suspected nobody expected it to end so ignobly. "It's far too dangerous in the shaft, let alone further down. The cavern is underwater." She looked to Gael. "There's no way to reach the tunnel. This is a dead end."

They all shuffled over to sit at the roots of the treasure tree, slumping heavily against the rough bark. Lola scraped the mud off her hands, longing for the times she used to get a monthly manicure.

Gael stood up, limping on his boot frantically. "This can't be the end. We were so close!"

"It was always a long shot," Nix said. She went to put her hand on Gael's shoulder.

"But we had gotten somewhere! You didn't see it, Nix; there *is* something down there." His eyes were overly bright.

"Treasure hunting is nearly always disappointing," Lola said. She wanted to wrap him up in her arms.

"But if we can't make this work, if there's nothing to find at the end of this, then I just have nothing." He spun away, nearly tripping over his boot. "It's not even about the money. Well, maybe it was at first, but"—Gael stopped and drew in a breath, blinking hard—"I just wanted to find something good, to go back and tell Diego. Before.... He's not going to pull through."

The group stood in motionless, Gael's pain raw in front of them. Then Nix let out a sobbing breath.

"And my mum hasn't slept in days, not that I helped." He gestured brusquely to his injured leg. "And I thought if only we could have found something, anything, it would be like a sign that something good was going to happen."

He leaned against the bark of the tree, eyes glistening, and Lola wanted to make it okay. She went back and crouched at the edge of the hole, staring in, contemplating diving into it.

He saw her look. "You said no one would be able to make it down there. Does that include you?"

With a heavy sinking in her stomach, Lola could tell where he was going with this, and it wouldn't end well. She gave an infinitesimal shake of the head, hoping he wouldn't continue.

Gael held Lola's gaze for a long time with a silent plea. Lola held up her hand to stop him before he said something he couldn't take back.

"What are you talking about?" Nix asked, looking sharply between the two. "She just said it's a death trap."

"I was just wondering if Lola, as a *professional treasure hunter*, would be able to go places where we couldn't."

Lola was shaking his head at him. "You have no clue how dangerous this is. It's not about finding a prize at the end. People could die!"

"I know people are going to die, Lola. And I realize I'm an idiot, but I thought if somehow I could find a miracle, then everything would be better. And then you came along, and I thought that was you."

It was as though he had kicked her in the guts. "I'm not a miracle, Gael." If she had tears to give, they would be spent by now. "I can't make everything all right."

She turned as though to leave them, but Nix stopped her with a hand on her arm. "Will somebody please tell me what's going on? You're acting like there's some kind of big secret here."

"There is so much you don't know," Lola said.

"Well then, tell me! I want to know."

"Do you?" Lola's gaze was fixed intensely on Nix's, as though she could peer all the way inside of her. "I can tell you stories that would make you never want to leave your house again. Sometimes it's better not to know."

Nix scowled. "You think it's better to leave me in the dark?"

Lola froze. Beau had stalked Nix just the other day. He wasn't going to leave her alone just because the treasure was impossible to reach. He would think it hilarious to kill her.

Lola had made all of them targets, and their ignorance made

them vulnerable. They would be dead within days if she didn't do something. They had to know how to protect themselves.

She shot a look at Gael. His eyes were wide with improbable hope.

Lola put her hands on her hips, staring at the ground while she counted off all the rules of men and monsters she was breaking. "Listen, this is going to sound impossible, but hear me out. There are...*things* in this world. Things you don't know about and probably wouldn't believe in anyway."

Nix groaned. "Oh god, you sound like Mrs. McInnes."

"She probably knows more about the world than you've ever imagined."

"Don't tell me you're one of those psychos too."

"No." Lola let out a bitter laugh. "I'm the thing the psychos fear. I'm one of the creatures." Walt and Nix stared at her in horror. "I'm a vampire."

There was a long silence, then Nix snorted. Walt gave a disbelieving laugh, and then they both started to snicker. Lola gave them a stern look.

"Okay, you're a vampire," Nix said. "And I'm a fairy princess. Now can you tell us what's actually going on?"

Gael struggled to his feet and limped to his friend. "This is for real, Nix. Lola showed me the other day, when we were down in the cavern. I would have died if it weren't for her. She carried me out of the cavern even as water was rushing in. No ordinary human, no matter how strong, could have done that."

Nix crossed her arms, looking Lola up and down. "So you're, like, the undead? How are you out in the day?"

"No sunlight." Lola pointed at the overcast sky.

"But all those times we've been digging during the day, it's... always been rainy. Okay, whatever, it's been a crappy spring. But you also...never eat anything." Nix glared. "Is this some kind of fetish thing? Are you goth?"

Lola shook her head. "I know it's hard to believe..."

"No, Lola. It's impossible to believe. I think you shook loose some brain cells down there."

"… but the world is full of dark creatures."

"Prove it," Walt said.

Lola looked at him, trying to see if he was being a bully, but his face was impassive. "You've asked us to believe in the impossible. But for us to understand, you have to show us something."

Pressure built behind her eyes. What was she, some kind of circus performer? She didn't want to put on a freak show for them. But if they saw, if they really understood the danger, it might keep them safe.

She took a deep breath, calling on her wilder nature. She closed her eyes and concentrated on the hunger that always lingered underneath. The subtle transformation washed over her. When she opened her eyes, the world looked slightly different: brighter, with less colour. She knew her eyes glowed, her skin was paler, and her canines were visible over her lower lip.

"Holy shit!" Nix stumbled back.

Walt paled until he looked like a vampire himself. He stumbled on the roots. "I didn't expect that," he said. "You are…" He reached out as though to touch her, then snatched his hand back. "This changes everything."

"I am *other*." Lola lisped around her teeth. "I am not the only one, and vampires are not the only creatures who prey on humans."

"How do we not know vampires exist?" Nix sounded cagey, like she was about to make a run for it. Her breath was coming in short gasps as she took in Lola's demonic form.

"Everybody knows about vampires. That's the beauty of it. We're everywhere, splashed throughout history in stories, books and TV shows. Everybody knows, and nobody believes. We hide behind the legends."

"So, what do you actually eat?" Nix asked. "If you're a vampire, does that mean you, like, suck blood?"

"I survive by drinking the blood of living creatures."

Walt paled even further; Nix looked revolted. Even Gael started to look queasy, crossing his arms over his chest as he darted glances at her. This was her fear: she *had* become a freak show.

Frustration fizzled through her. "What do you want from me? You asked me to prove it. Now you can't handle it?"

She shook her head, bringing human features back to the front, and both Nix and Walt relaxed visibly.

Her temper settled on Gael. "Don't go soft on me now. You don't get to be fussy about the details. Had you not thought what it meant to be undead? I am not human; I do not change or grow; I am stagnant, on the verge of rotting. The only thing that preserves me is a consistent supply of fresh blood. Was it only cool when you thought your girlfriend was super strong? *Now* it's gotten too real for you?"

"Girlfriend?" Walt's head whipped towards Gael.

Nix stood in front of Gael as though he needed protection from Lola. "Do you kill people?" she asked, her jaw jutting forward.

"I have. Humans are my natural prey. Now, though, I prey on wild animals. They work, but not as well as humans. Rabbits, mainly." Lola looked away, not wanting to be ashamed, but everything about her right now felt grotesque. Especially the way they were looking at her.

Beau was right. She would never belong with them.

"You eat bunnies?" Nix sounded outraged.

Lola narrowed her eyes. "What are you, a vegetarian? I've seen you eating hamburgers, so don't be a hypocrite. Duchesne Island has a nasty rabbit problem. It's about time they had a proper predator."

"That's what you are? A predator?"

"Yes."

"I..." Nix put her hand up. Her freckles stood out in sharp

contrast to her skin. "I need a minute. To process. I'm going to... go." She strode away without a backwards glance.

Lola thought about calling out to her, but there was no point. Their blossoming friendship was over. She watched her until she was out of sight, though, something crumpling inside of her.

"Do you breathe?" Walt asked. His eyes were brighter now, more fervent.

Lola turned back with a resigned sigh. "I don't have to, but my lungs work. Otherwise, I couldn't speak."

"What does being a vampire feel like?"

She shrugged. "For the most part, it feels..." *Lonely.* "Like being hungry all the time. Something inside of you demands you constantly feed, and it's never satisfied."

"How did you die? Were you killed by a vampire?"

Lola stared at him, her mouth open, feeling more freakish with every question.

Gael struggled to his feet. "That's enough. Walt, you're right; sometimes you ask weird questions."

"Oh. Sorry, Lola."

She let out a small, mirthless laugh.

Gael shook his head. "I'm sorry. I thought she would react better." He glanced in the direction Nix had disappeared. "She just needs time. She knows you're not a monster, deep down."

Lola wrapped her arms around her waist and hunched forward as he put his arm around her. Even through his grief and her misery, he could spark a bonfire of warmth in her.

"We should head out. There's nothing to do here unless conditions change."

"Right." He pressed his lips to her hair. "Don't think I didn't catch the 'girlfriend' you threw in there."

Lola tried to smile, to pretend like it was all going to be okay, but it wasn't. "Well, that was more for emphasis."

"Doesn't have to be." His beautiful mouth curled into a smile, and it did make her laugh. A little.

"Listen, we'll regroup and come up with a plan. Tomorrow."

"Yes, tomorrow." Lola brushed her hands over her face. She couldn't hide the whole truth from them, not when the whole point was to keep them safe. "Just...stay in the sunlight, okay? And once you're indoors, don't leave the house after dark. And don't invite strangers in."

Both Gael and Walt looked at her strangely, as though she had begun speaking a foreign language. She was already drawing the mist away from them, bringing it around her until she was enveloped in a cloud, drops clinging to her skin.

The boys gaped, now standing in dappled sunlight.

"Go home," she said. "Meet here tomorrow, if you can stomach it."

Still staring, Walt helped Gael to the ATV. Without another word they rumbled away. Only after they were out of sight did Lola allow herself to sink to the ground next to the hole. Whether they knew it or not, this hunt was over. So was their friendship.

Her legs dangled over the edge. It hurt that Nix didn't embrace her darkest secret and Walt thought of her as a science project. But, more than anything, it hurt that Gael wanted her to be his girlfriend, and that could never happen. She couldn't untangle her flooding emotions.

She stared into the hole instead, the suffocating walls coated thick with mud. She imagined forcing herself through the filth at the bottom into the lightless cavern. She didn't need to breathe, but she would be blind, helpless. If she could not get back up or find a way out, she could be stuck down there. She would transform into something else, more creature than person, forever in the dark.

She shivered. Whatever was down there, whatever power, it wasn't worth the risk.

She stayed that way until the sun set. Once the light had faded, she unleashed the cloud hovering around her. Lola lifted her head, letting the cool drops stream over her face. As it reached the hole, the mud dripped down the sides of the shaft.

Lola stared. With enough rain, the shaft could be washed clean.

She reached upwards. It started with a tingle over her skin. Above her, clouds from the ocean skidded across the sky to answer her call. They came, pregnant with water, and so she asked them to release. A bolt of lightning raked across the sky, and rolling thunder bellowed its answer, and the rain fell in a heavy sheet of water.

Spluttering and laughing, Lola rolled from the edge of the hole to avoid being swept in. She lay under the treasure oak, feeling the rain soak into her, watching the newly grown oak leaves play in the wind above. She had no idea what was coming next, but here she felt safe, sheltered.

She couldn't say how long she lay there, letting the rain pour over her. It felt healing. She idly formed a cloud of mist over her head, using her hands to sculpt shapes in it. A rabbit, a deer, a wolf. They morphed in the fog until they chased each other.

A gust of wind dissipated the cloud, and the playful mood shifted. The slant of the wind changed, buffeting into her. The gentle healing stream of water turned into violent lashes. An echoing laugh bounced around her, mocking her. She leapt to her feet, fangs slipping over her lips. She had forgotten for a moment she could be prey as well.

Twenty-One

The rain stung Lola's face as she waited, carried on the howling wind. The violence in the storm wasn't natural. Crouching against the onslaught, Lola readied herself.

"Show yourself."

The wind died suddenly, leaving total stillness, unsettling in a living forest.

Beau sauntered into the clearing as if he was taking a stroll in the park. His clothes were soaked, clinging to every sculpted muscle. His eyes glowed deep red in the darkness.

Lola remembered how her desire for Beau used to hit like a physical blow. In those early days, it would leave her weak with desperate longing to be near him, for a single smile.

But no more. She acknowledged the attraction, but he didn't have the same power over her. Somewhere along the way, she'd changed. She couldn't understand how she'd thought she loved him.

"Lovely day." He shook his hair from his eyes.

Cornered with her back against the tree, her gaze darted around the clearing. No easy escape route. She would have to brazen this one out. She huffed and crossed her arms. "Is that the game we're playing today?"

He narrowed his eyes and stalked closer. "I thought you liked the games we played."

"They're boring, Beau. You've become boring. I think it's time we move on."

His face hardened. "Move on to other things, chérie? Like warm, pliant flesh and pumping lungs?" He reached for her, his fingers grazing her cheek before she jerked away. His skin was hard and cold as marble. "He's only a plaything, after all. He'll get boring more quickly than me."

"I don't think so, Beau. You only have one move. Humans adapt; they change. *They* are interesting."

"Humans are weak, ruled by their emotions."

"It's their emotions that allow them to change! Their interest in others motivates them. It allows them to grow."

Beau snorted. "You've had your head turned by idealistic children. Give it time, and they'll be like all the rest. Humans are self-interested, greedy pigs. That's what makes them delicious." He placed a finger in his mouth and sucked.

She caught her breath. "Humans can be greedy and self-interested. But not all of them. Some are generous, and kind."

"Have you gone completely insane?" His eyes widened, the red showing clearer than ever, and he looked her up and down like he'd never seen her before. "I think the best *kindness* I could offer you is putting you out of your misery."

Lola braced herself for an attack, but after a moment he backed away from her.

He stepped to the edge of the hole and tutted. "What a mess. You intended to clean it out?" He glanced up, eyes gleaming. "What did you find? You're still here, so it must be more than a mud pit."

Lola narrowed her eyes. She'd rather rip out her tongue than tell Beau about the glowing tunnel. "Why are you here, Beau? At first, I thought it was to carry out Jacquotte's orders. You often play her errand boy." Beau glared. "Yes, I was there, Beau. I was on the yacht when she commanded you to *end* me."

Beau's face stretched tight with tension, but after a moment, he let his shoulders fall with a shrug. "So you know. It doesn't change anything."

"The fact you think that shows what a true monster you are. What confuses me is why you haven't followed through. Why aren't you obeying Jacquotte like the good little puppy you are to her? You're not doing much of anything other than making a nuisance of yourself. Why?"

"Why do you think?"

She raised her eyebrow. "Not for me? Because we're done. Why go through all the effort to follow me, if not to obey her command?"

He scoffed. "You were so obvious it was barely an effort. You left a trail a mile wide behind you. The stolen map? And do you honestly think I didn't know about your dealer in Havana? He was happy to let me know you were headed north, under the right pressure. It didn't take long to put two and two together."

"Yes, well, you didn't have to flee in a bikini."

"Was it that polka dot thing? I miss that one. Come on, Lola, why don't we forget all of this and go back to twilit beaches?"

"You agreed to kill me."

"But I haven't killed you. Yet."

Without warning, Beau lunged, but Lola was no longer there. She had darted to the side, out of reach.

Beau let out a shout of laughter. "Always faster than everybody else, isn't that right? Come now, chérie, it doesn't have to be like this. Hear me out."

"Hear you out nothing," Lola said, her voice throaty. "You're nothing to me."

Beau's mouth curved into a cruel smile. "Liar. I'm everything to you."

"You have to stop tracking me everywhere I go, Beau. I told you it's over between us."

"Things between us will never be over, surely you know that. You and I are connected. I knew it from the moment I saw you. You're mine, from here into eternity."

He lunged again, catching at her arm. She spun through the air and landed on the earth. Beau came after her, and she kept on rolling. She maintained the momentum until she flipped into a crouch out of reach.

"Amazing," he said. "There's never been anyone like you." He feinted to the side, then came straight at her. She jerked back at the last second. Their bodies brushed against each other, and she was reminded of how much larger he was than her. How much stronger. What chance could she possibly have against him?

Lola settled into a crouch, fangs fully exposed.

Beau swayed and laughed, drunk on the play and the heat of battle. "Always so goddamned fast, Lola. Too bad you can't keep up with me."

"Watching you spin in circles is hardly exciting. I did tell you you were boring."

He paused, resting with his hands on his knees. "That's not what I meant. I will always find you because, at the end of the day, you're not very clever."

"You don't know anything," she spat.

He lunged again, and Lola dodged easily. "I know you're hiding. You thought no vampire will set foot on this island. Not unless they're condemned, like you. I know you think finding the power in the Well of Souls will help you. But nothing will help you, Lola, until you rid yourself of your simpering humanity. It's turning you into an aberration."

Rage transformed his face into something twisted. His intensity shocked Lola, and she nearly lost her footing. Beau was on her in a second, forcing her back.

"You're jealous Jacquotte cares for me more than she'll ever care for you."

"Jacquotte doesn't care for you." A mad smile playing over his face. "Her obsession with you never made sense until she told me why you're different. You were an experiment. A failed experiment."

Beau struck. Lola, bewildered by his revelation, slipped in the mud. His fist slammed into her chest, bones crashing into bones. She was flung back, landing with a sickening thud. Her limbs lay at odd angles, and she tasted blood. There was a queasy tightness at her chest. Beau had crushed her rib cage and probably snapped her spine.

She wheezed, and Beau rushed to her side.

"Oh, chérie, I really got you, didn't I?" He brushed hair from her face as blood seeped from her lips. He looked genuinely remorseful. "I thought we were still playing. You're so fast, I never have to hold back. I never hold back with you."

The pain found her then, crashing over her. Her heart was punctured, bones stabbing into the muscle like a pincushion. She coughed, spattering blood across Beau's face like freckles. He didn't blink, gathering her into his arms.

If she had been human, she would be dying. Instead, the demonic energy flowing within her veins took over. With agonizing precision, her body stitched itself back together. Her organs shifted as her bones groaned.

She let out a howl, that of a wounded animal.

"Yes, let it all out, my love." Beau's eyes were lit with affection, with his love of pain. "I'll watch you put yourself back together."

"Get away from me," Lola gritted through her teeth. She screamed as something snapped into place, but she could move afterwards.

"I didn't come to kill you but to save you. We could be together, you and me, ruling over all the rest. All we need to do is find this power and control it."

Lola prepared to spit out a string of expletives, but she felt another presence. Straining, she caught a bright shot of copper in the mist. Nix.

Beau's bloodlust was up, and no human was safe near him. She couldn't let him know the girl was there. She grabbed his shirt at the front, bringing him closer.

"You...and...me," she forced out. *How long can I distract him?*

"Yes, chérie. Together, think about what we could do with the power trapped on this island, once we set it free. We could kill Jacquotte." His eyes glowed.

"Yes," Lola whispered. "I want...that. I want you." She moaned in pain as she forced herself up, using Beau as a lever. She brought her bloodstained face to his, peeking over his shoulder to make sure Nix was gone.

That was her mistake. Beau realized her attention wasn't on him. He stilled, and she presumed he'd caught Nix's scent. Desire and fury played over his features before he schooled them.

"That's what this is about? Another game?"

"No." Lola caught at Beau's arms, screeching in pain as her broken body fought her. They struggled, but Beau was much stronger than her at her best. He forced her down, holding her in place as he pressed a hard kiss against her mouth. She struggled, whimpering in pain.

"There will be time for that later, chérie. Right now, it's a race."

His eyes glowed, inhuman, before he jumped up and took off after Nix.

Lola let out a sob and rolled over, her arms flailing for something to help her stand. She would never get to her in time.

She squeezed her eyes shut, forcing herself to *move*. "Help," she whimpered, sending out a plea to nothing in particular.

She caught herself on the roots of the great oak.

Warmth from the bark spread through her palms, then flashed deep into her body like lightning. The scent of flowers, of green things, surrounded her, and she was infused with energy. Bones cracked into place, far swifter than she had ever done as a vampire before. She could move without pain.

She could sense the forest around her. Her connection to water seemed crystal clear, as though every raindrop waited for her direction. She let out a sigh of amazement as power crashed through her.

She flipped to her feet. "Thank you," she whispered to the tree and leapt down the path, swifter than any deer.

Beau had a head start and could jump through the wind. She had to slow him down.

Lola thrust her hands out, calling on the water in the air and earth to grab him. She had never done anything like that before. It was not in the nature of water to grasp but to flow.

To her shock, the water responded to her plea. It rose to her command, the mist swirling to obey her. She caught a glimpse of a dark shadow and physically pulled her arms toward herself as though to bind him. He tripped, pushed back by a wall of water. His growl of frustration ripped through the air, and a gust of wind shoved her.

"Nix, run!" Lola screamed. Her voice was whipped away by the wind. She reached out her hand, and the water formed a similitude of a hand. Before she had time to marvel at these magics, she clenched her fist, and the water fist grabbed Beau off the ground, throwing him down in a geyser. Beau sputtered as he strained to his feet, flailing against the waves she pounded over him.

A gust of air lifted her off the forest floor, careening into a tree. A cushion of water formed to soften her trajectory, and she landed on her feet. She sent the water crashing over Beau again, a tidal wave dragging him back.

The air around him filled with a swirling column of water, so he was suspended in midair, moving as though underwater. His eyes were incredulous as he opened his mouth, gurgling. It defied all laws of nature.

Raising her arms, she allowed the water to flow away from his face. "What is this?" he screamed. "How did you access such power?"

She had no idea. Now that Beau was confined, she stopped and stared at her hands. Previously, her control over water had been mild, simply bending some rules, but always remaining within the realm of possibility. This was unprecedented. Water responded to her very thoughts.

She raised a hand, water swirling in her palm. "*Incroyable,*" she said, watching it flow as though caught in the currents of her aura. "Like magic."

"Magic tricks." Beau spat on the ground. "Who cares?"

"You, I suspect. You've always been jealous of anyone with more power than you. That's why you hate Jacquotte. That's why you always wanted to keep me down. This must be killing you right now."

Beau sneered, as though he would deny it, but finally snarled. "But how?"

She let the whirlpool fall. As powerful as she felt right now, she was injured and tiring. She couldn't hold him for much longer. She flung her hands to the side, and Beau went flying through the air, landing on his back on the ground. She stood over him as he coughed.

"Leave the humans alone, Beau. Leave this island. Go find a hole to crawl into; otherwise, I'll find you."

He stared at her, and a slow smile spread across his face. His eyes gleamed. "You know, I think I'll do that."

A wall of wind shoved into Lola, making her stumble. When she righted herself, Beau had disappeared. She sprinted for Nix.

The energy the tree had given her was like medicine running through her veins. She caught up with Nix halfway through the town square, flaming hair streaming behind her.

Lola followed her, hidden in the shadows until Nix arrived at the shelter of the lighthouse. With her demonic senses she could hear the girl's heart beating wildly, and her voice shook when she called out a greeting to her siblings. But she was safe.

Lola's next stop was Gael's cottage. She lingered outside his door long enough to confirm he was inside, asleep and alone.

Lola needed to find Beau before he found another human target. She couldn't accept another casualty on this island, not when it was her that had put them in danger. She stalked back toward Port Despardoux, determined to ensure everyone remained safe this night.

Twenty-Two

Lola prowled all night, but there was no sign of Beau. She lingered until the sun's rays began to shine above the horizon, dashing for shelter ahead of the stinging heat.

She slept long, dreamless hours, recovering from her injuries and the new powers that crashed through her. When she woke, the first thing she was aware of was the ocean crashing against the rocks outside her window. It wasn't only the rhythmic sound or the bright salty smell; there was also the profound pull of the undertow, as though she was being dragged into the briny depths.

Lola sat, heart pounding. Something extraordinary had happened to her, though she didn't understand it. She had to get back to the dig site. The answer to everything was found tangled deep under the earth.

She squinted from behind the shade of her window. The rain had used itself up. The sun was high in the sky, disarmingly bright. Beau would still be sheltering; she knew he slept like the dead. He had no way to hide from the sun as she did.

She grabbed her leggings, washed in the sink and dried over the heating grate, and stole another sweater. It took a brief thought to summon a roll of mist from the bay to shield her from the sun.

Racing toward the forest, she hoped to stay out of sight. A moving ball of thick mist would attract attention – although it would probably be put down to the spirits that haunted the island. One more legend for Duchesne.

As she approached the treasure tree, she could sense Gael. She hadn't been expecting him and her heart jumped in her chest as she slowed.

The scent hit her, sharp and bitter. *Gin?* She leapt over a root and landed at the treasure pit; the edges had softened and wept inward. Gael stared into the hole.

"Gael?"

It was his baleful look that stopped her from approaching. He had been friendly last night; more than friendly. The person who glared at her now was someone else entirely.

"What's wrong? Did something happen?"

He snorted. "Did something happen? Let's see." He shifted his mud-streaked stabilizing boot, grunting in pain. "My brother is dying. They've given him a few days now. He's asleep and might not ever wake up." He sighed. "And the one stupid hope I had turned out to be a lie. Does that about cover it?"

"You mean the treasure pit."

"Should I mean something else?"

Lola approached cautiously. "Shouldn't you be in school?"

"Waste of time." He reached into his pocket to pull out a metal flask. He took a sip, pulling a face as it went down. Strong spirits wafted from him; he'd been drinking for some time.

His movements blurry, he held out the flask. "Want some?"

She crossed her arms over her chest. "Gael, what are you doing? This isn't like you."

He let out a bitter laugh and took another swig, holding her gaze the whole time. "I thought you liked bad boys."

"Bad boys?" Realization struck. Nix told Gael what she saw last night. Or what she *thought* she saw. If she had missed the fighting, then other things could be easily misinterpreted. Lola in Beau's arms, Beau kissing her. *Merde.*

"Nix told you about last night," Lola said carefully.

"Big guy, she said. "Very muscly" were her exact words. Nix isn't even into guys, but she was pretty impressed, so he must be something."

"Gael..."

"Oh, yeah, and something about glowing eyes and fangs?"

Double merde. "What Nix thought she saw wasn't what really happened. There *is* another vampire on Duchesne. He came for me, and we're *all* in danger. I suspect he has an interest in targeting you specifically."

"Why, because you put that target on my back?" He snorted. "I am so stupid. I made it so easy for you. You come waltzing into my life, all big eyes and tales of buried treasure. You convince me to dig, probably because it was easier than hiding from me. Although I suppose you could have killed me to get me out of the way."

"I would never kill you. I had my chance, and I didn't. You know that."

"What was even the point of this?" He made a drunken gesture between the two of them. "Was it a game? Did you go and laugh to your boyfriend afterwards at the stupid little boy who fell in love with you?"

"You were never a game to me, and he is *not* my boyfriend."

"That's not what Nix said."

"Nix doesn't know the first thing about what happened last night."

"You know him." His accusing finger drifted to the side.

"Yes, he was a part of the crew I travelled with."

"Crew?"

"Most vampires live in groups. We move together, hunt together."

"And you and he, were you...together?"

She pursed her lips, wishing she could just lie, but it wouldn't be fair to him. "Sometimes."

Gael scowled. "You must think I'm so pathetic. This docile little dupe, doing whatever you ask when you bat your eyelashes."

Lola reached out, but he jerked away, stumbling, and took another swig from the flask. Acid pain bubbled in her stomach. Because everything he said was true, wasn't it? She had used him, knowing he wanted her. That had been the *plan*, to dupe the local. How to explain how everything had changed?

"But now, Beau, he is my enemy. What I feel for you is real."

"Why should I believe you? You're a demon; you said so yourself." His voice broke.

Her eyes prickled as she stared directly at him, fury starting to boil. There were many things she'd done terribly wrong, but not this. "You should put that drink down."

He raised his head, glaring at her through narrowed eyes like a dare. "Don't think I will."

"Let me make this entirely clear. I am not with Beau. He followed me here, and it's a dangerous situation. What happened between him and me last night was me protecting Nix, something she clearly did not understand. Beau is in my past, but in the present, Gael, it's you I care for."

"You're not capable of caring."

The water in the air responded to her ire. It swirled around her as her fangs slipped down. She knew from the way Gael was looking at her, half-fear, half-awe, that her eyes glowed crystalline. "Be that as it may, I will do what I can to protect you." Her voice deepened and reflected off the swirling water.

It dropped in a sudden gush over Gael's head, leaving him spluttering. Lola let out a sigh, depleted, and turned to leave.

Gael staggered toward her. "Wait, Lola!" He sounded less fuzzy. Perhaps the dousing sobered him up.

She deliberately stepped out of his reach. "Go home, where

you'll be safe. Even with that boot, you can limp home before the sun sets."

"What about you?"

She growled, and he flinched at the vicious sound. "I need to eat."

TWENTY-THREE

Lola ripped a sapling out of the ground. She was as angry with herself as she was with Gael; after all, his accusations weren't without reason. She looked back at the trail of destruction she had cut through the forest with guilt. She had been hunting for hours, but it wasn't blood she craved. She needed to calm down.

Huffing out an outraged breath, she made her way into Port Despardoux. She would hunt down a cup of coffee instead. The sun had set not long ago and she would begin her rounds of guarding the town, starting at the café. The thought of slipping into The Pain Perdu warmed her. Faye was the only person who had been there for her, without fail.

The flashing blue and red lights drew her attention first, from across the town square, and her heart sank. She darted toward the café, suddenly sure of what she would find.

Two RCMP cars were parked in front of The Pain Perdu.

Lola reached the front door as an ambulance jolted to a stop in front of the café. Two uniformed officers guarded the front, one directing the scrambling paramedics, the other listening to garbled static on his radio.

"What happened?" Lola called, trying to get to the door. Dread washed over her. She knew Beau would target those she loved. But Faye was supposed to be safe; she never wandered the streets on her own. Tucked into her warm café, where she would... *invite any stray in off the street.* Her heart squeezed. He wouldn't, would he?

"Miss." The officer threw his arms out to stop her from entering. He smelled of stale coffee. "This is a crime scene. You need to stand back."

Lola quivered in front of him. The clear sky clouded over in seconds, and a loud crack of thunder sounded. The officer startled as rain splattered him.

"I need to see Faye. She's a friend."

"The best thing you can do is let us work."

The door swung open, and the paramedics descended the steps, balancing the gurney between them. Faye lay on the cot, eyes closed and skin pale, nearly translucent. A raw bloody gash on her throat was still bleeding, the medic working to stop it. Lola wished for the raindrops to stop splashing on her face because she couldn't brush them away.

The rain stopped suddenly. An underlying crackle of tension trembled in the air, like static electricity. Everyone darted glances at the sky, even the medics. Were they the same ones who had treated Gael? People she cared for had a high risk of trauma.

"Faye!" Lola called, but the officer caught her as she lunged to the woman's side. She sensed a very faint heartbeat, weak and thready. Faye was alive, but barely.

"Let me go." Lola whirled on the officer, barely able to control her human features.

"What's going on here?" A commanding voice rang out in the weird stillness.

Captain Greyson descended the café steps, face grim. His dark eyes bored into Lola's. "Lola Monteux. What are you doing here?"

"I came for a coffee. What happened to Faye?"

"Let her go," Greyson ordered quietly, and Lola fell forward as the arms holding her released suddenly.

"Is she alright?"

"There was an attack this evening. Right around sunset."

"Is she going to be okay?" Lola dug her fingernails into her palms, struggling to keep her voice level.

"Get her to the hospital; we'll be right behind," Greyson ordered the medics. Lola stood back, helpless, as Faye's body was passed into the ambulance. It careened away, sirens screaming.

Greyson turned on her. "I don't trust you. You showed up on the island right around the time the brutal attacks started. Know anything about that?"

Lola raised her chin. "You arrived at the same time. Are you a suspect?"

Greyson's anger was palpable, in the line of his shoulders and the clench of his jaws. "Faye may be taken in by you, but I know your type. Ready to take advantage of every kindness. If I find out you had anything to do with this..." He trailed off, clenching his fists.

"I would never hurt Faye," Lola whispered.

He pointed a finger in her face. "Soon, you and I are going to have a long chat. Don't leave this island."

Lola was left alone on the street, stunned by his vitriol. She had no intention of leaving the island. She was usually more than happy to get out of the way of trouble before trouble found her. Self-preservation demanded it. But she wouldn't leave now. Not until she had cleaned up her mess.

She sprinted to the hospital.

Spurred by worry, Lola arrived minutes after the ambulance had pulled into the emergency bay. Police cars blocked the front entrance, lighting up the sky.

Lola kept to the shadows, creeping around the side of the hospital until she found the loading dock unguarded. With the twist of her wrist, she broke the lock, the crunch of metal satisfying under her palm.

She slunk along the corridor, empty at this time of night. Once in the main hallway, she oriented herself. The emergency bay was on the other side. Sneaking into the central waiting room, Lola drew up short. Walt and Nix were there. Why were they there? Not for Faye; they wouldn't know about that yet. Who else had Beau hurt?

Nix paced the aisle between the seats with the coiled energy of a tigress. Walt sat on a chair, elbows braced on his knees. It must be Gael. How could she have let her anger get the better of her? She should never have left him alone, drunk and injured. A killer was stalking him!

Lola rushed into the room. "What are you doing here?"

Their heads snapped up, looking dazed. Lola grabbed Nix's arm. "Is Gael okay? Did something happen?"

"That hurts!" Nix shouted.

"Tell me what's wrong with Gael!"

"Nothing!" Lola dropped Nix, who rubbed her arm in outrage. "What is your problem, you psycho?"

"I'm not – please, can you tell me why you're here?" Lola rocked back on her heels, desperate for calm. Her fangs had slipped out and both Nix and Walt were staring at her. They slowly retracted.

"It's Diego," Walt said when Nix did nothing but glare.

Lola spun. "But he didn't tell me—" Except he had. He'd told her his brother wasn't going to wake up, and all she could focus on was Beau. She ran her hands over her face.

"Diego took a turn this morning," Walt said, his voice hoarse. "He's in intensive care. They put him on a ventilator. It...doesn't look good. Gael called us a few hours ago. He and his mum are with him now."

Lola's eyes flickered around the waiting room, trying to make sense of everything, when the crackle of radio static interrupted her thoughts. She tucked herself behind a tall magazine rack, which held outdated gossip rags. She could see Nix and Walt but was hidden from the police.

From the emergency bay, Captain Greyson stalked into the waiting room, followed by a uniformed officer. Their voices were low murmurs, but Lola could hear them clear enough. Nix and Walt had gone silent, Nix's eyes flicking to Lola's hiding place.

"She has the same marks as the other victims," the officer was saying. "Two stab wounds in the neck."

"We don't know if these are stabbings," Greyson replied. "But the puncture wounds tie these crimes together."

Nix's eyes went wide, and she found Lola, accusation piercing her. Lola shook her head, mouthing *no*.

The officer scribbled in a notepad. "What does this mean? We have a serial killer on the loose with a vampire fetish?"

Greyson tapped his fingers on the counter. "Shit, something fucked up is happening on this island." His voice lowered, the threat laden through every syllable. "I will make whoever's responsible pay."

Nix bit her lip, looking back and forth between the police and Lola. Walt stared at the linoleum floor.

Greyson turned on his heel, the officer following him into the rain outside. Lola melted with relief and crept into the open.

Nix pinned her with an accusatory gaze. Walt hadn't moved, but she felt his intensity.

"What did you do?" Nix hissed.

"Nothing. It wasn't me."

"Why are you hiding?"

"Greyson wants to question me, and I'm not in the mood to be questioned."

Nix peered at her. "Does he know you're a vampire?"

"No!" Lola was confident the no-nonsense man would not respond well to being told of the otherworld.

"He suspects you of a vampire attack even though he doesn't

know you're a vampire?" Nix's eyebrows were practically in her hairline. "What did you do?"

"I would never hurt Faye."

"You are a vampire." Walt's voice was expressionless. "And there has been a vampire attack. It stands to reason it was you."

"I'm not the only vampire on the island."

"That's right." Nix held a finger under Lola's nose. "There's also your boyfriend. I saw you together."

"Did you see him kick the shit out of me, or did you conveniently miss that part?"

Her finger lowered. "What?"

"You saw Beau, my *ex*-boyfriend, after he had broken all my ribs. Yes, I heal fast; it's a vampire thing," she said quickly to Walt, who looked like he might interrupt.

"Fascinating," he breathed, staring at her chest.

"Wait, your toxic ex-boyfriend? The stalker?"

"Yes. I shouldn't be surprised, but Beau followed me here. I don't know why, exactly, but he's causing trouble. I'm sure he's the one who hurt Faye."

"What about the two other murders?" Walt finally met her eyes.

"One of them must have been Graves," Nix said. "That creepy old man who lived by the water. Everyone assumed he'd drowned after a bender. Stab wounds don't sound like much of an accident, though."

"I don't know about that." Lola's hesitation betrayed her.

Nix whipped around. "Yes, you do!" Her eyes flicked over Lola, and she gasped. "Your stupid oversized fisherman sweaters. They're his, aren't they? What did you do, kill him for his sweaters?"

"Shh!" Lola hushed Nix's ever-rising voice. "Okay, yes, I killed Graves. I *am* a vampire. I had just arrived on the island and was starving, literally. He was near death, anyways." Her excuses sounded hollow, even to her ears. "I haven't attacked anyone since then. All the others have been Beau."

Nix rounded on her in disbelief. "You haven't killed anyone *since then*? What do you want, a medal?" She curled her lip. "And now you're squatting in his shack, aren't you, wearing his clothes? You're a ghoul."

"A vampire, actually." Lola held her head high.

"Let's focus," Walt said. "There have been three vampire attacks to date."

"Four, actually." Nix's eyes were narrowed to slits. "I've seen Gael's neck. That didn't happen in the fall, did it?"

"Drinking from Gael allowed me to save his life," Lola said, voice quiet. Shame washed over her, but she wouldn't lie to them anymore. "His human blood gave me the strength I needed to pull him out of the cavern before he drowned. But yes, I drank from him. Now, though, the danger lies with Beau. I'm going to put a stop to this. But first, I need to see Gael."

"Leave Gael alone." Nix's voice was mean. "He has enough to deal with, without killer vampires trying to get off with him. He told me he doesn't want to see you ever again. He thinks you're a monster."

Walt glanced at Nix, a troubled look spreading over his face, but Lola hardly cared. Something inside of her broke. "Right. Fine. I'm going to clean up my mess. Then I'll leave. Could you tell him goodbye for me?"

"Absolutely not," Nix hissed. "Nothing good can come of you."

Lola reeled as though she had been punched, but she couldn't defend herself. "Right, *c'est ça*. Stay in large crowds, okay? Near the police is better. Don't go outside alone."

"You must be stunned. Get the hell out of here."

Lola whirled, fleeing the hospital waiting room, brought low by a pint-sized pixie-girl who faced her with no fear. She ignored Walt as he called out for her. She had no right to be around them.

She checked outside for the police, then darted into the darkness, staying out of the light. Gael thought she was a monster, and he was right.

A car door slammed, and Lola's head shot up. Greyson strode to one of the cars, speaking into the window. "Look for the kid," he said. The kid, presumably, being her.

She sidled along the building, pressed against the brick wall. Her heart thumped as she waited for Greyson to re-enter the building.

Next to her, the bright light from a window made a yellow square on the ground. Shadows flickered inside, and despite the danger, she peeked over the edge.

Gael entered the waiting room, limping toward his friends. His broad shoulders sagged, and his leg dragged heavier than before. They went to his side as he gave a shake of his head. His face crumpled, and Nix rushed to put her arms around his waist. She held him up despite being nearly half his size.

Walt stood next to him and patted him stiffly on the back. Gael reached up, briefly squeezing his hand. Lola's fingers pressed against the window, her chest wrenching open. She was so sorry, for everything.

Unable to stop herself, she crept down the side of the building. There were only a few lit windows. Three rooms down, she found Gael's brother.

His frail body looked more like a withered mummy than a boy. He barely made a wrinkle in the bedding, tubes stretched out of every part of his body. Lola read the flashing screens: his heart continued to beat slowly as the ventilator did the work of squeezing air into his body. But by all counts, this boy had lost his fight. Gael's brother likely wouldn't live another day.

Next to the bed, Anita held her son's limp hand, staring at the wall. She didn't brush away the tears that trickled down her face, rolling along the lines of grief grooved into her skin.

What thoughts whirled behind those blank eyes? Did she think about every lonely day that stretched ahead of her, her youngest son cooling in a grave? Did she wonder how she would survive the pain? Or was it nothing but a blank void, emptiness so deep there were no thoughts at all, only suffering?

Lola looked away. She had no right to intrude on such personal moments. Grief was more intimate than love, more exposing than hate. And yet, she needed to witness this. She moved toward the last lit window along the row. She knew who she would find there.

Faye was laid out, similar to Diego. Her eyes were closed, sweet face drawn and ghostly pale. She looked younger here than when she was in her stronghold, sashaying through the café. Around her neck was a thick white bandage, and connected to her elbow crook was a bag of dark red fluid.

Lola's fangs slid out at the sight, and she loathed herself. She turned to flee the hospital, but movement stopped her. Greyson entered the room. He spoke with someone in the hallway, but his professional demeanour collapsed when the door shut behind him. With burning eyes, he reached for Faye. He stopped himself before he touched her, his hand flexing as though the gesture had been involuntary.

Beyond her grief and shame, something else stirred inside of Lola. It protested that she must crouch outside in the shadows, always looking in at life but never allowed to join. For decades she had observed life taking place, like a spectator to a show.

Enough of that. She was going to make things right. Or die trying.

She raised her hand to the window, mouthing *Stay well* to Faye. The movement caught Greyson's attention, who frowned and moved to the window. Lola was already long gone, heading deep into the night. Her fangs were fully extended.

TWENTY-FOUR

Lola returned to the café and caught his scent, bright and spicy like pepper, with the underlying rot of old blood. He had lingered near the scene of his crime, probably watching her.

She followed his scent straight through Port Despardoux, finding Beau in the gazebo of the town square, staring moodily out toward the Atlantic.

With every step, she increased her speed until she was sprinting. With all of her strength she barrelled straight into him. They both crashed over the railing, landing in an undignified sprawl in the sodden grass.

"Lola, what the hell?" Beau sputtered before she reeled back and punched him in the face. His nose crunched under her fist.

He shrieked in pain as he rolled over, holding his face. Black-red blood spurted through his fingers. Lola aimed a kick at his side and missed crushing his ribs by inches as he continued to roll into a crouch. He moved like a cat, startled to realize the mouse was more than a plaything.

"You piece of shit." Lola's voice broke. "You nearly killed her!" She allowed the demon inside to sweep over her, glowing as her cursed nature shone through. She landed a hard kick to the side of his knee as he started to rise, answered by a satisfying crunch and his groan of pain.

"What's it to you?"

"What's it to me!" Lola screamed. "You have no right to take her away from me."

"Ah." Beau was arrogant even as he jerked his knee back into place with a hiss. "So that's it. Suddenly this is all about *you*?"

She flung her arms out. "Isn't it? Why did you attack *her*, specifically, if it wasn't about me?"

"Why does it matter, Lola? She's a snack. That woman is not your mother. Neither is Jacquotte, but that's an issue for another day. The sooner you accept it, the sooner you'll find peace."

She stopped dead, staring into his demonic face. "Peace? You have no peace."

"Of course I do. There is purity in the hunt, instincts taking over, knowing where you stand. The effort you spend, all the while knowing you are going to win. Because if you don't, you die. That is the most profound peace I know. Can you honestly tell me you don't feel it?"

"I don't." Her response was sharp, and a lie. Even as he described it, the thrill of the hunt pounded in her veins.

"Liar." Beau's voice rang like crystal in the night air. "I can taste your longing. I've seen you when you let go, and you are magnificent." His eyes glowed. "This is why I follow you, Lola. Not for the sentimental weakling that you are, but because of what you could be once you are finally free. A goddess, with the power of oceans inside of her."

She wanted to fall into the pull of his words. She longed to be free of her suffering. What would happen if she just let go, allowed the demon to take her wholly?

He sensed her softening and smiled in triumph. "That's why we need to find the Well of Souls."

She blinked. "What? The treasure?"

"Of course. I know you don't have all the information." His voice was smug and grated over Lola's nerves.

"What are you talking about?" She circled him, and he watched her carefully, tensed for another attack.

"About the true nature of what lies beneath. You stole the map, Lola. But did you forget that I was the one who discovered it in the first place?"

Lola stopped, body so still she could have been a statue. She remembered well the night she'd fled from Jacquotte. How could she forget, when her creator condemned her to death, and her former lover agreed to carry out the execution? She'd cringed in the shadows as Beau stormed past, murder scrawled on his face. And she'd spied on Jacquotte as she slammed her fist down on the table, before grabbing a tankard of rum and heading below deck. Lola snuck into the cabin, knowing it would be the last time she'd ever enter it. She wasn't sure what she was looking for. A memento? A miracle? And then, she found it, tucked away in the top drawer. A map of the Well of Souls treasure, the only thing that could give her enough power to survive her enemies.

Beau had been the one to find it in a crypt in Lebanon, and Jacquotte had nearly lost her mind that he had brought it to her. Duchesne Island was the one place all vampires were forbidden to go – unless they had nothing left to live for.

Lola's mind worked in overtime, but she kept her face still, her eyes unblinking. "When you found the map, was it intact?"

His eyes glowed as he reached into his coat, pulling out a scrap of paper. Brittle and yellowed, it matched the map Lola had stolen from Jacquotte, the parchment torn in half. But while Lola held the map of Duchesne Island, Beau's part was scrawled with markings. She itched to snatch it out of his hands, but she waited with the deep stillness of a predator.

"The nature of the treasure. I take it we're not talking pirate gold?"

Beau snorted. "What is gold compared to power? You already

knew it wasn't anything so prosaic or you wouldn't have come. We've all heard the legends. But you never knew exactly what it was. I tore this off so Jacquotte would never lay eyes on it. I've been trying to show it to you, but you keep attacking me." He sounded deeply hurt.

"You keep trying to eat my friends."

"They are not your friends." His rusty eyes glowed, deadly serious. "They are your mortal enemies. They are your prey. And if they had any idea what you were, they would kill you in an instant."

Lola wanted to deny this. But all she could hear was Nix's voice ringing through her head: *He thinks you're a monster.*

"What does it say?" She snapped her hand open for the parchment.

Beau hesitated as he handed it over, his grip tightening slightly. She read his misgivings on his face and jerked it away. She glared at him before angling the paper to catch the light.

Her heart caught in her throat.

There were more arcane symbols, constellations like the ones from the map. Like the ones from Gael's fireplace rock.

She stilled her hand, so no trembling betrayed her excitement. Most of the parchment was written in Greek, which she scanned quickly before letting out a huff. "I can't translate on the fly. What does it say?"

Beau crowded closer to her, reading over her shoulder. Lola breathed in his familiar scent, all pepper and cloying blood. His body emitted no heat; it was as if he wasn't there. It was the warmth of a person that marked their presence. She wondered if her friends felt the same emptiness when she was near them.

"I can't figure out these symbols." He pointed to the arcane markings. "But I translated the Greek here. It speaks specifically of the Well of Souls." He indicated two passages. "And here it refers to the greatest power known to the world, a life force. And here it speaks of a cleansing power, a purge for power, something like that." He paused, letting her take it all in. "It all comes back to power. Think of the power and control over your element you've gained spending time near it. That's proof right there. We go into the Well of Souls, we will become more powerful than we've ever imagined."

"It might be a touch more complicated than that." Lola pursed her lips. "How can we even get down to the treasure? The hole is a death trap."

"We're already dead, Lola. We have nothing to fear."

"The flooding was only the first of the traps, I'm sure of it. There are some truly horrible things waiting for us there."

"And we'll get through them together. Lola, have you lost your spirit of adventure? *This* is the greatest prize we've ever gone after. You've never balked before."

Lola turned to look him in his eyes. He glowed in triumph. She twined her body into his so they were all but embracing. "If we do this..." she whispered.

Beau pressed into her eagerly. She leaned into him.

Then rammed her knee into his groin with all her might.

Beau slumped over her shoulder, momentarily voiceless. Lola shoved him off her, sending him sprawling in the mud. She leaned down to his ear before he recovered. "It's a race," she whispered.

His reedy scream followed her, but she was miles away, the parchment clutched tightly in her hand.

———

She spread the paper over the table. Gael's house was a safehold for her; Beau had not received an invitation to enter. That legend was true. Demonic creatures could not step over the threshold of the home of a living person without an explicit invitation. It had always been that way.

She knew Beau wouldn't be able to resist her challenge. As soon as he could, he would head into the Well of Souls. That kept her friends safe and put him where she wanted him. Down there, it would just be the two of them. And only one of them was going to come back up to the surface.

But she needed a moment to clear her head, to know what she was dealing with. She focused all her attention on the ancient symbols, which she had seen recently. She shifted her gaze to the matching etchings on the rock in Gael's fireplace. Whoever had made the etchings had also made the map – or at the very least, used the same language.

She rustled through the drawers and found a paper and pencil. She sucked the end of the pencil as she studied the parchment. She couldn't decode the arcane symbols. It was like no other language she had seen before. She suspected both were dire warnings, cautioning anyone who proceeded of their imminent death. The flooded cavern had already proven the way was deadly.

But the inscription in Greek gave her pause. None of Jacquotte's crew knew the extent of her ability with languages. Greek came to her far easier than it did to Beau. She scribbled out her translation, scratching out words here and there as she struggled to get the meaning. She looked at the results and laughed. Beau would have done well to hire a translator because he had done a poor job.

She stared at the passages Beau said meant great power and life force. He wasn't far off, but the details made all the difference. There was something he had missed, and in it, Lola found her atonement. She circled the words unsteadily: *Elixir of Life*.

Muttering to herself, she paced the tiny living room, her feet passing next to Diego's abandoned Lego set. Did she have this right? At the end of the Well of Souls was the Elixir of Life: a liquid that had the ability to heal and regenerate.

The treasure at the bottom of the well wasn't power, it was *life*. No wonder no vampire should enter there; it was inimical to them.

Her pacing came to a halt in front of a family portrait, Gael with his family. It had been taken several years back. Gael was shorter and rounder, with a full set of braces on his teeth. She smiled at his likeness, finally seeing what he said about being an awkward kid. She imagined this boy reading *Great Expectations*, and her heart softened like butter.

Oh, but they were happy. The family sat on the grass, captured in a moment of uproarious laughter. Gael was doubled over. Diego lay across his mother's lap, head upside down, his broad smile showing several gaps. Anita held her son, eyes squeezed shut in laughter. The photographer captured a tear on her cheek.

Lola brushed her finger over the tear. How fragile it all was.

She flipped over the paper, leaving a note at the base of the photograph.

I will do my best to make things right.

Twenty-Five

It was the darkest hour of night when Lola arrived at the treasure oak, when even the starlight lost its lustre. She studied the dig site. Beau's scent lingered in the air, pepper and blood, and his boot print was pressed into the mud. She peered over the edge of the hole, checking for glowing eyes, but it was empty.

She stared into the bottomless shaft until she was dizzy and not entirely sure what way was up anymore. She imagined suffocating in mud, trapped forever. *What if I never make it out again?*

She pressed her palm flat on the earth, grounding herself until her panic subsided. It was time to see what she was made of. If she was right about what waited for her, it would be worth the risk. It would be worth everything.

The tree rustled above her, standing sentinel. Lola reached for the nearest root.

"Wish me luck," she whispered. Was it wishful thinking, or was there an answering pulse of warmth? It steadied her. She glanced up in gratitude to the old tree, and something caught her eye. A branch was sticking out of the trunk the wrong way, glowing ever so slightly.

It came away in her hand as she grasped it. It wasn't a branch but a stake, gnarled and long and wickedly pointed on one end. She gasped, giving the tree a sharp look.

The leaves rustled as though to hurry her along. "*Sacré bleu.* You're a murderous tree, aren't you?" Lola put the stake in her bag. It contained laughably little: some rope, some climbing equipment, a water bottle. A bag of Spanish doubloons. A sharpened branch to murder her ex-boyfriend.

She readied herself for the descent, settling herself at the edge of the hole. A surge of excitement washed over her, the thrill of the chase in her veins. "Happy hunting," she said out loud and slipped over the edge.

Gliding down the ladder, she ignored the dread that mounted with every foot she dropped. She wouldn't be destroyed by mud.

Perching on the edge of the wooden platform, she fastened one end of a long rope to the metal ladder. She took the other end and looped it around her body. She needed a way to climb out of the cavern.

The water that had flooded the cavern had receded enough that there was a gap between the platform and the black lapping water. Inside, it smelled of dark things. Over the surface, a sparkle shimmered. She glanced up, seeing the tunnel lit up on the other side. Waiting for her, daring her to enter.

She dived in. Icy stabs of cold prickled over her skin. She broke the surface with a gasp, spluttering, and kicked hard for the tunnel. The rope at her shoulder uncoiled as she went.

An elemental shiver passed through her as she moved through unknown waters. What else swam with her? Creatures, who lived in darkness, had crawled through these tunnels for aeons, all teeth and scales. She shivered and kicked out against an imaginary tentacle.

She chastized herself for her fear. Was she or was she not an immortal vampire? If there were any monsters in the water, they should be afraid of her.

Steeling herself, she thrust forward with a smooth breaststroke to reach the side of the cavern, then climbed towards the light source.

Viewed from the shaft, the distance between the water and the ledge to the tunnel entrance hadn't seemed very far. But scrabbling up the slippery rock proved impossible. Lola slipped back, again and again. She sought handholds in the slick wall, trying to jam her nails into the rock itself. It angled away from the tunnel, so she needed to crawl up at a steep backwards angle. She splashed into the water again.

She slapped the surface in frustration. She couldn't force her way up.

"*Merde*!" The sharp sound echoed through the cavern chamber. She swam back, trying to get a different perspective. Maybe she was looking at this the wrong way. Instead of trying to force her way up, she needed to go with the flow.

Closing her eyes, she glided her hands through the water, caressing it. It was refreshing against her skin. The essence of the element welled inside of her until they were joined together. Lola was made of water, or it of her.

With a thought, the water swelled, forming a gentle wave that lifted her to the edge of the tunnel. She settled onto the stone ground, surging with power.

The water fell back with a playful wave.

"Thank you," Lola whispered. Beau was right. Being inside the well made her powers stronger. But did that mean he was more powerful too?

She shook off that unsettling thought. She would deal with Beau when the time came. Jamming a bolt into the wall, she used her force to screw it in deep. Unhooking the rope, she threaded it through the anchor, pulling it tight. Now she had a way back to the hole, her escape route. Assuming she survived the Well of Souls.

Lola turned to face the tunnel and peered into its depths. What lay ahead of her? The lights started to twinkle and she stepped forward.

The chatter of voices halted her, muffled by mud but still audible to her ears.

"*Non.*" This could not happen.

"Lola!" Nix screamed. "Lola, are you down there?" She was at the bottom of the hole, yelling into the cavern.

"What are you doing?" Lola yelled. "Go back up! It's dangerous down here."

"Oh thank God, she's there. Lola! Wait for us!"

Lola threw up her hands in horror. "Wait for you nothing. Do not come in here, or I swear on all that's unholy—"

A cry sounded, and an instant later, a splash. Nix bounced to the surface of the water, sputtering.

"*Merde,*" Lola said through clenched teeth. She ripped another rope out of her bag and tied it to the line she'd already secured. Then she dived into the water.

"*Imbecile!* Of all the stupid things you could have done!" Lola reached Nix, who was swimming toward her. "You have to go back!"

"How?" Nix gave her a wide-eyed look, and Lola cursed. Part of her considered leaving the meddlesome little pixie to drown, but she couldn't do that.

"The wall is nearly impossible to climb." She guided Nix toward the rope. "Can you manage it?"

With a great deal of cursing and slipping, Nix clinging to the rope and Lola hefting her up, they made it to the ledge of the tunnel.

Nix flopped onto the stone. "How did you do that on your own?" she asked, panting.

Lola shrugged. "Vampire tricks."

"Thank god for those," Nix said.

Two beams of light bobbed into the tunnel.

"Lola?" she heard Gael's voice.

"Gael, listen, you can't be down here." She was pleading with him now. "Go back up before it's too late."

"She's attached a rope to the tunnel entrance," Nix called out to them, voice trembling with the cold. "Try crossing on that."

"No, don't do that!" It was too late. The lights entered the cavern, swinging along the rope line. When Gael got close, Lola reached out to grab him by the shirt, pulling him to safety. He tried to hug her, but she shoved him away and then grabbed Walt. A moment later, the three of them stood in front of her in a row at the threshold of the tunnel. Her blood boiled.

"I have never known a greater group of idiots in my entire undead life." Her voice quaked with the effort to control her fury. They were going to get themselves killed.

"The way was clear," Walt said. His head swivelled to hers and the headlamp beamed into her eyes, momentarily blinding her.

"Turn that *maudite* light off!"

"Sorry." The lights clicked off, and the darkness was soothing. Lola blinked, finding her night vision again. When she could finally see, she surveyed the three, none of them looking remotely sorry for being there. Walt carried a large bag over his shoulders, likely full of the highest-tech equipment for cave exploration.

"What exactly are you doing here?"

"Gael said you'd be here," Nix said.

Gael stepped forward, his foot still heavy with the stabilizer boot. He held the note Lola had left at his house. "I went home to get a change of clothes, and I found this. I knew where you were going, and I came to help." He let out a long breath. "I'm sorry. I shouldn't have said the things I did. None of that matters now."

Lola felt a flicker of grief. "Is Diego...?"

He shook his head, lips pressed into a flat line. "No change. His body is giving out. The doctors say he might hang on for hours or days. But he won't wake up again."

Her voice was hoarse when she responded. "I'm so sorry. About everything." She let out a bitter laugh. "I think I'm a monster, too, for what it's worth. But I never wanted any of this to happen to you."

Gael's brows drew in. "What are you talking about? I meant our fight earlier. God, that feels like days ago. I shouldn't have been drinking, and I shouldn't have said all that about you using me. I was angry, but not at you."

"Oh." Her forehead wrinkled. "But you said I'm a monster."

"Um." Guilt played over Nix's face in the dim light. "That was me, actually." Her face hardened. "I still think you were using us and taking advantage of Gael, but the stuff I said he said...he didn't say. He was asking for you in the hospital." She hung her head. "Sorry."

"Gael never said you were a monster," Walt said. "And when Nix told him about what happened to Faye in the hospital, he defended you, saying it couldn't have been you. He said you were a good person, and he would never believe it."

Lola hadn't looked away from Gael. "You believe me?"

"I've never doubted you, even when I was acting like a complete idiot. I know you would never hurt Faye; you care about her."

"No, that was Beau. My ex," she specified at his questioning look. She glanced uneasily down the tunnel, wondering if he was listening to them. "He's a vampire, but much meaner than I am. He's been killing on the island, and he attacked Faye to hurt me." She looked at each of their faces. "Thank you for telling me. This was dramatic and unnecessary, and it means the world. But you need to go home. The sun will be up soon, and you'll be safe. You should be with your family." She nodded at Gael. "Your mother and brother need you right now."

He held up the note she left him. The other side was covered with her scribbled translations. "Lola, the thing that's down there, the treasure. It's not gold, is it?"

"No, I lied about that. Creatures like me, we call it the Well of Souls. The treasure we seek is legendary in the otherworld. I thought it would bring me power, but I was wrong about that. It is a substance that can heal living creatures."

Gael let out a long breath. "But can it help my brother? Is that why you're going after it now?"

She wanted to lie to him. He didn't deserve promises she couldn't keep. "It probably won't, but I'm going to follow the tunnel to the end to see what I can find."

"We're going with you," Nix said.

"Absolutely not." She spread her arms as though to bar their way. "You're not going any further. Odds are you all die. I don't even know if *I'm* going to make it out."

The three of them shared mulish looks, and she growled. "Don't you understand? I am the undead, and I'm terrified. I can't let you."

Nix crossed her arms over her chest. "Try and stop us."

Lola swallowed the cry of frustration building in her throat. "There is a blood-thirsty vampire down here who can easily tear all three of your throats out without blinking. And I'm not even talking about me."

Gael bristled. "That asshole is going after the treasure? He can't have it. It's mine!"

"Gael, he'll kill you if he gets the chance. He will kill all of you, horribly, one by one. You have to go back!"

Her voice carried down the tunnel, and bounced back to them, echoing weirdly. They looked around, uneasy, as the ground started to tremble.

"Earthquake!" Nix cried, and they pressed in tight together, throwing their arms over their heads.

But it wasn't the Earth that was shaking. Thick dark roots ripped themselves out of the stone walls, rapidly tangling around each other. As they watched in horrified fascination, the roots wove together, forming a web, blocking their exit from the tunnel. Soon the water-filled cavern was no longer visible.

Once they stopped moving, Lola reached out to prod at the

tangle. She could feel the familiar warmth there, the pulse of life. The roots were utterly unyielding. They were trapped in the tunnel.

"How could you?" Lola whispered, feeling betrayed by the oak tree. It wanted to keep them down here, and she didn't have time to fight through this mess. She turned to the other three, who still clung to each other. "Okay, you'll have to stay here. I'll be back as soon as I can."

"I'm not going to let you go alone," Gael said.

"There's also every chance that your ex-boyfriend returns this way and kills us here," Walt said, raising a shoulder. "I think we're in danger no matter what we do. Might as well have an adventure, right?"

Lola spun on him. "It's not an adventure! This is deadly. You make a mistake, you die. Do you understand me? This isn't some video game, and you need to stop behaving like children!"

"We're not children," Nix said, her eyes sparking.

"We know what's on the line," Gael said.

"Besides, I'm going to follow you anyway, and there's nothing you can do to stop me."

Lola glared at Nix for a second before throwing her hands up against their insanity. Short of maiming them all, which was starting to sound awfully appealing, she couldn't stop them. She kicked the side of the wall. "I suppose we have no choice." Her words sounded like a sentence.

A shadow flickered in the lights around them. They all stared down the tunnel.

"Lola?" Gael asked.

A blood-curdling shriek echoed from deep within the tunnel. Every hair on her body stood up at the inhuman sound.

Twenty-Six

Lola dropped to a crouch in front of the others, baring her teeth, waiting for an attack. For long minutes they stood paralyzed, dripping water the only sound.

"What was that?" Nix finally whispered, her eyes popping out of her head.

Lola listened for an approaching threat. There was nothing. "We'll find out soon enough." She met their eyes, finding differing levels of fear and resolve. "Follow me, and be extremely cautious. If I tell you to do something, you obey without question."

She waited until they nodded agreement and set off down the tunnel. They splashed through puddles, their footsteps bouncing off the stone walls in eerie echoes. Their way was lit by the inhuman glow that emanated from the tunnel, the greenish light casting ghastly shadows over their skin. Every so often, a shadow would flicker across the bare stone walls, making a chittering noise that crawled over Lola's skin. The air here was musty, but a current of air gusted past them that smelled of salt.

Lola took the lead. Her dread of what lay ahead weighed heavy on her chest, mounting with every bend in the tunnel. Nothing jumped out at her, and there was no sign of Beau beyond his scent that showed he'd passed through here already, but her nerves screamed that something very dangerous surrounded them.

Gael was directly behind Lola, every other step accompanied by a soft gasp of pain. She slowed her pace so he could keep up without struggling. She reached back, taking his hand in hers. He squeezed gently. The pressure was soothing.

"How are you doing?" she whispered.

"I'm doing really good. Actually, I'm happy to be here."

Lola glanced back at him, frowning. It was an odd thing to say, because why would Gael be happy? His face was lit in the glow, but the light was warmer here, less ghoulish. A slow smile spread over his face. The longer she looked at him, the more she realized he was right. She was happy, too, light-hearted. Why not let herself feel this way? Everything was going to be okay. "Yes. This was the right thing to do. I'm happy you're here with me."

The way ahead became easy, the ground flat and smooth, inclining upwards. Lola wasn't stressed; the tunnel was a good place. She stopped checking around every bend. Nothing would hurt them here.

The glow brightened, a kaleidoscope of pink and orange lights. Spread out above them like a star map were thousands of points of light.

"The roof of the tunnel is emitting a bioluminescence," Walt said. "I can't see what's causing it, though. I've never seen anything like that."

"Bioluminescence," Nix said, and chortled. "Walt, you are such a nerd."

Gael ran his hand over the roof, making the lights flicker. "It looks like something out of a dream," he said, eyes fluttering closed.

"No, it's bioluminescence." Lola's lips sounded out the word, enjoying how it felt. She giggled. The air changed as they rose, warm and fresh. Soon she no longer dripped with dampness, and she stopped to stare at a pattern of lights that looked nearly floral.

She had lost track of where they were going. "Wait, where's Walt?"

Walt was gone and this struck her as hilarious. She let out a whoop and doubled over in laughter.

"We better go and get him," Gael said between belly laughs. They found Walt had stopped up the path, fascinated by an outgrowth of lights.

"It's a fungus," he said, running his fingers over the roof of the tunnel. This made them scream with laughter.

This was wrong. The thought popped into Lola's head, but she pushed it away. She wanted to feel bliss for once. Why was she always so stressed? She wanted the tunnel to continue forever. She looked at Gael. Nobody had ever been as beautiful as he was at that moment. She held her hand out to him as she skipped ahead teasingly.

He smiled as his gaze followed her. Then something changed.

For an endless second, his face sagged into an open scream of horror. He reached for her.

Lola's foot hit nothing but air. She crashed forward under her own momentum, over the lip of a yawning pit the tunnel opened onto. All her levity fled as she tumbled into space.

A wide shaft had been carved out of the rock. The bottom of the pit was lined with long iron spikes, the length of a man's spine.

A tug at the back of her shirt slowed her propulsion forward, enough for Lola to throw herself to the side. She grappled for the side of the rock wall, gripping with her fingertips, using every ounce of her supernatural strength to slow her fall.

Gael, who had grabbed at her shirt, overbalanced and plummeted over the edge. Lola screamed, lunging for him, knowing she couldn't keep him from plunging to certain death.

A black shape swooped from the other side of the opening, grabbing Gael. He crashed back into the tunnel, a black figure encompassing him.

"Gael!" Lola scrambled to get back to the tunnel, propelling herself out of the trap to see Beau crouched over Gael. His fangs were out and ready to bite.

"Get away from him!" Lola leapt on Beau, forcing him off Gael, toward the pit.

"Okay, okay!" Beau backed off, stumbling a few steps. He glanced over his shoulder, ensuring he didn't trip into the pit himself. "I wasn't going to – I saved his life!"

"*You?* Saved a human's life. How stupid do you think I am?"

"Look at him! He's fine. Not impaled at all."

Lola risked a look back at Gael, keeping her body between Beau and her friends.

Gael rose, grimacing. "I'm all right." His voice was shaking. "That was close."

"See? You're welcome." Beau sounded sulky, and Lola turned back to him, eyes narrowed. Why would Beau save Gael's life?

He hunched in on himself. His face was drawn and splattered with blood, and his eyes darted around the tunnel. He had none of his usual swagger, and beneath his usual spice she caught a whiff of the acrid scent of fear. But that couldn't be right. No matter what they had faced in their long years together, Beau was never scared.

"What happened to you?" Lola asked. He was covered with filth and cradled his arm against his chest. She peeked over the edge of the pit. One of the iron spikes was drenched in blood. Beau's blood.

"Bad luck," she said and tutted. "It really got you, didn't it? Was that you we heard? Horrifying screech of a vampire being impaled?"

"I couldn't help it," Beau said, voice reedy with pain. "It hurts."

His wound was still weeping. "Why haven't you healed?"

"Poison," he said. "On the spike. It's slowing the process. If I were human, I would be dying right now."

"The impaling probably would have gotten you first."

Beau laughed, then winced in pain. "They do a thorough job

of killing you here. Weird place. It gets under your skin. You feel all good, you're looking around at all the pretty lights, and then..."

"It's a defence mechanism," Walt said, running his hands over the twinkling ceiling. "Maybe releasing gases that affect our senses. It's designed to make you look up, so you don't look for...that." He gestured at the ugly iron spikes.

"I don't like it." Beau scratched at the back of his neck. "Making me feel things..."

Lola was still trying to process Beau calling something "pretty."

"It makes us happy," Nix said. She glared at the ceiling, betrayed. "So happy we don't pay attention."

"But *who* designed this?" Lola asked. "I understand digging a hole and sticking some spikes in it. I've seen it before. But this is unlike anything I've seen." She gestured at the phosphorescence. "This is organic."

"It's as though the Earth herself wants to stop us," Gael said.

"Or only the truly worthy can make it through." Beau's eyes burned from his pale face. "Come on. We've seen some horrors before, haven't we? Remember that mine in Peru?"

"Yes, but that was man-made."

"Still harrowing. We only got through it because we had each other's backs."

Lola narrowed her eyes. What was Beau playing at? "This is different. This is supernatural."

"So are we, chérie." Beau flashed his cuspids. "How about it, for old times' sake? Let's get through this together. We'll share the treasure at the end."

Nix cleared her throat noisily. Beau's eyes flickered over the others. Despite his arrogance, desperation creased his face. Lola wasn't sure which had rattled him worse: being impaled on an iron spike, or being made to feel happiness.

"Why would you share with me?"

"This is a nasty place, and it's going to get nastier. You can help me; I can help you." Beau's eyes flickered over the cavern again, and she read fear in the tension of his arms, the set of his shoulders. A shadow flickered around him, playing over the surface of the tunnel.

Nix gasped as Lola held out her hand. "We'll work together. But all of this is off the second you try to bite anyone."

"Lola, no!" Gael thrust himself next to her, glaring at Beau before facing her. "Do you actually trust him?" His eyebrows were knit together, and she sensed his rage. At Beau, certainly, and maybe at her too.

"Of course not. But right now, he's either our ally or our enemy. I don't want him as my enemy."

"But..."

"Trust *me*, Gael."

He turned to Beau, arms crossed over his chest, lips pressed paper-thin. But he didn't say a thing when Lola put out her hand again.

"We finish this," she said as Beau's eyes glowed, "and then we never see each other again."

Beau's smile was smug, but the speed that he reached for her belied his unease. "Deal." As their hands touched, a dark growl rippled through the air. Lola snatched her hand away from his touch.

No one else responded to the growl. Had she imagined it? Lola inspected the tunnel again, uneasy, but there were no more flickering shadows.

"Fine then. How do we get across?"

"You could make a bridge." Beau gestured to the side of the tunnel. "You have ropes? One to walk on, one to hold. Even the edibles could shimmy across."

She eyed him uneasily. How could she possibly trust him? But what if it was the only way to survive?

"How did you make it across?"

He shrugged. "It's not hard if you're paying attention. It's only a problem if you come skipping along the path, staring at the ceiling like an idiot. I deserved it."

"Why wait for us?"

"I told you, I want to do this with you. We need each other." He sighed. "I need *you*, Lola. Your pets can go to hell."

At Lola's narrowed eyes, he put up his hands. "But I accept them."

Lola stared for a long moment before nodding. "Walt, let's make this happen."

With her strength and Walt's gear, Lola sank anchors into the wall on their side of the pit. Then she and Beau crawled across the tunnel edge, clinging to the rough rock walls.

As Beau helped her to the other side, his hands lingered on her waist.

"You could leave them," he whispered into her ear. "They're only going to slow you down. They're not going to survive this. You'd be doing them a favour."

She considered her friends on the other side of the gap. "Lola..." Gael said.

She shook her head. They couldn't get out the other side. They were trapped down there; the only way out of this tunnel was forward. She hoped.

She also didn't trust anything Beau wanted. "Piss off," Lola told him over her shoulder. "I'm going to make sure they survive. Throw me the rope," she called.

Gael let out a breath, doing as she'd instructed. After Lola had secured the cord to another anchor, she did the same with another at shoulder height. She shimmied out onto the rope bridge, bouncing with all her weight.

"It feels secure. Come over one at a time. Hold on tight."

Gael came first. His jaw was clenched as he shuffled foot by foot along the rope until reaching solid rock, hampered by his boot. He let out a deep breath, holding tightly onto Lola's outstretched hand, palm slick.

"Scared?" Beau gave a scornful laugh.

Gael looked down at him. "Not looking to impale myself on poisoned spikes. They didn't do you any good."

Lola laughed as she watched Nix pass next. She was swift and surefooted, dancing over the cords. No fear there.

Neither with Walt, who peered into the pit as he shuffled across. "Fascinating."

Once they were together, Lola turned to Beau, who was busy sneering at the humans. "Did you go any further? Or have you been waiting here for us?"

"I went a bit further, but..." Beau refused to look at her.

"But what?"

"I got spooked, okay?"

Nix snorted, and Beau spun on her, truly looking at her for the first time. "And you're so brave, little girl? Why don't you lead the way?" His fangs gleamed, but Nix raised her chin.

"I don't have a problem with that."

Lola grabbed Nix's arm before she could pass her. "*I* have a problem with that. Beau goes first."

"I'm not scared!" Nix protested.

"It's not you I'm worried about. I want him where I can see him."

Beau smirked. "Can't take your eyes off of me?"

Gael tensed, but Lola put her hand up. "I don't trust him to not start snacking on you when my back is turned. It's non-nego-tiable," she said firmly when Beau started to argue. She raised an eyebrow. "And make sure you watch where you put your feet."

He glared, but finally stormed down the tunnel into the unknown depths. The tunnel twisted ever downwards.

"What's on the ground?" Nix pointed at black stains splashed over the rocks.

Lola sniffed, recognizing the scent. "That's Beau. He bled a lot."

He glared over his shoulder at her. "I was impaled on a spear!"

If he had bled out that much, Beau would have to feed. Soon. She watched him nervously. This was a mistake. But, down here, what choice did she have? Even weakened, he could best her in a fight. Then the rest of the group would be helpless.

How was she going to keep everyone alive? She curled her fist around the stake in her bag. He wouldn't expect it, not right now.

Beau glanced back at her then and smiled. It was such a familiar look, the shared thrill of the quest. A headache began to pound in her temples, and she released the stake.

They travelled in taut silence until they reached a point where the tunnel branched, two dark holes leading away from where they stood.

Lola turned to Beau. "What way do we go?"

Beau hesitated, eyes flicking from one side to another. "I... don't know. I think this is a test. Guess right, and you get the treasure. Guess wrong, and..." He gave an elegant shrug.

On the ground was a pool of his blood. How long did he stand there, weighing his options, before he came back to get them? She didn't delude herself he did it for any reason other than his own self-preservation, but he must be terrified.

He caught her look and sneered. "Don't go feeling things for me, chérie. I wanted a second opinion, is all. There is a malevolent force down here, and I'm not sure we'll survive it. Not even us."

"Very comforting," Lola said. "Any suggestions?"

They stared at the crossroads, hearts thumping hard as their lives hung in the balance. The left tunnel twisted to the side, while the right sloped downwards.

"There's more phosphorescence in this one," Walt said, pointing to the right. "Do you see how these tiny trails lead into bigger ones, like veins? It's like a capillary network. Something is feeding off the earth."

"Like some giant monster? No, thank you." Nix scowled at the tunnels, then stepped to the left. "The air feels warmer here. And,"

—she sniffed—"It smells like the ocean. And maybe a bit like… bread? Does anyone else smell that?"

Lola leaned into the tunnel. It smelled more like buttery croissants mixed with chocolate. Exactly like Faye's patisserie.

"It's that one." Gael pointed to the right tunnel with grim certainty.

"How can you know?" Lola asked. She longed to follow the tunnel full of chocolately good smells.

"Because I don't smell baking or the ocean. I smell my mother's chipotle burritos."

Lola and Nix both swung to him while Beau let out a mocking laugh.

"Also, the smell of a wood fire."

"Your favourite things…" Nix said slowly.

"And Nix, you love the smell of the ocean and fresh-baked bread. But this place isn't trying to help us. It's enticing us *away* from the treasure."

"It's a ruse," Beau said, stepping to the left tunnel. His face was tinged with sadness, and Lola wondered what he smelled. "The edible is right."

"Are you sure?" Nix leaned toward the left tunnel. Unshed tears gathered in her eyes as she lingered there.

"I'm sure. Look." Gael pointed at the right tunnel again. A tense silence built as they stared into its depths. Finally, a shadow skittered over the roof of the tunnel.

Nix and Walt started.

"What was that?" Nix whispered, fear creeping into her voice.

Gael's voice was hard and flat. "I don't know, but it scares the hell out of me." His skin rippled with gooseflesh. "We need to go toward the scary thing."

Lola finally spoke into the silence that followed. "Gael is right. We never thought this was going to be easy."

They nodded, some more reluctantly than others. "All right,

then, Beau. After you." Lola gave a sugary smile, mainly to cover the hammering of her heart.

With a sour look, he ventured into the tunnel. Lola followed him.

The tunnel narrowed until their shoulders scraped the sides. The network of lights glowed blue and green, casting sickly shadows over their faces. The only sound was the breath of the living, coming out harsh and shallow. The tunnel twisted and looped back in on itself, always downwards. How far underground were they now?

Beau held out a hand to her. "Doing okay, chérie?"

She stared at the outstretched hand. "I'm fine." His tender tone annoyed her more than his presence.

"I know. You're always at your best the harder things get."

Lola chewed on her lip, contemplating him.

A sharp clicking of stone on stone sounded. As the earth rumbled, panic spread to the tips of her fingers.

"Everybody down!" she screamed, throwing herself back and knocking Gael to the ground.

TWENTY-SEVEN

Screaming rocks enveloped them with an explosion of dust. Somebody howled in anguish.

As suddenly as it started, the sound stopped. Lola lay still, blinking dust out of her face as it settled around them. She tried to turn over but found something was holding her down, rigid and unmoving. She thrashed, but her body was trapped.

She wiggled until she was face-up, wildly trying to see what imprisoned her. Long iron spears had been thrust through holes in the side of the tunnel, creating a maze of metal rods barring the way. One had come out a hairsbreadth away from where she had fallen. If she'd been any slower, she would have been punctured. Pinned down as she was, a frenzy of horror built inside of her. Her thoughts scattered like static, and she wanted to scream.

She had to calm down, she couldn't fall apart. She repeated the thought until she believed it. She coughed dust. "Is everyone okay? Gael?"

"I'm okay," he rasped, not far from her although she couldn't turn to see him.

Another howl came, this one ending on a whimper, as though someone was trying to hold it in.

"Walt's been hit," Nix said, her voice trembling.

"Is he okay? Walt, talk to me."

"I'm...here." Walt whimpered again.

"Walt, buddy, where did it get you?" Gael asked. He grunted as though he was trying to get out of his prison.

"My shoulder."

A wrenching groan sounded deep in the wall. The iron spears shrieked like a blade on a whetstone as they were reeled back by some unseen mechanism. The spike above her scraped along Lola's skin, and she held very still. The tip glinted green. *Poison.*

As soon as she was free, she flipped to her feet and spun to find Walt. He was dragged back against the wall, skewered by the spear as it ground back to its hidden hole. He writhed as the spike was agonizingly pulled out of his shoulder.

His scream caused them all to cringe. Lola leapt over Gael and Nix, still prone on the ground, to drape him over her shoulder. His breaths were heavy rasps, and his weight was heavy enough she was sure he had passed out. But after a moment of silence, he let out a huff that could have been a sob or a laugh. "Well," he wheezed. "That was...interesting."

Lola let out a low laugh. That level of pain could kill, and he was making light of the situation.

"You're going to be okay," she said. "I need to look at your wound."

"Lola, we must have tripped a mechanism," Beau said, mounting anxiety in his voice. "It could happen again. We need to get out of here." Without waiting for them, he scrambled down the passage.

"He's right," Lola said, her gaze sweeping over the ground. Some stones were darker than the others. Under the dust, she could see the hint of carvings. Like the otherworldly language found on Gael's chimney stone or the map of the Well of Souls. "We need to move, but watch out for those stones, there. The darker ones. I think they'll set the trap again. Walt, if you lean on me, can you make it? Gael, can you manage?"

Gael grunted, bracing himself against the stone as he stood. He stared at the holes in the wall with dismay before limping forward as quickly as he could, Nix tripping right behind him.

Lola half-carried Walt, relieved when he began to get his feet under him again. She hurried, listening for stone mechanisms.

They negotiated a curve in the tunnel, and the way widened. No more holes in the walls threatened them. They crowded together, all of them covered in grime and nearly indistinguishable from the walls, hacking up dust.

Lola eased Walt to the ground. She needed to know how much damage had been done. He hissed as she tore open his shirt collar to get a look. She bit her lip in dismay at his mangled joint. The spike had ripped through the bone.

"Walt, this is bad. You should stay here."

He shook his head adamantly. "No," he croaked.

"This could get infected. If this is treated, you might be able to...have some use of your arm..." She broke off. Trails of green spread from the wound. The poison was working its way through his system already.

Walt glanced at the wound, wincing when he saw it. "You and I both know what's going to happen if I stay here," he whispered. He gritted his teeth and pushed himself up with a bellow of pain. "What's done is done." He took a step and was able to support his own weight. "I can still walk, so we might as well keep on going."

"Walt, don't be crazy." Gael hovered, wanting to support his friend while fearful of hurting him. Dread and sadness grooved his face.

"You'd leave me here to die alone?" Walt's face was so fragile, his control like glass as he gazed at his once-best friend.

Gael shook his head, fighting back tears, and held out his palm to him. "No. I won't do that."

Walt forced himself to look at the wound, gangrenous already. "This is probably my only chance to go on a real treasure hunt. Don't tell me to stop just when things are getting good." His eyes shone with fevered determination. "Besides, this thing we're looking for, it could help me. Right?" Walt blinked back tears, betraying how desperate he was. "I'm not giving in. If we make it to the end, maybe I can make it, too."

"He's right," Nix said slowly. "We have to get to the end of this bloody tunnel!"

They turned as one at the sound of rustling to see Beau returning. His eyes burned red in the dark.

"He's going to slow us down," he said, running his eyes over Walt. "He'll be in horrible pain. You'd be better off putting him out of his misery."

"Don't you dare," she hissed. "I'm not giving up on him."

"His heart is going to give up on him before long. Lola, you need to watch out for yourself."

"Like you did?" She snorted, contemptuous. "I noticed how quickly you fled like a rat."

"They'll weigh you down, these humans."

"Touch a single one of them, and I will kill you myself."

"And how are you going to do that?" Beau looked amused. "Hold me down and cut off my head with your nails?"

His suggestion sounded enticing. "If I have to."

Walt straightened, coughing and choking, but managing to put his head up. "Keep walking," he panted.

Beau raised an eyebrow but turned down the passage, leading the way.

They began moving again, in fits and starts. Nix came to Walt's other side, and the two women supported him. Gael's leg dragged more and more, and he used the wall to help pull himself along. Lola's stomach sank. The chances they were going to make it out at all were becoming smaller and smaller.

"Cheer up," Nix said, panting under Walt's weight. "Think of the story we're going to have."

"That's the spirit," Gael said.

Lola smiled, grateful for their courage. Even if it wouldn't make a difference in the end.

The tunnel twisted in sharper spirals, heading ever downwards. Beau was out of sight, but she could hear him whistling.

"Beau?" she called, voice echoing ahead of them. Something was off. "Beau, where are you?"

"I'm here!" His voice bounced toward them, full of wonder. "You have to see this!" A wind rushed by, playing over their skin and rustling their hair.

Around another bend, the tunnel opened to a cavernous chamber. The ceiling stretched high above them, glowing like the night sky. It seemed to go on forever, straight up to heaven.

They came to a stop in the middle in a reverent hush. Lola glanced at Walt, staring at the sight as though he could memorize every pinprick of light. Tears streamed down his face, and she didn't know if it was from pain or wonder.

Gael stumbled and fell to his knee with a grunt. Her attention pulled from the awe-inspiring cave, Lola rushed to his side, getting her shoulder under his arm. As she got him on his feet, that sense of wrongness pulled at her again. The cavern was designed to make them look up. Instead, she forced herself to look down. Her own warning came back to her. *Watch where you put your feet.*

Among the rocks at the base of the cavern were small splashes of black blood. Beau's blood. Only he stopped bleeding some time ago. That meant...

She looked up in shock to find him at the edge of the cavern, the red light in his eyes stronger than ever.

"But that means you've already been here," she said out loud.

A mischievous smile played over his face. "Guilty." Beau raised his foot over a stone. Inscriptions were etched across it. Another trap. He slammed his foot down, jamming the stone into place. With a sharp click, the ceiling began to rumble.

"No!" Lola screamed. Walt and Nix were too far away. She could only grab Gael, shoving him out of the way with all her might.

TWENTY-EIGHT

Boulders crashed down around them. An enormous slab struck Lola's back, and she cried out as she fell forward, brought to her knees by the terrible weight.

The air filled with sediment. Lola could only focus on keeping the rock from crushing her entirely. It was as though the earth had decided to devour them. She screamed against the strain.

Blood dripped down her arms, forced out of her skin through the unbearable pressure on her system. She felt it slick on her face, crying tears of blood. She didn't know she could do that. The thought passed, disjointedly.

After endless minutes, the storm passed with a final trickle of stones. All was muffled, silent. Lola was entombed in the earth; this would be her cairn.

Fury rose from deep within her. She would not end here. Though she thought she had no strength left, she found it in herself to press against the slab holding her in place. Screaming again and again, she used everything she had to push until the rock budged.

Something shifted, and she strained even more. A howl was ripped from her lips. With agonizing slowness, the slab lifted, angling and falling away from her in another shower of dust. Faint light trickled through a hole she had made, large enough to crawl through.

Slipping on her own blood, she emerged to witness the devastation. The starry lights were gone, nothing but a pile of rubble up to the ceiling. It had been another trap, designed to seduce until it was far too late.

Light emanated from the tunnel ahead of her, orienting her. She was on the treasure side of the collapse. She could still make it. As she crawled forward, she let out a bitter laugh. There was no sign of Beau or of the others. She was alone.

"Hello?" she said, her voice hoarse with choking grit. "Is anyone there?"

"Lola?" The voice was weak. Her heart leapt, beating at a gallop.

"Gael?" She barely dared to think he could have survived this.

"Here." She saw the disturbance in the dust as he crawled out of the hole she had made. The whole time she had held the roof up off him, keeping him safe. She let out a sob.

"Gael!" She scrambled toward him, slipping on loose stones. She found his hand and followed it to the rest of him. "*Dieu merci*, you're alive!" Lola launched herself at him, grabbing him in an embrace that pulled him free.

"Whoa!" he said as he stumbled forward, but Lola was there to catch him. Her hands were on his face, his lips, brushing dirt out of his hair. Pressing her hand to his chest to feel his still-pumping heart.

"Are you okay?"

"I think so. I don't know how, only that you saved me. You kept the rocks from crushing me."

She flinched when he reached for her, ashamed of how monstrous she must look. Her hands were slicked with blood; her face must be the same. But Gael pulled her back to him. He trailed his fingers over her face and wasn't horrified.

"The others." Her voice was hoarse.

Anguish swept his face, and he turned to face the wreckage. It was hard to make sense of it. She couldn't imagine anyone else surviving.

"Walt! Nix!" They screamed until their voices cracked, but there was no answer.

Behind them, the tunnel twinkled, continuing to lure them onwards, the ghost of a laugh floating in the air.

"Beau did this," she said. "He arranged it all, waiting until we were right where he wanted us, and then..."

Gael stared at the boulders, no doubt thinking about the bodies of his friends trapped forever beneath them.

Lola shook her head. "I am so stupid! I should have never trusted him. He is a master at bringing you in, then unleashing the hurt."

"Like the tunnel. They deserve each other."

Anger coiled inside of her at the thought. "Beau doesn't deserve anything but a nasty end. He doesn't get to win."

Gael turned to her, desolate. "Lola, he's already won."

They both stilled at a quiet sound in the room. A rock near the ceiling shifted and bounced down the incline to their feet. Then another one. And another.

Lola stared at the moving rocks, then bounded up the steep incline, slipping on shale as she scrambled to reach the top where the roof of the cavern met the rubble.

At the summit, Lola scrabbled at the small loose rocks, digging to the other side. A shower of dust blinded her as the rocks shifted. She blinked and continued. Gael struggled up the incline, a look of frantic concentration hardening his face, even as he grimaced in pain.

"Come on, come on," Lola repeated under her breath. A boulder blocked the way between them and the exit, and she grabbed it. Bracing her feet on the stone pile, she used herself as a lever to move it.

Her nails tore off as she yanked, but she didn't let go. Finally, the rock began to give. She sobbed, pulling harder until the boulder ripped away from the pile.

She fell back, then attacked the hole that appeared, scooping out armfuls of shale. There was light on the other side, as though the cavern opened up to the surface now.

"Walt!" she screamed into the dust. "Nix!"

A hand appeared through the hole. "Lola?" A white face peered through the opening.

"Walt, you're alive!" Lola crumpled with relief.

"Walt?" Gael had made it to the top. He reached out to take Walt's hand, and they clung to one another. "Where's Nix?"

"She's…" Walt glanced back over his shoulder. "She's alive, but not conscious." He looked away. "It's probably better that way."

"Walt," Lola said. "Can she survive this?"

His eyes were wild with panic. "I don't know if she'd want that. She's caught under the rocks."

Gael let out a sob and Lola closed her eyes. They had trusted her, and look where she had brought them.

But it wasn't over yet.

"Walt," she said with urgency. "How's your arm?"

He tried to laugh, but it came out as a sob. "Still attached." Fear and grief tinged every word. "It won't be long."

"Stay with Nix. Try to make her comfortable, and try to keep her here. And hold on. Nobody goes anywhere, do you hear me?" Her eyes glowed so much she could see the light reflected in Walt's widening eyes.

He gave a slow, disbelieving shake of the head. "Nobody's going anywhere."

"Good." She turned to Gael, holding out her hand. "Let's end this."

Gael reached out blindly through tears and caught her. She felt his warm pulse under his skin. There was life in them still, and they would keep on fighting until the end.

They slid down the rockslide together. Gael's face was grey, so she draped his arm over her shoulders and half-carried him along. She was terrified to bring him any further, but she also was terrified of what would happen if she didn't. There were monsters here, in one form or another, and she couldn't leave him.

"It's not much further." Her voice was low and soothing.

Gael's eyes were half-closed. "How do you know?" he gasped. "What if the tunnel never ends?"

He would still follow her. Lola was certain she could lead Gael to the depths of hell, and he would still trust her. They were about to find out.

"It will end, Gael. All things end."

She followed the skittering shadows that continued down the path. If she hadn't been sure they were approaching the treasure chamber, the concentration of these shadows would have convinced her. Flickering green lights like eyes sometimes flashed. They were being watched. Judged.

Pressure filled her head, a crushing force within her. The watchful eyes seemed to peer inside her, combing through her mind and lingering on the tangles inside. The greed and cowardice. The violence of her long undead life. So much pain and suffering.

Her earliest memories were a wash of blood and gore. She did terrible things and never gave them a second thought. Now, somehow this place was forcing her to revisit them, to understand the stain that she had been on this Earth. She bowed under the pressure of the shame.

Gael seemed to be twisting under the weight of the gaze, getting heavier with every limping footstep. He must be suffering as Lola was, reliving horrible moments, only she was certain he wasn't experiencing the same thoughts as she was. She pulled him tighter against her. "What is it?"

"I can't get these thoughts out of my head." Gael panted like he was having a full panic attack.

"Maybe if you told me." She tried to smile, the effort leaving her light-headed. "Sometimes it's best to tell a complete stranger what's going on in your messed up head."

He remembered her words from when they first met and gave a weak huff of laughter. The moment seemed to lighten something in him, and he took a part of his weight back. "Not a stranger, Lola. Not you." He shook his head. "He left me, you know. He left *us*."

"Your father," Lola guessed what he was talking about. She had wondered what had happened to him. Gael had never spoken of him.

Gael nodded. "I don't really remember much. There was a storm that night, an early hurricane. I was tucked in bed, and my mum stayed with me because I was scared. She was pregnant with Diego then. We didn't hear him leave, but he sailed right into the storm." He shook his head. "They said he must have capsized, but they never found his boat or body. I think he just kept on sailing and never looked back. I always wondered what it was about me that was so lacking that he'd rather drown in a storm than spend another second with me."

Lola swallowed the lump in her throat. She had only known abandonment, so she couldn't speak from experience. Instead, she spoke with all the dreams and wishes she was never supposed to have. "No, Gael. If that is what happened, then he was the one who was lacking. You deserve so much better than someone who leaves his family."

"I don't know about that." He was silent for a long moment, his face strained under the weight of his torment. "Diego never even met him. He never had a father."

"He had you. And he was better for it. Look at you now. You are walking into hell to save him. How many people have that in their life?"

Gael swallowed hard and stood straighter. The pressure unleashed her mind then, allowing her dark past to fall away behind her.

Had this gauntlet, being forced to live through their worst moments, everything that caused them shame, been one more test? Another trap, designed to torture them on the inside. Whatever it was, it released them from its grasp.

They walked through the tunnel together. The green luminescence brightened to white. They turned a corner, and the source of the light was revealed.

The tunnel ended with an arch, inscribed with the same constellation carvings found on the map and the hearthstone. A galaxy of stars stretched across the rock face, lighting up with silvery light so brilliant Lola had to cover her eyes with her hands as she passed under the archway.

Inside the cave, the air was warm and humid. A low humming sounded all around them, as if they stood on top of a mystical source of energy. Parts of the walls were twisted and knotted, wood rather than stone. Lola reached for the rough bark and felt a familiar pulse of warmth.

They stood under the roots of the ancient oak, only far below. She should have known the treasure oak sat guard over this sacred well. It was the Tree of Life. They had travelled miles and ended back at the same place where they started.

At the centre of the cave, a stone fountain was carved into the floor of the cavern, constellations of messages surrounding it. Water bubbled over the sides, and steam drifted from the top. The silvery light of the markings bounced off the water, causing the cavern walls to glow.

Standing on the other side, red eyes lit by the glow, was Beau.

His eyes flicked over Gael with disinterest. "I was positive the cave-in would have ended your ridiculous edibles. But one survived. And look, it's the most useless one."

"You bastard!" Gael lunged for him, and Lola caught him. "You destroyed them!"

Beau scowled and turned away from Gael. "Why do you attach yourself to such anchors, Lola? I had thought it would be you and me, tasting this power together. Instead, you bring him with you. I'll have to kill him myself." His fangs slipped out.

Lola stepped in front of Gael, her hand jamming into her bag to grab the stake. But Beau's steps were hesitant, sluggish, and he didn't attack. What had he felt in the tunnel? Had he been judged?

She turned her gaze to the fountain, hoping to distract him. "The water of life. That's what we've been chasing all along. Only you need to be dead to survive the treasure hunt. Ironic, don't you think?"

"This water will feed us all the power of this Earth. *That's* what we've been chasing." Beau's muscles tightened, as though he was struggling to get close to the fountain.

Lola tilted her head. Despite his brave words, Beau's gaze seemed steeped in dread. "You came all the way here on your own, but you didn't drink. Instead, you went back. Why?"

"For you, Lola. I love you."

She snorted. "You don't know what love is. You feel obsession, desire. But you have no understanding of the generosity and compassion it takes to love. You serve only your own interests. So I'll ask you again. With all the power laid out in front of you, why didn't you drink?"

Beau's face turned sulky, and Lola smirked. "You're scared, aren't you? Immortal demon like yourself, and you're scared of a puddle."

"It burns," he said. He placed his hand above the bubbling liquid, pulling it back with a hiss when a drop sizzled on his skin.

She snorted. "Of course it burns. Don't tell me you're that naïve. You sought ultimate power but weren't prepared for the sacrifice it would take. Surely you understand you must give something in return? What's a little pain compared with everything you've ever desired? Would you give your arm, your eye, your very heart?"

"Yes. Anything for the power!" His eyes glowed brighter.

"And yet you still waited for me, not because you want me by your side, but because you wanted me to go first." She gave him a lopsided smile, knowing the truth as she spoke it. "You wanted to see what happened."

She stepped forward, knowing what she had to do. "You'll get what you want. I'll go first. And once I have tasted ultimate power, what's to stop me from ending you, the monster who used and betrayed me every chance he got? You and I both know there can only be one. And you didn't have the courage." She reached for the fountain.

"Get back!" Beau shouted, and leapt at them.

Lola forced Gael into the twining roots, his warmth at her back.

Beau stumbled to the fountain, still hesitating after all that. Lola bit her lip to keep from crying out, to keep from warning him of what would come, despite everything. The shadows flickered and gathered close, rearing like a cobra readying to strike.

Beau met her eyes, as though she was the lifeline tethering him to this place.

He gave a half-smile. "Bottoms up." He closed his eyes and plunged his cupped hands into the water.

Twenty-Nine

His scream ripped from his throat. His eyes bulged from his skull as his flesh that touched the water bubbled and disintegrated. His body was racked with tremors, and he forced his hands closer to his face, even as he fought with himself. He looked wildly at Lola. She gave an encouraging nod.

With a jerk, he brought the caustic substance to his mouth and drank. Only a dribble got in before his hands flew away from his face, and he was seized by massive shuddering spasms, screams flying as he convulsed.

His body flared, boiling from the inside, glowing red. The surrounding shadows swirled into a tornado that descended on Beau, devouring him whole.

Lola turned away from the heat and pressed her face to Gael's. They braced against the hot wind that blew through the cavern. It went on for an eternity. She gripped a root, holding them in place so they wouldn't be whipped away.

When the wind and the shadows finally subsided, Beau dropped to a heap on the floor of the cavern.

Lola peered at his body, diminished and broken. He had fallen for it. It gave her no pleasure to have won. She understood Beau's greed and desire for power; he wouldn't recognize the danger when all of that was being offered to him. He would always try to take something away from her.

The shimmering of the water brightened, calling her to it. The Elixir of Life, a magical substance that could heal both body and spirit. It could purify the demon from this body. It was anathema to vampires because it would kill the demonic force that energized them.

She took a step toward the fountain, then looked back to Gael. He gazed at her with a dark, searching look, sensing something was amiss. "Lola—"

"Listen, Gael, everything is going to be okay. I have something for you." She reached into her bag, pulling out the sack of gold doubloons she had found in the shipwreck. "I should have given this to you ages ago; forgive me for taking my time. I wanted to keep on giving you a reason to dig. A reason to spend time with me."

"What is this?" Gael pulled out the ragged sack, drawing out a golden coin.

"It's our cover story," she whispered with a mischievous smile. "We came down here looking for treasure, and we found it."

"Lola, is this real?" His voice broke.

"It's a fortune. Your family can use it."

"No, I don't care about this. I don't need money. You need to come back with me." He tugged her away from the fountain. "Lola, stay away from there. We've made a terrible mistake."

"No. Beau was the only one who was mistaken. He sought only what he would gain, never imagining the sacrifice."

She gestured to the fountain and the roots around them. "I understood once he showed me his part of the map. The Well of Souls is a holy place, more than anything else I have ever known. This is the Elixir of Life." She put her hand on the root again, finding comfort. It was like being called home.

"I don't understand. What is the Elixir of Life?"

"To a human, it is healing; it is regeneration. It will replenish your forces, revitalize you. Repair wounds and save a little boy who needs to be with his family now."

Gael's eyes filled with tears, and Lola wished hers could as well. "And to vampires?" he asked.

"Demonic energy is the antithesis of life. The Elixir will purify my body of the affliction, leaving behind that." She nodded her head at Beau's tortured form.

Gael gasped. "You can't do this."

"Gael, it will heal me." She placed a hand on his cheek. He was so beautiful, racked as he was with grief and suffering. His body would break, and one day he would die, but that was the marvel that made life so exquisite. "For more than eighty years, I have existed in a half-life. I don't want to continue like this forever, hiding in the shadows, forever staving off the rot of my own decay.

"Pity the monsters that go on forever, for they will never know, never understand, the meaning of this." She took Gael by the hand and led him to the fountain. This time he followed, reluctantly. The pool brightened his face, but she could sense the gathering shadows at her back. She reached into her bag, pulling out the water bottle she had brought.

"I don't think you're supposed to take much. Just enough. Take enough for Nix and Walt and for Diego, and for Faye, and never say a word about it. It is a great secret, the greatest, and no one can ever know. This place would be destroyed by greed."

Gael stopped her when she moved to touch the water, his warm hands over hers. "Lola, I don't want you to die."

"I died more than eighty years ago, Gael. Today, I will be free." She stared into the pool, mesmerised by the flickering light. "Tell Faye I'm safe, will you? Thank her for her generosity. It gave me the strength to get where I needed to go." She met his gaze, eyes dark with grief. "Take some and go, Gael. I don't want you to see this."

Gael shook his head, lips set in a tense line. "I won't leave you, Lola. I don't want you to go through that alone."

All the emotions swirling through her collided into a single pinpoint. "Gael. I..." Her throat closed over. What she felt for him was impossible, and overwhelming. "Goodbye," she whispered.

The shadows swirled, forming a single entity that towered over her. Green eyes glittered with unimaginable knowledge. She acknowledged the presence with a bow. "There is no light without darkness. There is no life without death." She smiled into the monstrous abyss. "*À ma santé.*"

She dipped her hands into the water.

White-hot pain shot through her fingers, up her arms, through her veins until her entire body was on fire. She closed her eyes against it, her teeth grinding together to keep from screaming. A part of her fought it, tried with all its might to get her to release the water. It wanted to cower in the corner and lick its wounds. It lashed out. Her fangs grew, and her face twisted into an ugly snarl. She desperately wanted to throw the acid aside and launch herself on Gael instead. She would take his throat deep and vicious, letting his hot blood splatter over her tongue.

But the other part of her, the spark that lay dormant within, welcomed it. She concentrated on that, the spark growing inside of her. She steadied her hands and stared down the snarling beast within. Lola bent her head and drank the scalding liquid, as much as she could take in before the blackness consumed her.

Thirty

It was as though she no longer had a body, as if she had become nothing but an amorphous entity of fire and pain. She may have screamed, but she couldn't tell. The sound mingled with the howling wind, rolling thunder, the baying of hounds. She hung in purgatory, lashed by suffering, forever it seemed. She couldn't move; she could only burn.

Eventually, though, even the soul fire was consumed. In its wake came something else, a refreshing flow like water. It washed through her until the pain was relieved, and she felt nothing but the vibration of energy.

Everything was connected, and she was connected to everything. At that moment, Lola was starlight and oceans and planets colliding, and the tree standing sentinel for millennia and flowers opening their buds to sunlight. She was all of life.

She stared into a vast galaxy. Next to her was the shadow. Within the shadow was a glowing light, the purest white, and it moved toward Lola.

Recognition lit as something within her flared in joy. The missing piece of herself; she had grieved for it all this time. She opened her heart wide to welcome it. The white light entered her, joining with the spark that had always been there, broken apart, hidden away this whole time, waiting to be recognized. Within Lola's demonic form, part of her soul from another life had remained. The light seamed within her, and with a soundless explosion, Lola was finally made whole, two pieces of her soul reunited.

There was no more fear or suffering. Lola knew only the endlessness of love.

The shadow opened its hand to her now. It no longer threatened but rather invited. Lola had the choice. She could stay here in a wash of love, vast and unending. Or she could accept what the darkness offered her.

Her hand formed in front of her as she reached for the shadow, her body reforming on a thought. She placed her hand into the shadow's outstretched one. All was black again, and she fell into it.

———

Lola awoke slumped over the pool of water. She blinked. Her eyes were gummed and fuzzy.

Her hand dangled in the pool, but the water caused no pain. She wiggled her fingers, delighting in the warm bubbles that traced over her skin. The skin was pink and flushed: a mortal hand.

She laughed out loud, thrilled by the vibration in her chest. Blood pulsed through her veins, her own blood, not the life force she scavenged from others. She took in a breath of air, her lungs expanding. She ran her hands over her face. She was alive.

"Lola?"

In the strange light of the cavern, it was difficult to discern anything. Everything was softer with human eyes, hazier. But she found Gael. He braced against the roots of the tree, eyes open wide, tear tracks lining his face.

"Gael." Lola's voice was lighter, no longer a threatening growl. She took a hesitant step. Her body did not have the predatory grace it once did. Unsure of herself, she wobbled, holding her arms out as she relearned balance.

Inside of her, a buoyancy grew. Skipping and falling over herself, she found a way to his arms. He reached out and caught her to him, pulling her up until they were pressed against each other. She breathed him in. He still smelled like cinnamon, but he no longer made her hungry.

"I thought you were gone. I thought you died." He breathed into her hair. "You disappeared into the shadow."

"It was death," she said. "I had to face death, accept it would be a part of the deal. To become mortal."

"Mortal?" He held her out at arm's length.

She laughed. "I'm human. I had my soul restored to me. This pool gives life and purifies the demonic. The demon inside was washed free."

"But then, what about him?" Gael pointed to Beau's ravaged body, limp on the cavern floor. "Why are you standing and he's ripped up on the floor?" He ran his warm hands over her arms, sending shivers rippling through her whole body.

"I believe a part of my soul lingered in my spirit when I was made. It's always been there and it allowed me to connect with my humanity. With who I was...before." She pressed against her chest fondly, thinking of the spark that had stuck with her through all those years. "I *wanted* to become human."

"You told me you were going to die." Gael let out a laughing sob.

"I thought I was going to. I didn't know I would be offered this choice. When my soul was rejoined, there was a place that was..." Tears spilled over her cheeks. Real tears, she was crying! She laughed bright and clear. "It was so beautiful, Gael. A part of me wanted to stay. But a bigger part wanted to come back. The other place...it's waiting. And I will go there someday."

Lola let out a sigh, her own breath moving through her body.

"Then, you are as you were before?"

"Before I was a vampire. Except, I don't remember her. Only... no." She stumbled as memories trickled over her, more and more, until it was a flood of bloody images. Of waking up as a vampire; of feeling nothing but hunger. Of being surrounded by bodies. So many bodies, lined up through the years. She was responsible for so much death. She doubled over.

"No." Lola breathed through the pain. Her soul quaked as she relived the suffering she had caused. There were memories of her young days as a vampire when her strength was new, and she gloried in her power over others. Jacquotte next to her, encouraging her, building her into the monster she would become. When she and Beau travelled the world, powerful and forever young, leaving a trail of devastation behind them.

"What have I done?" Lola groaned, collapsing, hunching over her weakened body as pain crippled her. The fire had been easier than this. "I shouldn't have come back. How did I dare?"

"Lola, it will be okay." Gael knelt, cradling her.

"It's not going to be okay!" she shrieked. "They're dead; they're all dead and gone." She yanked at her hair.

Gael wrapped her tighter in his arms, pressing her face to his chest. "You are strong enough for this." Gael pressed his lips to her hair. "There is a reason you came back. And those that are gone, they're in that beautiful place. They're at peace."

"That doesn't make it better. I am evil, I had no right."

"Lola, there was something inside of you that made you different. You saved me. If you truly were evil, without a chance of atonement, you wouldn't have done that."

Lola drew in a painful breath, then another. The only thing that kept her from falling into madness was Gael next to her, talking her through her rebirth.

"I had forgotten what it is to feel. It is so much more than I remembered. *I* am so much more." She stared at her hands. This is what Jacquotte wanted to keep from her. Humanity. To spare her or to keep her captive? What was it about this place that frightened her so? Would Jacquotte be able to face up to the suffering she had caused all her long undead life?

Lola took a deep breath, then another. She reached out blindly for Gael and he was right there, his face in her palms. His gold-flecked eyes took her in, solemn, and he traced a thumb over her cheek. "You can do good, Lola. You can be good. But you have to get up and try. Don't waste this second chance."

She nodded. The pain receded. The guilt was still there; it would always be there. But perhaps it wouldn't crush her.

They rose to their feet, and Lola stumbled. He helped her up, keeping her close against him, and brushed the tears away. "You're warm, Lola. I can feel you."

She grabbed his hand, pulling him. "Gael, we need to hurry. We need to get to the others."

Gael glanced over her shoulder, and his body went rigid.

Lola whirled and overbalanced. Beau was moving, groaning from deep within his chest. He writhed on the ground. She stared, horrified, as he staggered to his feet, his mouth opened wide in a silent scream. His eyes were brown, flat normal *human* brown, bulging out of his face as though he was still trapped in the burning place. He ripped at the skin of his arms with his nails as if something tortured him from the inside.

"What have you done?" His gaze fell on her, unfocused. "What have I done?" He ended on a long, lingering wail.

"Beau, it's me. Do you remember?" Lola took a tentative step toward him, like approaching a rabid dog.

Beau looked at her with such abhorrence that she cringed back. "What is this? Stop it." He sobbed, clawing at his chest as though to dig his heart out. "Take it out! Take it out!" He screamed and reached up to dig his fingers into his eyes. Lola grabbed him.

"Beau, no, stop!" she sobbed. "I didn't mean for this. Give it time."

"Time?" Beau reared away from her, snarling in disgust, wiping his hands over and over on his pants. "There is no time.

There is only disgusting flesh. This is unbearable. You did this to me!"

"This was you, Beau. You sought power; here it is. Life is the ultimate power."

"No!" He shrieked. The sound echoed in the chamber. "Make it stop!"

He lunged for Lola, who stumbled, no longer as fleet on her feet as she once was. Beau, equally graceless, heaved into her, and they slammed to the ground. Her breath was ripped from her in a painful wheeze.

Gael tackled Beau. They wrestled, rolling over the floor, neither finding an advantage over the other.

Beau no longer had a demon's strength, but he was driven by manic energy. He roared in fury, his eyes lit in pain and desire. "I want it back!" His fangs didn't lengthen, but he thrust forward, sinking his teeth into Gael's neck. Eyes bulging in horror, Gael screamed and tore himself away, a gaping wound at his throat.

Beau scrabbled at him, trying to get at his blood. Lola didn't have the strength to stop him on her own, but Gael was going to be ripped apart if she did nothing. She tore open her pack and grabbed the stake, hand shaking so hard she almost missed. It fit in her hand.

Before he could get to Gael's throat again, Lola leapt onto Beau, thrusting the stake deep into his back where his heart was, flinging the entire force of her mortal body into it. Because Beau was no longer a vampire, it didn't offer him an easy death.

Beau seized up with a gurgling choke. He coughed, a cloud of blood spraying from his mouth as he turned to look at Lola, eyes wide. There was fury there, but also relief. He opened his mouth to say something, but only blood came out. He collapsed on Gael, eyes still staring.

Gael roared, holding his neck while trying to push Beau's corpse off. Lola sobbed as she pulled at Beau, rolling him away into a heap on the ground.

"It's okay. It's okay," she said. Blood pumped out over Gael's hand, and he trembled in shock. He didn't have long. She dashed to the pool, taking the warm bubbling water in her hands. The blood on them melted away, disappearing into the pool.

She brought the liquid to Gael's lips, a thin stream running past his lips. He drank, body shuddering, holding her gaze the entire time. He shimmered with a white glow. As she watched in awe, the shadows flickered over him, lingering in his aura.

Gael closed his eyes and breathed easier.

The gaping wound at his neck stitched itself back together, pulled by threads of light. The lines on his face smoothed, and she could tell the pain was gone. The light flared bright as the sun, lighting up his body with an inner flame. A soul worth saving.

Gael's eyes fluttered open. "That was incredible."

"What did you see?"

"Only light. I felt peaceful." He sat, hand going to his neck. "This is gone."

She peered along the line of his neck, nothing but smooth skin. "There's not even the slightest scar."

"Lola, you saved my life."

Lola brushed the hair back from his face. "Gael, you gave me mine. But there's still miles to go before we can rest."

Gael's eyes widened. "What are we doing here. We have to get to Nix!"

"Easy," Lola said, cautious of him, but Gael bounded to his feet. His legs held firm as he tested his bad ankle.

"This stuff is incredible."

"The true water of life." Lola took her water bottle and held it over the fountain.

The cavern rumbled as though something ancient was displeased. The shadows skittered along the walls, faster and faster, eyes glittering malevolently. An unearthly screeching rose in warning.

Lola looked at the shadow creatures gathered on the ceiling

above her. "I wish to take a small amount with me, to save the lives of my friends who hang now in the balance. I pledge to protect this fountain with my life."

The shadows screeched as one and a green light flashed. She blinked away the light spots, to see the shadows fading into nothing.

Lola dipped the bottle into the pool, filling it. "Thank you," she whispered.

"What was that?" Gael asked, his terrified gaze on the empty space where the shadow creatures had disappeared.

"A guardian. Or guardians, I'm not sure which." Lola held out the bottle. "This is more valuable than anything in existence. If the wrong person found out the Elixir of Life truly existed, it could destroy everything." She looked at the flickering shadows. "The world, maybe."

Gael nodded. "We never tell a soul."

She looked at him, dizzy with the freedom that stretched out in front of her. "What are we waiting for? Let's go save some lives."

THIRTY-ONE

Lola had forgotten what being human felt like. She was hypersensitive to everything – the air on her skin and the roughness of the cave wall under her fingertips. She caught herself staring at her hand before Gael took it in his.

"Come on."

He glowed with health, cheeks flushed as he bounced on his feet, as though remaining static was impossible. He plunged up the tunnel filled with boundless energy.

No longer slowed by injury, no longer weighed down by grief and fear, it took them short minutes to find their way back to the caved-in chamber.

"Walt!" Gael yelled, lunging up the slope, scrambling as the rocks under his feet shifted and slid. As she tackled the climb herself, Lola let out a slow hiss of breath. *Merde*, it was hard. Her body was slow and graceless, and she sliced her finger on a sharp rock as she made her way up. She lagged as Gael desperately threw stones down the incline. Nothing moved.

"Walt!" Gael screamed. "Nix!"

"I'm here." Walt's weak voice floated from the dark cavern on the other side. "I'm with Nix."

"Is she okay?"

There was a very long silence.

Lola pushed up to the hole. "Walt, is Nix still alive?"

"I think so. I didn't want to leave her alone." His voice was very young and very scared. "I can't...I can't move."

Gael banged at the rocks, cursing when a boulder refused to shift. Lola hit a rock, used to things moving when she demanded it, but all she did was graze her knuckles.

She sat back and eyed the hole. "Gael, give me the bottle. I can make it through."

Gael eyed it dubiously. "I don't know, Lola. We should try to get a few more out of the way. With time, these rocks will shift."

"We don't have time. If you help push me through, I can do this."

"Okay, I got you."

Lola took a deep breath. There would be very little wiggle room. She didn't think about what would happen if she got stuck. She shook out her hands, then crawled forward.

Her head and arms eased through it. But at her chest slid through, she got caught. She could see the opening right in front of her, but she couldn't get any grip to push through. She gasped, her ribs compressing in the small space. Panic reared up inside her.

"Gael!" Her legs flailed against nothing. Then his hands were on her ankles, under her feet, pressing her forward. She used the pressure to push as hard as she could, launching herself through the hole.

There was nothing to stop her on the other side, and she slid face first to the bottom of the rock pile. She lay there, stunned. Her body was battered and bruised, and some of her new human skin had been scraped off.

She heard a weak groan and made herself get up. "Walt!" She choked on dust. Her fall had stirred up a cloud, and she couldn't see anything. "Where are you?" She stumbled forward.

"Over here." His quiet, calm tone spiked her anxiety. Arms

out, she headed in his direction. The dust settled. Light came in from above on this side of the rockfall, and she could make out two lumps among the rocks.

Walt sat with his knees tucked to his chin. With his good hand, he held Nix's limp one.

Lola's hands flew to her mouth. If Nix was still alive, she had no idea how. Most of her body was crushed, bones stuck out at grotesque angles, other parts flattened. The back of her head was caved in.

Tiny and fragile, her skin was pale to transparency. Walt was right; she would never wake up from this. The miracle was her heart continued to beat.

"Brave spirit," Lola whispered. She took the bottle and unscrewed the top. Very carefully, trying hard not to move Nix in any way, she let a few drops fall onto her lips, then a few more.

The world held its breath.

Lola's throat tightened. What if she was too late. No, Nix...

A swirl of colour vibrated under her deathly pale cheek. It began small, then grew and stretched and whirled to the rest of her body. Golden sparkles shimmered above her as her skin glowed white.

As the glow spread to the fingers he was holding, Walt gasped. He gaped as the broken fingers under his hand straightened and healed.

Nix's body inflated like someone had blown air into her. Her head filled in, and the colour continued its sweep over her. Her brows snapped together, and she moaned, twitching and shaking her head as though trapped in a bad dream.

The glow increased to a crescendo of light pouring out of every pore. Lola, no longer able to look at her, shielded her eyes. She waited until the blinding glare pulled back. When she peeked her eyes open, only a beam of light emanated from her chest. Then even that reeled in, and Nix sat up.

Her blue eyes were bright as the Atlantic on a summer day as she looked over Lola and Walt, curious. She glanced where Walt still held her hand. He noticed and blushed, putting her hand down with a pat.

"I told you it would be okay." His voice was a hoarse whisper.

Nix gave a smile that shone in the gloom. "You did. I heard you. You told me Lola would save us."

Darkness passed over her face. Lola shivered. Had Nix been trapped in that broken body, racked with pain but unable to speak?

There was a crash and a curse from above, and in a landslide, Gael skidded onto the ground a few paces away. Nix laughed as Gael pounced on her, sweeping her into a dusty bear hug. "You're alive!"

Walt tried to move toward them but fell back with a gasp of pain. The skin of his face was tinted green.

"Your turn." Lola held out the bottle. "A sip is all you need. Make sure there's enough left for the others."

"What is it?" Walt asked.

"A liquid that can heal you."

He raised an eyebrow. "Really." He took a swig. He kept his head bowed as the white light passed over him, concentrating on his shoulder and chest. It was different from how it was for Nix, without flashes of gold, nor with the shadows that enveloped Gael.

Walt breathed in, and then once more. "Fascinating," he whispered as the light pulled into him. He held the bottle up. "How does this work?"

"Does it matter?" Lola asked, taking it back.

He frowned, his gaze following the bottle. His eyes were bright, but doubt lingered behind them. "I guess it shouldn't," he said. "But a part of me can't just accept that it was *magic*." He said it like a dirty word. "There must be a logical explanation. Only, I have no idea what it could be." Then he shook his head and gave a broad smile, one Lola hadn't seen before. He seemed younger, less weary of the world, more like the boy who played *Star Wars* with Gael years ago. "It ends up being the same."

He uncoiled and stretched to his full height. Nix stood, too, only to be swung up into Gael's arms again.

"You scared me," he said into her hair as he held Nix tight. Nix wrapped her arms around him, tears squeezing from her shut eyes.

"I scared myself. It's good to be back."

Gael set Nix down carefully, and the girl turned to Lola. "You need to take the potion, too! You're bleeding!"

Lola glanced down. It seemed every exposed part of her skin was somehow bruised or scraped. She looked at her fingers, flexing them, admiring them even as she hissed at the sting of a cut.

"I've already been healed."

Nix stared. "You're bleeding."

"I know, it's okay. I'll keep my little wounds."

"No, I mean, you're bleeding red. Like a human."

"Yes." Lola broke into a grin. "I'm human."

"No shit!" Nix's grin was huge, and she wrapped Lola in a hug as well. She was a few inches shorter, but her grip was fierce, and Lola let herself be held. "You feel different. Before, you were like a Greek statue or something. Now you're all warm and bouncy, and"—she waved her hand around Lola's face—"A little messy, to be honest."

Behind the rockslide rose an inhuman shriek, and the ground trembled. Growing shadows skittered toward them.

"We've overstayed our welcome," Lola said, steadying herself against Gael. "The guardian wishes us to leave. And I want nothing more than to return to the surface."

"How are we going to get out?"

They paused as realization settled in. The way out of the tunnel was blocked. Nix let out a bitter laugh, and Lola knew what she was thinking. They'd found their treasure at the end of their quest, and now they were trapped. They would die down here. One last trap for the seekers of the Well of Souls.

Lola looked up to the trickle of light coming in. "I think the cave-in might have opened up the earth above us."

They all looked up, blinking. "That's awfully high up," Nix said. "How are we going to get there?"

"We could yell. Maybe somebody will hear us." Gael held out a hand to Lola. "We have to try, right?"

Together, they made their way up the sliding rocks, keeping each other steady until they had reached the top of the slope. Even from there, the top of the cavern was a long way off and the trickle of light weak.

"Hey!" Gael called, cupping his hands around his mouth. "We're down here!"

"Help us!" Nix screamed. They all started to scream.

Lola braced her hands on her knees. She caught her breath, gazing at the cavern. For the first time, she was uneasy about her decision to accept mortality. She had sacrificed her strength to become human. She wouldn't be able to save the others the way she did before; couldn't slam herself into situations and use brute force to make it all right. Nobody could count on her as a weapon.

Lola cocked her head. Above them, a green glow lightened the endless darkness. She squinted, trying to make out what she was seeing. As the glow brightened, she could see it running like veins through the rock. It was a root system.

The Tree of Life's roots stretched all the way down here. It had blocked them in. Maybe, now it could help them find a way out.

Reaching up, Lola concentrated on the root nearest her, thinking of the connection she had felt with the tree. The air rippled as though it recognized her. The earth rumbled again, and the others cried out, grabbing each other to keep them from sliding down the rock pile.

"The rest of the roof is going to fall in!" Nix braced herself against Gael and Walt, holding her arms over their heads as they crouched.

"No, it's the oak tree that stands next to the treasure dig. We're underneath it, and the roots go all the way to the surface. If they could just stretch a little further." Lola closed her eyes and made the plea, for a bridge between this otherworldly place and the human world above. She was ready to step into the sunlight.

The ground grumbled and the air shone with green lights as thick roots ripped from the soil, showering them with earth. When the air had cleared, a massive gnarled root descended right in front of them. It was thicker than Lola was wide, and the rough bark had plenty of handholds to help them up.

Lola eyed the very long climb ahead of them to reach the surface.

Walt and Nix began to climb first. Energized from their healing, they bounded up the root bridge towards the surface.

Gael waited next to her. "Regretting your choice?" he asked, as though reading her thoughts.

Lola turned to him, stepping onto the root so they were face to face. "No. Because I get to do this." She leaned in and kissed him, lips grazing soft and tender and sensitive. She let out a laughing breath as he pressed his lips to her neck. "And I get to feel that."

She took a deep breath and began climbing, her muscles protesting, her body dripping with sweat. The root path angled through the earth, leading upwards towards the thinnest crack of golden light from the now-risen sun above them.

Lola held her breath and hesitated, then reached for a sunbeam. Her fingers brushed through it. There was no burning, only the warmth she had dreamed of for eighty years. She climbed into the light and let it claim her.

THIRTY-TWO

Lola squinted in the sunshine, trying to make sense of the crowd of people. They stood around the edge of the earth that had fallen in on itself, exposing the ancient oak's root system. They had travelled so far only to get back to the place they started. Lola climbed out of the hole and placed her hands on the tree's bark, in gratitude.

Nix was wrapped in the arms of a redheaded woman. "Arabella! What were you thinking?" Nix laughed and pulled a face as she tried to escape her mother's grasp. A shaggy man embraced them both. His eyes crinkled in his weathered face, looking over his daughter with evident relief.

Walt had lost his look of wonder. He stood aloof, face shuttered, next to an impossibly thin woman. She must be Walt's mother. She held herself so tight Lola wondered she could move at all. She gazed at the Nixes' open affection, disapproval pasted over her rigid face.

Anita broke out of the crowd, her lovely face creased with worry. She cradled Gael's backpack in her arms, and Lola's heart broke. Anita thought she'd lost another son. But she was going to make sure she didn't lose any.

Anita grabbed Lola's arm, shaking her. "*Mi hijo!*" she pleaded. "Where is my son?"

"He's here," Lola said.

Anita's head snapped up as Gael emerged from the hole. "*Mi amor*, how dare you! You could have gotten yourself killed!" She lunged for him, pulling him into her arms.

"Mamá!" Gael picked her right up until her head was under his chin. She shrieked and sobbed, trying to hug him and curse him at the same time.

Lola stood to the side, alone. She had nothing in this world. She could take a few steps away from this crowd and disappear into the forest. No one would miss her.

A figure approached her slowly.

"Lola Monteux," Captain Greyson said, lingering on the vowels. "Once again, I find you in the middle of a shitshow."

Lola simply stared at him, wondering how this was going to play out. For once, she didn't hold any power. This man could make her new life very uncomfortable.

"Walk with me." He brought her away from the crowd to the site of their original dig.

He stepped to the edge of the hole and whistled. "That's a pretty intense pit. I'm sure there's some kind of violation of public property."

"This is Gael's property. He has a permit to dig for treasure here."

He let out a weary sigh. "No one seems to be injured. But things could have gone very differently."

He had no idea how right he was.

"What were you doing down there?"

Lola couldn't help her cheeky smile. "Looking for buried treasure."

"Did you find anything?"

She was saved from answering when Faye came bundling toward her. She wore blue hospital pyjamas, her feet shoved into flimsy slippers. Her face was white and drawn, but her eyes sparkled with defiant fire. "Lola! I was so worried about you!"

"Faye, what are you doing out of bed?"

"Try to stop her." Greyson's eye roll was barely held back. But the way he stood protectively near her, Lola could tell how much the attack had spooked him. "I got the call some kids went missing while I was in her room."

"But how did you know…"

"Pssht." Faye huffed dismissively. "I know everything that happens in this town. You think I didn't know Gael Smith was digging the old treasure shaft with you? Now, honey, tell me truthfully. You look beat up, but underneath it all, are you whole?"

Faye reached out and cupped Lola's face. Lola's eyes pricked at the words. *Whole.* She couldn't put into words how she felt.

"Faye, how are *you*?"

Faye's face creased. "I'm okay. I had a blood transfusion, and I feel much stronger."

"You need to rest." Lola wanted to hustle her right back to the hospital. "You were near death."

"I lost a little blood is all. I've always bounced back quickly enough."

"Well, what happened?"

"A young man was lurking at the entrance of the café, and when I told him to come in, he leapt at me." She shivered. "They think he might have been the person committing the murders around the island. How horrifying."

Lola took her hand. "He can never hurt you again."

Faye's face opened in surprise at Lola's certainty. But after a moment, she nodded and squeezed her hand. "That's nice to hear."

Greyson eyed Lola as though he somehow knew she was to blame. She didn't meet his eyes.

Anita still cursed Gael. "What were you doing? I come home to find you gone. You could have been killed!"

"Mamá." Gael pulled away. "How is Diego?"

Anita sagged. "He is the same. He will not wake. He might fade away naturally, or we might have to…" Her lips twisted, and she looked away, unable to speak her impossible choice.

Gael nodded. "I want to see him. Can we go to the hospital now?"

"Good idea," Greyson called to the group. "Everyone who climbed into this messed up hole goes to the hospital to get checked out."

"Ridiculous." Walt's mother spoke for the first time, her clipped voice as chilly as the rest of her. "Walt is perfectly fine."

"Ma'am, you can't know that."

She sniffed. "I'll have him looked over by his private physician. Officer, I trust you to handle this mess." She turned away, nose tilted in the air.

Anita and Faye both stared at Walt's mother. Lola removed herself from Faye's protective arm, and she grabbed Gael.

"Here's the Elixir," she whispered, handing him the bottle. "Try to give it to him when no one is looking. And don't forget about the gold."

He brought the sack out of his pocket. "This doesn't matter, now."

"It will when it gets us out of trouble. Watch and see."

She winked and left Gael holding the bottle in one hand, a sack of gold in the other, watching her go.

Anita approached. When she saw what he held, she let out a strangled gasp. "What is this?"

Greyson raced over at her alarm. "What's going on?"

"I…" Gael glanced at Lola. "I found some gold pieces at the bottom. They look really old."

Greyson looked over one of the pieces and whistled. "Son, I think you solved Duchesne Island's mystery. We'll have to register this." He glanced at the hole again, and his face softened. Lola could see dreams of adventure and pirate treasure playing over his features. Then it closed again, the lines hardening. "And I hope you found it all, because these holes are hazardous. They will have to be filled in. No one is allowed to dig here again."

"I have no problem with that."

Anita fingered a gold piece. "This could be 18th century," she whispered. "Do you know what this is worth?"

Gael looked directly at Lola. "Yeah. I do."

Lola jerked her head in the direction of the forest path. *Go,* she mouthed.

"Mamá, we need to see Diego."

"I'll take you," Greyson said. "Faye, Officer Davids can take you back to the hospital." He gave a long, searching look at Lola, then ushered the Smiths to the RCMP ATV.

The Nixes were already moving out of the clearing, wrapped around each other. Nix looked back at Lola, complicated emotions playing over her face, her eyes very bright. Her brows drew sharply together. "I'll see you later, understand?" she called, her voice muffled by her mother's arm. "Don't go anywhere."

Walt's mother let out another huff and stalked away. Her delicate heels were not made for the uneven forest ground, and she wobbled, scowling. Walt gave a small salute, following her silently.

Lola and Faye stood facing each other in the clearing. A blanket wrapped around Faye's shoulders, cheap thin material. She must have grabbed it off the hospital bed.

"How are you doing?" She asked in such a tenuous way, as though Lola was about to shatter. She was right, of course.

Lola blinked away tears. She brought her hand to her face as they flowed. Fresh human tears, no blood in sight. "I'm cold," she said, and laughed in wonder. It was true. She had been cold as ice for decades, but now that her core was warmed by spirit, her skin trembled.

"Of course you are." Faye removed her blanket from her shoulders, wrapping it around Lola's exposed skin, tutting over her scrapes and bruises. "But what I meant is, how are you, as in your situation? I've been trying not to pry, which is hard for me, but it looks like you could use a hand. Do you have anyone?"

Lola shook her head. "I'm alone. My parents died a long time ago."

"Do you have anywhere to go now?"

Lola squinted at the sun, riding high toward noon. It was so gloriously bright. No, she had nowhere to go, no plan. For the first time in a very long time, she was free.

"I have everywhere to go."

ACKNOWLEDGMENTS

Seeing this book brought to life is a dream come true for me. Above everything else, I have to thank Zach, because without his unflagging support through all the good times and the bad, I don't know if this would have become a reality. I know you got my back, and it means the world to me.

To my incredible editor Marilyn Boake, thank you for having such a fine eye for detail and for giving me the guidance to get this manuscript to where it needed to be.

I also want to thank Sarah Johnson for her initial review of the manuscript. Your enthusiasm certainly helped me continue on my path.

To my entire family, whose support has been strong from the very beginning. And a shout out to Heather Grab, my first editor, who has read through some lemons throughout the years. I hope you like this one.

About the Author

Cordelia Kelly has been a lawyer and a journalist in past lives, but finally settled on writing stories and drawing illustrations after all that. She writes mainly horror and fantasy for young adult and middle grade audiences. The Well of Souls is her debut novel. All of her work can be found at cordeliakelly.com.

Her anthology of horror stories, *Then She Said Hush* is available. Several of her short stories have been published, and she was the 2019 winner of the Geneva Writers Literary Prize in Fiction.

9 781738 863365